Beneath a Beating Heart

by

Lauri Robinson

Beneath a Beating Heart

Cover Art by *RJ Morris*

The Wild Rose Press, Inc.
PO Box 708
Adams Basin, NY 14410-0708
Visit us at www.thewildrosepress.com

Publishing History
First Fantasy Rose Edition, 2018
Print ISBN 978-1-5092-2112-7
Digital ISBN 978-1-5092-2113-4

Published in the United States of America

Her heart landed in her throat

as he leaned forward. Liz closed her eyes and held her breath as the charged vibration between them grew stronger, and stronger.

Tingles of anticipation washed over her.

But there was nothing more. No pressure. No meeting of lips. No kiss.

A wave of regret, of disappointment, of why me, why now, was so great she wobbled and grabbed the stove to hold her upright.

As her equilibrium returned, he whispered, "Let go of the stove, Elizabeth. Hold your hand up."

Drawing a fortifying breath, she did so, copying how he held his up. She watched, as did he, as they both slowly brought their palms closer. Her fingers trembled. It may have been her imagination, but it was as if a halo, a faint golden light, formed around their hands as their fingertips grew so close they should be touching. Yet weren't. Or were they? Her fingers vibrated, and heat spread up her arm.

Their eyes met, and the smile on his face was about the most wonderful, and dangerous thing that could have ever happened to her. The heat generating at her hand, running up her arm, hit her heart, where it pooled and then spread out into a radiance that went deeper and deeper inside her.

"Can you feel that?"

Convinced there was something there, she nodded. "Yes, can you?"

"Yes. It's as powerful as ever."

"What is?"

"Our love."

Dedication

For Nancy.
Here's your ghost story—finally!

Chapter One

1901, Cody, Wyoming

Rance Livingston fit the final two pieces of black stove pipe together and secured them with a few taps from the hammer before stepping back to admire his handiwork. It took up the entire wall and had set him back a fair amount, but the smile on Beth's face when she saw the blue and white cook stove, trimmed in shiny chrome and decked out with two top warming ovens and a glass temperature gauge on the oven door, would be worth the cost of a hundred stoves. The dozen of kisses she'd bestow upon him were worth far more than years of profit. Money could never compare to the loving they'd share when she arrives home.

In the twenty-nine years he'd walked this earth, he'd never once fancied himself a marrying man, but it had happened in a remarkably short amount of time. Along with the ring on his finger had come more love and joy than any one man should have a right to experience.

Beth had insisted upon the ring. Said she wanted the whole world to know he was hers and would be forever. He had the same sentiments, except, to him, forever wouldn't even be long enough.

Smiling to himself, for there was no one else for miles around, though he really wouldn't have cared who saw him grinning like a fool, he returned the hammer to his wooden tool box and hoisted it up by the handle to carry out to the tool shed. Hell, if he didn't have a skip to his step. Webster had promised the stove would be here, but Rance hadn't completely believed it would happen considering Webster's past promises of freight arriving on time.

The old man had come through, and just in the nick of time. Beth would return home from visiting her family in Billings today—in a few hours actually—and his heart thudded at the thought. Knowing she missed him as much as he missed her promised her homecoming would be amazing.

After three months of marriage, he should be able to be parted from her for a few days without feeling like he was only half there. Maybe that would come in time—the ability to be separated from Beth and not miss the very dickens out of her. Perhaps after forty or fifty years of marriage. Up until then he'd go right on missing her, and loving her. That he'd do until he hit the grave, and beyond. He'd pledged forever, and meant it.

Rance returned to the kitchen and hands on his hips admired the stove once more. He could almost see Beth standing before it, her blue eyes sparkling as she examined each little part of her surprise. The warming ovens, the water reservoir, the temperature gauge, the handle that lifted the burner plates, the fire box. He grinned again. She was going to be surprised.

She wasn't the type to ask for anything, and she'd probably say he shouldn't have bought it and surprised her, all the while being tickled pink he had. He was going to love every moment of it, and in between kisses, assure her that they could afford it and that she was worth it. She was and they could. Life was good, and he couldn't see a way for it to get better.

With that thought warming his insides, he collected his hat and headed for the barn to complete the morning chores before it was time to hitch up the buggy and head into Cody in order to collect Beth from the railroad station. The morning sun was big and bright and already casting down heat that was intense for May. Beth would appreciate the shade of the buggy's awning, and he'd appreciate the privacy. There was no way he'd be able to resist stealing a kiss or two on the way home.

The smile on his face slipped away as a chill tickled his spine. He spun around, toward the house. Seeing just the empty porch, he turned and scanned the barn, the yard, the hills.

There was no sign of anyone, anywhere.

He could have sworn he heard Beth shout his name. Call for him. He took off his hat and shielded the sunlight with his hand. After gazing down the long and vacant road for a time, he put his hat back on. It must have just been the wind.

Thinking he'd heard her voice hung within him the next few hours, making him lonelier than the past five days put together. He felt empty without her, and that made it hard to concentrate on the horses, the chores.

A nagging sensation still hung with him a few hours later. He'd just hitched up the buggy when approaching hoofbeats had him walking around the barn instead of toward the house. The rider was approaching fast, and he waited, watched, until the single horse traveled beneath the overhead board he'd erected after burning the name *Rocking L* deep in the wood. Beth had said the sign was beautiful, and that it would make her smile every time she returned home. It made him smile every time he looked at it.

He wasn't smiling. Recognizing the rider, a quiver vibrated up his spine and caused a frown. Although they'd been friends for several years, the sheriff rarely traveled out to the ranch in the middle of the day. "What are you doing out this way?" he shouted as the man rode closer.

Cliff Dixon nodded as he pulled his horse to a stop and didn't say a word while dismounting, which had Rance's nerves picking up on an eerie undercurrent. An even stronger chill than before coiled around his spine.

"What are you doing here, Cliff?" There better not have been a bank robbery or some such dastardly deed. He couldn't ride posse, not with Beth returning today.

Cliff took off his hat, looking in every direction except directly ahead. "There's been an accident, Rance."

His nerves kicked in, drumming a fast and erratic beat beneath his skin. "What type of accident?"

"A train accident," Cliff said. "Shortly after it left Billings this morning."

Rance's entire being turned cold, except for the ball of fire that landed in his throat. Sucking in air through his nose and refusing to think the worse, he asked, "Was anyone hurt?"

Cliff nodded and then turned to face him. His eyes were glistening, and red. "There were no survivors. There was a storm. The bridge collapsed, and Beth—"

"No." Rance grit his teeth together, refusing to listen any further. "No," was all his thick throat would let out as his teeth clenched against the fiery tightening deep in his chest.

"I'm sorry, Rance," Cliff said. "So, so, sorry."

Chapter Two

2018, Billings, Montana

Liz Baxter slipped on her sunglasses against the bright summer sun with one hand and slid her cell phone into the cup holder with the other. This would be the longest drive she'd taken the Mustang since purchasing it more than two years ago, and that in itself felt good. She felt good. Right. A hundred miles wasn't a major road trip, but for someone who'd only left Billings a handful of times, it was significant.

"Call me—"

The ringing of her cell phone interrupted what the woman standing outside her car had been saying. Liz punched the decline button and grinned out the driver's window. "I'll call you when I arrive."

Vivi Anne lifted a finely drawn on brow. "Someday you're going to have to answer that thing."

"When someone worth answering calls, I will," Liz said.

"Your old boss again?"

"Yes. Dusty's been hired by the new company that took over Cell One and wants to hire me back." A hint of guilt twisted her stomach, but as always, she told herself she didn't care.

"You worked there a long time."

"Only because I believe customers should get what

they pay for." Which didn't mean she cared, only that she was honest. Even when it came to Mrs. O'Toole who called the first of every month, mainly just to share the latest escapades of her cat. A brief thought of calling Mrs. O'Toole had formed while cleaning out her desk, but company policies forbade it, which was best for everyone.

Vivi Anne grinned. "Maybe it's not just a job he's trying to offer you."

As much as Liz enjoyed working for Vivi Anne at the antique store, and enjoyed the friendship they had, she wasn't open to Vivi Anne's *other* vocation. At least not in *that* sense. "He's not my long-lost soul mate so get off that track right now."

Vivi Anne shrugged. "The universe gives back what we put out there, whether we're conscious of it or not. Sometimes we may not even know who or what we're looking for. It's based at a time and place our minds don't recall, but our hearts do."

The tiniest of tingles zipped just beneath the surface of Liz's skin, an anticipation of sorts, and it had nothing to do with her old boss. "Your matchmaking skills are lost on me. I worked with Dusty Wayne for almost seven years. Trust me; I'm not searching for the likes of him." With a grin, she added, "I'm not going back to work at Cell One. Ever. But I am going to Cody, Wyoming." She started her car. "And I'll call you when I arrive."

Liz put the car in drive and waved as she pulled out of the parking lot. She buried all thoughts of Cell One as excitement pumped through her veins. Maybe someday she'd be like those two guys on TV who drove around the countryside searching small towns and old junkyards for forgotten treasures.

Traffic was minimal, even on the interstate, and became practically non-existence when she exited onto the highway that went south into Wyoming. A few miles later, she approached the railroad crossing where her parents had died. She'd been on this road a couple of times since that night twenty years ago, but had never stopped, never wanted to, until today.

She pulled the car to the side of the road. The tracks were no longer used. The white and black crossing bars little more than piles of rubbish on both sides of the roads. If the crossing bars had been present years ago, they might have saved her parents' lives. It had been storming fiercely, and her father must not have seen or heard the train coming with all the hail and lightning.

Liz climbed out of the car and crossed the ditch to see where the railroad bridge met land. Grass grew over the ties and rotting boards hung sporadically amongst the huge trellises that supported the bridge over the river far below. The bank was steep, and from what she'd been told, their car careened down it, into the water. She couldn't remember any of it, nor anything about her parents. The only memory she did recall, which was very, very faint, was of horses. Lots of them.

Or perhaps those recollections were nothing more than childhood fantasies.

The authorities had searched far and wide for relatives but had come up empty-handed. The story was her father worked for a construction company out of North Dakota, and they'd only been in Montana a short time. Liz and her mother had been the only family the company knew about, and in all the years since, no one else had ever surfaced, certainly no relatives with horses. Years of searching had provided nothing more than a birth certificate. Other than that piece of paper stating she'd been born in Missouri on August 8, 1990, Elizabeth Ann Baxter may never have existed.

Liz stood there for several minutes, as if waiting for something. Anything. A memory. A sign. Nothing came. Not even a car on the highway.

As her gaze settled on the brown, murky water, a faint and faraway sense said there was more beneath that water than anyone could fathom.

Shaking off a shiver, she returned to her car and drove forward over the tracks. Long ago she'd accepted her rather non-existence past, and her life. Nothing had changed. No reason to start wishing things were different.

Instead she should be grateful for all she had. For the journey she was on this very moment. If not for Vivi Anne, Liz had no idea what she'd been doing right now. Selling tacos at the Taco Hut would have been an option, she supposed. That made her grin, and she turned on the radio. Her own laugh echoed inside the car as a ballad of country roads taking someone home came through the speakers.

"Vivi Anne's favorite singer. Fitting, don't you think, Esmeralda?" It was a silly name, but as soon as she'd seen the car, that was the name that had come to her. Turning up the volume on the radio, she sang along to the words about the radio reminding of a home far away.

The song ended, but her smile didn't. All in all, she was glad she'd met Vivi Anne and was glad to be on her way to Cody. All that *felt* right.

She rolled into Cody before noon and took a scenic drive down the main street, catching a brief glimpse of all the shops catering to tourists and the historical buildings, before getting back on the highway and taking it to the edge of town where the old west village sat. If she hadn't been looking for it, she might have driven past. There was only one faded sign for the area that looked more like a ghost town than a tourist attraction.

Parking next to the fence that surrounded the dozen or more old log cabins, she noted another faded sign indicating the attraction was open daily, nine months out of the year.

There was another log cabin, larger than the others and not inside the fence. She assumed that was Buzz's residence. Vivi Anne said he lived on site and was the only employee of the village. Since it was during open hours, she walked through the entrance gate and into the building marked office and gift shop.

"Hello," an old man greeted. "You must be Liz. Vivi Anne's friend. I just hung up with her."

The building was old, made of square, chinked logs. "Then there's no reason for me to call and say I made it. Yes, I'm Liz. It's nice to meet you."

"You, too," Buzz answered, making his way around the long glass counter with the aid of a knobby tri-colored cane. "I've left a message on Lou's cell phone, just waiting to hear back so I can send you on out to the ranch."

Assuming Lou was the land owner, she took a brief glance at the usual tourist knick-knacks of colored shot glasses, key chains, spoons, and thimbles. "So," she said, having seen enough. "How do you know Vivi

Anne?"

Buzz settled on a chair near the door. "Met her a long time ago, she was friends with one of my daughters. I couldn't believe it when she stopped in this spring. Glad she moved out this way."

"Does your daughter live around here, too?"

He shook his head. "Dolly passed on some time ago. Same year as my wife. Cancer took them both. Damn stuff."

"I'm sorry." Hating these types of uncomfortable moments, she looked around again, wishing something would draw her attention.

"Thank you," Buzz said sincerely. "It was some time ago, but one never gets over the pain."

Liz glanced around again, still unable to come up with something to say. She had nothing to compare to his loss. No compassion to draw upon. Yes, both of her foster parents had died, and she'd been sad, but death was a part of life. She figured her somewhat callous feelings, or lack of feeling anything, was because of losing her parents so young. Who would want to remember something so painful? No one in their right mind. She was thankful she'd realized that long ago. "Vivi Anne said there's a story behind this house I'm here to look at, what is it?" She flinched slightly, hoping the change of subject didn't sound as abrupt as it felt.

"The *Rocking L* is kind of a local legend. You know, where the story has been added to over the years until it's a bit unbelievable."

Sensing a hint of reluctance, she asked, "But there is truth behind it?"

Buzz lifted a hairy brow. "You don't give up, do

you?"

She shrugged.

"Yeah, there's truth behind it." He waved to another chair.

A hint of excitement flared as she sat.

"Years and years ago, around the turn of the century, the twentieth century, a man named Rance Livingston raised and trained horses for Buffalo Bill. Story goes, Rance and his new wife built the house, and shortly thereafter his wife died in an accident." He sighed while resting both hands atop his cane. "Seems old Rance turned into a hermit after that. He continued to raise horses but never remarried. When he died back in the nineteen sixties, he willed everything to his friend's grandson."

She wondered if that was the Lou he'd mentioned, but didn't ask, sensing he'd continue.

He grinned. "That was Riley. Riley Dixon. His granddad, Cliff, had been the sheriff around here and Rance's best friend. Riley was a good man. I knew him fairly well. He and his wife had two sons, but they both died in the army. Sad. Anyhow, Riley's only family left were Nate and Lou, and when Riley died last year, the two cousins inherited everything. Riley's place and the Livingston place. They sold Riley's place quick enough, but…" Shaking his head, he shrugged. "Some claim the *Rocking L* is haunted, and that's why it hasn't sold. It's rumored Rance still roams through the house, waiting for his wife to come home."

Never affected by stories, not sad ones, sappy ones, or scary ones, Liz wondered why her skin tingled and her stomach fluttered. Excitement? Fear? The initials on the hand-tooled leather tack Vivi Anne had already purchased from Buzz were R. L. That had to be Rance Livingston. Needing more information, Liz asked, "Why would he be waiting for his wife to come home? Didn't you say she died in an accident?"

"I did. Story has it she died in a train accident up by Billings, but they never found her body, therefore, Rance never believed she'd died." He laid his cane across his lap. "Very few people have seen the inside of the house, but from what I've heard, it looks just like it did in nineteen-o-one when Beth died. Riley was rather closed-lipped about it all, but I know for certain he inherited money to keep the house in good standing, even had a new roof put on it a few years ago."

Beth Livingston. B.L. were the initials on the half-finished saddle in Vivi Anne's storage room. Excitement bubbled. "Really?" Ghosts, like psychics, intrigued her.

His eyes sparkled as he grinned. "That's why I called Vivi Anne. I knew she wouldn't be afraid of ghost tales, and I hoped she'd get here quick. Nate's asked the fire department to perform a scheduled burn out there this coming weekend."

"Nate? I thought you said you called Lou."

"I did. Lou and Nate are cousins."

"That's right, sorry." She should have listened better to the family history lesson he'd given rather than focusing on the initials. Vivi Anne had mentioned the scheduled burn. "What about Lou? Does he want the place burned down too?"

"He wanted it left standing, just like Rance's will requested, up until lately."

There wasn't necessarily hesitation in his voice, but she caught something. "And that surprised you?"

Buzz shrugged. "Yes, it did. But it ain't up to me, and that's a lot of property to just let sit there. I'm just glad Lou agreed to let the antiques be appraised."

The jangle of a phone interrupted any response she may have had, and hearing his response to the caller had a thrill zipping beneath the surface of Liz's skin.

Hanging up the landline phone that could almost be considered an antique, Buzz climbed to his feet using the aid of his cane. "Lou will meet you at the gate." He waggled one finger. "Gotta warn you, Rance didn't like folks snooping around." With a somewhat serious gaze, he added, "Even when he was alive."

If the old man was trying to scare her, it didn't work. The excitement humming through her was electrifying. "When will Lou meet me?"

"Twenty minutes." Buzz tore a slip of paper from a tablet and drew a sketchy map. As he handed her the paper, he said, "You be careful."

She gave him a nod and a smile. "Don't worry. I'm always careful."

Little more than fifteen minutes later, she clicked on the blinker and turned onto a gravel road. Oddly she hadn't needed the map full of the little landmarks Buzz had indicated. She parked next to a locked gate made of pipes, complete with an old cattle guard beneath it and a red and black *no trespassing* sign wired to a post.

Beyond the gate, a long dirt road snaked up a hill and disappeared. A sense of déjà vu had the hair on her arms standing up. She rolled down both the driver and passenger side windows before turning the car off. The breeze that blew through was reminiscent of something, too, but she couldn't say what.

The lonely, yet, steady ping-pang of the wind

fluttering one corner of the sign against the steel caused a wave of sadness to strike. Maybe it wasn't déjà vu. The land didn't look a whole lot different from what she'd seen on her trip down from Billings. Maybe she just felt sorry for Rance Livingston, having wasted so many years waiting for his wife to come back.

Chapter Three

1901, Cody, Wyoming

It had been two months since his life had changed in less time than the length of a heartbeat. Rance wasn't in much better shape internally than that day, but he had managed to train and deliver the order of horses to Buffalo Bill Cody for his shows. Bill had been out to the ranch a few weeks ago, saying he'd understand if the order couldn't be completed, all things considered. Rance had said he'd deliver them. Training horses, working until he was too tired to think, was all he had to keep him going.

Having lost his own loved ones, Bill said he understood that, and as soon as the horses had been delivered to his ranch several miles south of Cody, he'd ordered more, lots more, claiming he was going to take his Wild West Show to Europe again next year.

Rance agreed to provide all the horses Bill would need. Training horses had been his life for over ten years. Herds populated his acreage, some were wild and others were breeds he was raising. Every spring he rounded up the two-year-olds and brought them closer in to start training and would continue to—for now. He hadn't lost his mind, just his heart, which meant he was merely going through the motions like a locomotive on a rail line. Following the tracks until they ended and then turning around to head back the other direction.

Unless, of course, a bridge collapsed.

With Beth at his side, he'd imagined a successful life. Big barns full of horses, kids, several of them, helping with the animals as they grew older, taking over the *Rocking L* when he and Beth eventually grew too old to do much more than sit on the front porch.

All that had changed. He no longer dreamed of children, no longer imagined a big barn full of horses. No longer imagined growing old. That he felt. He might as well have been eighty with one foot in the grave for all the lack of drive inside him. He'd keep trudging forward though and never give up hope. Until he had something to prove Beth had perished in that train wreck, an article of clothing, her trunk, her, he'd keep on imagining she was still visiting her family in Billings.

Call him crazy. Call him stupid. Call him whatever the hell anyone wanted to, he wasn't giving up. Not on Beth.

As thoughts of her overtook his mind, he glanced over his shoulder, beyond the corral, past the front yard, to the house. Quicker than a rattler strikes, a shiver gripped his spine.

He squinted, trying to pin-point exactly what was out of place. When he found it, he leaped off the horse. He hadn't left a window open, yet one was open. A curtain fluttered outside of the frame, catching the breeze in an upstairs bedroom.

His bedroom.

Beth's bedroom.

The one he hadn't slept in since the day of her accident.

Stomping through the corral, he searched the yard for a horse or rider. Surely someone hadn't walked all the way from town. The onslaught of visitors leaving kettles and baskets full of food on his porch had slowed lately, but he hadn't been upstairs for days. Someone else had opened that window.

He scanned the yard and roadway as he made his way to the house. Whoever it was would get a piece of his mind. He was tired of intrusions. Of people thinking they knew what he needed. Saying what Beth would have wanted.

He knew what she would have wanted—to live with him until they were both a ripe old age.

The instant he threw the front door open, a vast and powerful awakening said someone was in the house.

And he knew who it was.

Running, and breathless due to the racing of his heart, he bounded up the stairs three and four at a time, shouting, "Beth! Beth!"

Their bedroom door was open, but as he rounded the doorway, the woman sitting on the edge of the bed had his heart skidding to a stop at the same time his feet did. He caught himself by the door frame and held on to keep from toppling over.

She was staring at him with a blank frown.

He stared back.

It was Beth. But it wasn't. Or was it? Once long and a gleaming chestnut, her hair was chopped short, just below her ears, and full of blonde stripes, and she was wearing britches. Blue ones and a shirt with no sleeves that was so tight his eyeballs stung because he was unable to blink.

"Beth?" His whisper was so raspy it burned his

throat.

Her frown increased, and she tilted her head. Her blank stare seemed to go right through him instead of at him.

"Buzz?" she asked inquisitively.

"No, it's me, Rance," he answered, questioning himself for the briefest of moments. This was Beth, his insides said so. His Beth. Then why was he hesitating? Why wasn't he running across the room? Why wasn't she running into his arms? Why was she looking through him, not at him? Why were her eyes so different? They were blue, but there was no shine in them.

He waved a hand, but her gaze never wandered.

"Beth?"

She shook her head, as if checking her hearing, and then stood. Setting the magazine in her hand on the bed, she started walking toward him, her gaze still fixed on his chest, or *through* his chest, like she couldn't see him.

"Mr. Dixon?"

Dixon? Why the hell would she call for Cliff? Or was she calling him Cliff? Rance opened his mouth to respond, but the breath shot out of his mouth with a swoosh. He grabbed one side of the doorway with both hands, fully shocked by what had just happened.

She'd walked through him.

Right through him.

Not past him.

Not around him.

Through him.

He pushed off the wall, stumbling slightly. "What the hell is going on?"

She spun around from where she stood in the hallway. Staring at him again, well, through him again, she tilted her head as if listening. When she took a step toward the room, he jumped out of the way, not wanting to experience that weirdness again.

He grabbed his opposite forearm and squeezed, just to make sure he was awake, and then ran his hands over his chest and stomach, checking the firmness of his own flesh.

Too bad he wasn't a drinking man. He could use a shot of whiskey right about now. He was definitely awake, and as solid as ever. How had she done that?

She'd walked back into the room and was rubbing her arms as if chilled.

"Beth," he said, trying once more. "It's me, Rance. Your husband." Or was he? Was this a lost stranger and he was so lonely for Beth he was imagining this woman looked like her?

She walked to the window and pulled the curtain inside before she stuck her head out. "Buzz? Mr. Dixon?"

A stranger wouldn't know Cliff. "Why the hell are you hollering for Cliff, and who's Buzz?" Rance yanked the hat off his head and scratched at his tingling scalp. Had he lost his mind? Was he seeing things? Hearing things? He rubbed his eyes and blinked several times.

He wasn't imagining things. He knew that rump. The one inside those blue britches that had stretched tight while she bent out the window.

"Beth!"

She pulled her head in and glanced around the room.

Why the hell wasn't she answering him?

Her frown had grown, and there was an eerie wariness in her eyes. When she bit down on her bottom lip, a thickening happened in his throat. Beth always did that, but as his gaze wandered back to her eyes, the back of his neck tingled. Those were Beth's eyes, but they weren't. Something was missing, and not just their sparkle. How the hell could that be?

He glanced around, and that's when he noticed the crate on the floor. The one he'd put beside the new stove and had filled with wood. Now it held— "What the hell?" Everything off Beth's dresser was in the crate. Her comb, her brush, her mirror, and hair-pins. The picture of the two of them on their wedding day.

Cursing, he stomped forward.

Still rubbing the chill that had consumed her body and searching for the source of the strange hum she'd heard several times, Liz froze as her heart clawed its way into her throat. The brush and comb in the crate near the bed rose into the air and then floated across the room, landing back on the dresser where she'd found them earlier. The hand mirror and glass bowl full of old hair pins followed moments later, and finally the ornate silver picture frame. The items shifted slightly until they were in the exact positions as when she'd entered the room.

"Holy shit," she whispered. Glancing toward the age-old magazine, she waited, expecting it to move back to the table beside the bed.

When it didn't, she scanned the room again, the hair on the back of her neck and arms standing stiff. This place *is* haunted. She'd thought the rumors Buzz had mentioned where just that. Rumors.

Slowly looking back at the dresser, she swallowed around the lump in her throat. Where was Vivi Anne when she needed her?

That wouldn't help. Vivi Anne was a psychic not a ghost hunter. No, that wasn't true either. Vivi Anne claimed she merely used her insights to assist long lost loves become reunited. That certainly wouldn't help when it came to ghosts.

Liz took a deep breath and juggled her choices. Running seemed like a good idea, but the house was full of antiques. Pristine and gorgeous antiques. More importantly, she wasn't afraid.

Freaked out, yes.

Afraid, no.

Hadn't she always wanted to meet a ghost? Hadn't she secretly hoped it would happen since walking through the door?

Sort of, but now that it was happening she was doing some serious reconsidering.

Like there was time for that.

She drew in a deep breath. "M-Mr. Livingston?" Shivering at how squeaky she sounded, she tried once more. "Rance?"

The faint, almost notes-on-a-breeze echo she'd heard earlier, sounded again.

"Is that you?" She rolled her eyes at her own ignorance. "That was a stupid question, of course it's you. Who else would it be?"

How did one communicate with a ghost?

Introductions?

Couldn't hurt.

"My name is Liz Baxter. Elizabeth Baxter actually, but I go by Liz."

A hum filled the air, as if he, the ghost, was answering. A long answer. She waited for the hum to stop, all the while processing what she should say next, and wondering if he could hear her, or if her voice was a hum as well. Either way, raising her voice just in case, she said loud and clear, "I'm not here to hurt you." She moved to the dresser. "I'm here to preserve some of your things." Picking up the mirror, she added, "Your wife's things, before Mr. Dixon demolishes the house."

The humming noise came again, louder than before, and the mirror in her hand jiggled, as if someone tried to pull it from her grasp. She tightened her hold, but as she glanced down, she screamed. Scared out of her skin, she let go of the mirror.

Her entire being shook, and she stared at the mirror floating face up and flat in the air before her. The reflection showed the ceiling, but a moment before she'd seen a man in the glass. A young man with an angry scowl.

A hint of common sense told her that hadn't been possible. Testing that theory, she cautiously reached out and touched the handle again, only to pull her hand back when the image of the man appeared again.

"That's crazy," she whispered while pressing the hand that felt as if electricity had shot through it against the erratic beat of her heart. Its racing beat thudded against her chest, and a zing-zang tingling shot all the way to her toes.

Unable not to, Liz reached out and touched the mirror again with just the tip of one finger. And again. Watching the flashing image appear and disappear.

It wasn't until the fourth or fifth time that she realized the humming stopped when she touched the mirror and she heard a voice. Testing her ears, or perhaps her sanity, she tapped the mirror handle with her finger tip several times.

Yep, she heard a voice. Like a scratched CD skipping in and out. The image kept flashing in the mirror, too.

"Holy Hannah." Her entire being trembled, but with as much excitement as trepidation. Drawing a deep breath to fortify her nerves, she grasped the mirror handle fully, half expecting it to electrocute her, or something along those lines.

"What the hell are you doing?"

Liz swallowed and forced her hold to remain on the mirror, image, angry shout, and all. "I can see you," she whispered. "And hear you."

"I can see and hear you, too," the voice said.

She let go of the mirror and waited a full minute, at least it felt that long. Her heart had certainly raced through sixty beats. "Can you hear me now?"

When nothing but a hum sounded, she grasped the mirror again.

"You," was the only word she heard.

"Could you see me, hear me, when I wasn't touching the mirror?"

"I just told you, yes."

The reflection in the mirror grew clearer, and despite the frown pulling his brows tight above the bridge of his nose, his eyes weren't inhospitable.

A friendly ghost? She could hope.

She glanced up, trying to figure out where he was standing, where his head might be. There was no way to know how tall he was, and it seemed odd to talk to thin air, so maybe the mirror was better. She looked back at the reflection. "I can only see and hear you when I'm holding the mirror."

"What are you talking about? What do you mean?"

She searched for an answer, but her thoughts stopped as a complete head to toe man gradually appeared directly in front of her.

"Holy shit." Her hand slipped from the mirror.

The man disappeared.

She grabbed the mirror again and held her breath, hoping, praying. Slowly, he reappeared. Completely. Head to toe. Standing right before her.

All of him, not just a reflection in the mirror.

Her heart thudded so hard it affected her breathing. Gasping slightly, she repeated, "Holy shit."

He was dressed in turn of the century clothing like she'd seen hanging in the elaborately carved free-standing wardrobe closet, complete with boots and a dusty hat. The little lines at the corners of his dark brown eyes said he was older than she originally thought, and he was looking at her as if she'd lost her mind. Maybe she had, for this couldn't be Rance Livingston. He'd been in his eighties when he died. She was a terrible guesser of age but went with late twenties, early thirties for her ghost.

Her ghost. She pressed her free hand to the fluttering in her stomach. She was standing next to a ghost. A real live ghost. Or a real dead one—however it worked. And all she could do was guess his age? How crazy was that? How crazy is this?

Dang, he even had whiskers. Well, the shadow of them. He was handsome for a ghost. That thought caused her heart to skip a beat as a unique vibration shot through her.

Ignoring it and stopping her appraisal before it went any lower—again—than the unbuttoned top of his shirt, she released the mirror to test her theory one last time.

He completely disappeared. Instantly. No fading. No lingering mist.

"Wow," she whispered. "This is mind-boggling."

The hum echoed again, and Liz took a hold of the handle. He was back. And frowning. Questioning one more thing, she said, "Let go of the mirror."

"Why? So you can steal it?"

"No." The warmth of a blush covered her cheeks. "So I can see something. Let go."

"What? See what?"

"Just let go," she insisted.

He disappeared, and the mirror grew slightly heavier as the other end of it tipped downward. She tightened her hold to keep from dropping it. Small, the mirror wasn't heavy, but the added weight was enough to say he'd been holding it up, along with her.

"Okay," she said. "Take a hold of the mirror again."

No hum sounded. No image appeared.

The hair on her arms and neck stood again. "Hello? Are you there? You can take a hold of the mirror again."

Nothing.

No image. No hum.

Had she imagined it all?

Surely not.

Her imagination wasn't that good.

She glanced around, searching to see if anything moved, floated. Turning back to the mirror, she looked into the glass, seeing only her own reflection.

She wobbled the mirror.

Nothing.

"Damn."

The mirror jiggled at the same time "Boo!" resounded in her ears and the image suddenly appeared.

Screeching, she dropped the handle.

Once she caught her breath and was assured her heart was still in her chest, she grabbed the handle floating before her. "That wasn't funny."

"I thought it was," he said, laughing.

She completely lost her breath all over again, this time because of his laughter, how young and alive it made him look. As his laughter died, she regained her ability to breathe while watching as a slightly lopsided grin settled on his lips.

Leave it to her to find a ghost with a sense of humor.

"You must love Halloween," she said.

"Not really."

"Don't get many trick or treaters, do you?" Without waiting for his response, she shook her head. "I can't believe I'm talking to a ghost."

He frowned and shook his head. "A ghost?"

"Yes, you're a ghost."

"No, I'm not."

"Yes, you are. That's why I can only see you, hear you, when I'm holding the mirror. That's odd, even for a ghost, I guess. But it's true, you're a ghost."

His frown had deepened, and his head tilted slightly as if pondering what she'd said completely.

After a few stilled moments, he shook his head. "You aren't seeing a ghost," he said. "I am."

"Nope," she insisted. "You're the ghost."

"I beg to differ. I'm very much alive."

"So am I."

"Oh, how I wish you were." Sadness filled his eyes. "I've missed you so much."

A tenderness ballooned around her heart, as unique and foreign as talking to a ghost was. "You can't have missed me," she said softly. "We've never met before."

Misery seemed to consume his entire face. "So you don't remember me?"

"Remember you?" The urge to take his hand struck her. Not only was that very unusual for her, it was impossible. She settled for shaking her head. "How could I remember you? I don't even know your name."

His eyes practically bore holes into hers for several long moments. He sighed then, a heavy, almost heart-wrenching sigh. "It's Rance. Rance Livingston."

"You can't be Rance Livingston," she said. "You're too young." Or could ghosts choose what age they wanted to be?

"Too young?"

"Yes, you died in nineteen sixty-six."

The weight of the mirror increased as he disappeared, and her heart stopped. "Don't, please! Please don't let go of the mirror."

He reappeared. "Nineteen sixty-six? That's sixty-five years from now. I'll be ninety-four. I sure as hell hope I'm dead by then."

There was no humor in his voice and none in his eyes either. "What year do you think it is?"

"It's nineteen-o-one," he said. "Everyone knows that."

She shook her head.

He frowned. "What year do you think it is?"

"Twenty-eighteen."

"Twenty-eighteen?" He stretched each syllable out.

"Yes, and I was born in nineteen-ninety." She had no idea why she chose to add that. Maybe because she'd never argued with a ghost before. Getting past that, she asked, "You're really Rance Livingston?"

"Yes, I am, And you certainly have an imagination. I'll give you that."

"No, I don't. You've been ambling around in this old house for so many years you don't know how long it's been."

He shook his head, but the hint of a smile on his face made her want to smile.

"Still think I'm a ghost, do you?"

"I know you're a ghost," she insisted.

He disappeared. The mirror was heavy again. She held it tight as the picture was lifted off the dresser and floated across the room, directly toward her. When it stopped before her face, a hum sounded.

"You have to hold the mirror," she reminded him.

The mirror grew light as he reappeared, picture in hand.

"Look at this," he said.

She didn't tell him she'd already examined the picture thoroughly before putting it in the box earlier. The frame was gorgeous, and pure silver she'd bet, but the picture inside was small and rather grainy, making the identification of the people impossible. "What about it?"

"That's you," he said. "And me. On our wedding day. Six months ago."

Liz's stomach fell to her toes. She let go of the

29

mirror, and leaving it and the picture floating in the air, took a step back. Attempting to collect herself, she shook her head. She hadn't found a humorous ghost; she'd found a delusional one. Then again, maybe all ghosts were delusional. They sort of had to be.

Cautiously, she reached out and gripped the picture, waiting for him to appear. He didn't, and she pulled the picture closer, feeling when he let go of it. Scanning the image, she concluded there might be a resemblance. Maybe. In size. The faces were so tiny it was impossible to tell. Considering it was on the dresser in his bedroom, he very well could be the man in the picture. Rance Livingston, but the woman wasn't her.

A wave of grief, or guilt, rose up inside her, as if she didn't want to have to tell him the truth. Sighing, she took a hold of the mirror again. "This isn't me," she explained as soon as he appeared. "This woman has long dark hair."

He took the picture and glanced between it and her several times. "You cut it."

"No." She clamped her lips shut and contemplated how to restate that. "I have it cut all the time. I've never worn it long."

"Why?"

"It's easier to take care of. It's—" Seriously? She was arguing with a ghost about her hair. This is beyond crazy.

The weight of the mirror increased at the same time he disappeared. She watched the picture float back to the dresser, where it was stationed perfectly amongst the other items. When the mirror didn't jostle as she expected, she glanced around the room. "Rance?"

Nothing. Not even a hum.

A wave of panic had her shouting, "Rance! Rance!"

The mirror grew light. "I'm here." He fully reappeared. "Sorry."

"Don't do that," she scolded as her heart settled down again. "Don't let go of the mirror."

"I don't understand that. I can see you whether I'm touching the mirror or not."

"There you have it," she said.

"Have what?"

"Proof that you're the ghost. Not me." Emotions weren't her thing, but logic always had been. "I can't hear or see you unless we're both holding the mirror."

A thoughtful expression overtook his face, and he nodded toward the window. "What did you see when you looked out that window?"

"Nothing." She changed her answer. "Other than the barn, corral, and my Mustang." Watching his frown growing again, she added, "And grass and gravel."

"You remember your horse, but not me?"

"My horse? I don't—" Understanding hit. He raised horses. "My Mustang is my car. Not a horse. Well, it does have horsepower, but not the four-legged kind."

He was frowning again and took a step. Her hold on the mirror increased.

"I won't let go," he said. "Come to the window with me."

They crossed the room side by side and each pulled back one of the old and sun-faded curtains as they gazed outside.

"Tell me what you see," he said.

"I already did. My car is in front of the house, on

the gravel. The barn is straight over there, along with the corral full of tall grass."

"There's no grass in the corral, there are a dozen horses in the one on the left, and one horse, a buckskin still saddled, is in the one on the right."

She glanced at his profile, noting the seriousness of his forward gaze, before glancing back out the window. "I only see one corral. On the left."

"How can that be?"

A shiver rippled her spine. "I don't know. Do you see my car? It's blue."

"A *blue* mustang?"

A flicker of hope lit up her insides. "Yes."

"A mustang is a horse," he said.

"And a car," she insisted. The idea he thought he was in nineteen-o-one hit her. The word car may not have been used then, other than train car. She wasn't certain when cars first became popular in Wyoming. "You know, an automobile, a horseless carriage. It's right there, just below us. It's blue."

"I don't see it," he said.

"You don't?"

"Nope."

"How can you not? It's—"

"I don't see it, Beth."

Everything before her eyes turned blurry, and her heart started to race. She'd had panic attacks. Each time she'd seen the old trunk in her foster parents' attic. The one they claimed she'd been draped over when rescuers had pulled her from the river as a child. Unlike when she'd seen the trunk, there wasn't the darkness or the gloom, but she was shaking and couldn't catch her breath. "I-I need to-to sit down."

"All right," he said gently. "This way."

The room started to spin, and her knees wobbled. Fearing the overwhelming panic that was sure to come, she whispered, "Don't let go of the mirror. Please."

"I won't."

They arrived at the bed, sitting down at the same time, and together lowered the mirror onto the quilt between them.

The strange swirling inside her wasn't as strong as she remembered. In fact, it had already eased considerably, and no panic squeezed her insides. Her vision cleared gradually. The room no longer spun, and it didn't hurt to breathe. She'd never recovered this quickly from a panic attack before. There hadn't been that many of such attacks, mainly because she avoided them at all costs. The few she'd had in the past were far more than enough.

"This is really strange," she whispered.

With his free hand, he removed his hat and ran his fingers through his dark brown hair. "Unbelievable."

Completely out of her norm, she wanted to giggle. A minute ago, she was about to pass out, now she wanted to laugh. How crazy was that? About as crazy as the pulse of electricity surging through her. She was sitting here talking to a ghost. A real flipping ghost. Totally unbelievable. She couldn't look at an old trunk without freaking out, but she could sit on a bed and converse with a ghost without so much as a shimmer of fear. She'd always been the odd duck, but come on. This was mind-boggling.

"So," she said, trying to get a grasp on things. "It's nineteen-o-one in your world right now."

"Yes, and it's twenty-eighteen in yours?"

"Yep," she said. "Pretty freaky, isn't it?"

He shifted slightly, angling to look at her. "That picture is small, but you look just like her, my wife, other than your hair. Hers was a lot longer, and not—not striped."

A brief giggle escaped. "They're called highlights." Women didn't have highlights put in their hair in nineteen-o-one, she was pretty certain of that. "They bleach certain strands."

"Bleach?"

She nodded.

"Why?"

"Why not?"

His baffled look made her grin. So did the craziness of all this. "To make us look prettier I guess."

"You sound like her, too, even your laugh. And your smile..." He closed his eyes for a moment. "Your smile. It's hers. But your eyes, they aren't quite the same. I—" He turned away.

Her heart trembled, going out to him, the hurt she saw in his eyes. "I'm sorry," she whispered. "But I'm not her. That would be completely impossible."

"And being a ghost isn't?"

She shrugged. As much as she wanted to comfort him—something she had little experience in—she couldn't lie. Not to him. "I'm not a ghost, Rance."

As he nodded solemnly, a great bout of sorrow rose up inside her.

"But I am," he said quietly.

She nodded. "I'm afraid so." She wasn't afraid, but she was sorry. Sorry for him. For his loss. For the wife he genuinely must have loved beyond all else.

They sat side by side, quietly, for several minutes.

She couldn't think of anything to say. She could sense his sadness, his loneliness, which made her heart ache like it never had before. Love was something she had absolutely no experience with. She couldn't even say she believed in love. At least not in the 'nothing but love matters' sort of way. There were a few people she'd grown fond of over the years, such as her foster parents and Vivi Anne, but that was about it. She'd truly never been struck with an overpowering emotion that filled her so completely nothing else mattered. That was train-wreck thinking at its core. Being that dedicated, that committed to something was destructive.

She had seen that. The world is full of people who love money, power, even other people to the point they became obsessed. They lie, cheat, even kill over that one thing they love. To her, that was evil at its finest.

Good grief. When had she become such a philosopher?

No, she wasn't a philosopher. She was a realist. And honest. Deep inside, at the very core of her soul, she'd experienced the pain, the all-consuming torture and fear of never seeing a loved one again. Although she couldn't remember, it had to have formed when her parents died and was the reason she chose not to care, not to love. Ever.

A shiver rippled along her skin as she glanced at the image in the mirror. Him. Seeing a ghost probably inspired all sorts of deep thinking for people and brought all sorts of insights to the surface. Seeing a ghost was a strange phenomenon. Unbelievably so.

Eventually, he turned back her way. "What did you mean about Cliff demolishing the place?"

"Cliff? I don't know a Cliff."

"Cliff Dixon. You were calling for Mr. Dixon—"

"Lou Dixon," she interrupted. "Not Cliff." As she said the name again, her conversation with Buzz filtered through all her crazy thoughts about love and ghosts. Buzz had said the sheriff back then had been Cliff Dixon, and Rance's friend. "Lou Dixon, and his cousin Nate inherited this place from their uncle Riley Dixon. I think Buzz said Riley was Cliff's grandson. Lou wasn't interested in demolishing the place, but his cousin Nate was, and evidently, Lou now agrees with Nate." She stopped herself from explaining how people thought the house was haunted. By him. "That's why I'm here, to appraise the antiques, anything of value. That's what Buzz said, anyway."

"Who's Buzz?"

Explaining Buzz, Vivi Anne, and *Here for Now,* the antique store Vivi Anne owned would be more information than he needed right now. She shrugged. "Buzz is a friend who told me about this place."

He eyed her suspiciously, as if he knew she wasn't telling him everything.

"This place is my home," he said. "I live here."

"Not in twenty-eighteen," she whispered.

Chapter Four

Maybe he'd lost his mind. It happened. People went insane for many reasons. That's why they had asylums. Surely he would have felt that coming on. One didn't just go from sane to insane. Did they?

One didn't think his wife was a ghost either.

He rubbed his forehead and his temples. A good case of the jitters had him wanting to get up, but he'd promised he wouldn't let go of the mirror. And wouldn't. She'd gone white a few minutes ago, over by the window. As if she'd seen a ghost or something.

Maybe she had.

Him.

That made no sense. He wasn't dead. She was.

Beth was.

Aw, hell. He wasn't prepared to let that thought in, may never be, no matter how many strange women entered his home.

But this wasn't a strange woman. Despite the few minor differences, she was Beth. How could that be? People didn't all of a sudden have a few minor differences.

"This Lou," he said, chasing aside ghostly thoughts for a minute. "You said he's Cliff's relation?"

She pinched her lips together as she nodded. That was a classic Beth move. She always tried to make things sound simpler. As if telling the entire truth would take too long. Not that she'd ever lied to him. Not a once. Something told him this gal—this woman who looked too much like Beth to make him comfortable—wasn't either. Because she was Beth.

Stopping his mind from continuing to turn on that wheel, he asked, "A feller named Buzz told you about this Lou?"

"Yes. Lou and Nate. They're cousins."

"Why did this Buzz tell you about them?"

She sighed. "Actually, Buzz called Vivi Anne, a friend of mine, about the antiques here. Vivi Anne couldn't drive down to Cody because she had to meet a guy from Helena, so I drove down. That's when Buzz said they, Lou and Nate, inherited this place."

He was far more interested in her than anyone inheriting his place, now or a hundred years from now. "Drove down from where?"

"Billings."

His heart jolted even though he'd had a gut feeling that's what she'd say. This was Beth. Maybe she hit her head during the accident and couldn't remember. The accident had been two months ago. He'd gone up there as soon as he'd heard about the accident and searched the banks of the river. Others had been there too. Her mother and father and sister. Strangers had set up camp like he had, searching for their loved ones. Maybe one of those people found her, took care of her, cut her hair. She could have been unconscious for an extended amount of time and when she awoke, couldn't remember things, but knew this was home.

He sighed. And maybe he was a ghost. Hell, none of this made sense.

Her brows pulled together as if she was trying to

remember something—just like Beth used to.

His heartbeat kicked up its pace.

"Cliff was the sheriff, or is, in your time, right?"

Trying to decide if any portion his rambling thoughts made sense, Rance absently answered, "Yes, Cliff's the sheriff." He stopped shy of asking if she remembered Cliff.

"Okay, so, I think Buzz said Cliff's grandson was Riley. He said so many names it was hard to keep track, but I know he said that you left this place to someone named Dixon, I think it was Riley, along with enough money to pay for its upkeep."

He hadn't made any plans of leaving this place to anyone, but, without Beth, without a family, Cliff seemed like the obvious person—when the time came. Beth would have known that. Cliff would know it too. Shortly after he'd returned from Billings, Cliff had ridden out. Not in the mood to see anyone, he hadn't been very friendly, but that hadn't stopped Cliff from making him sit down and eat the food his wife Nan had sent out. Cliff had also pointed out that if the things had been different, that if he'd been the one to die instead of Beth, that he'd have expected people to step in and help her. Bring her food. Make sure she was getting along.

Cliff had been right. There wasn't an ounce of doubt inside him that he'd have expected people to help Beth, or in the fact that they would have.

"You never wanted this place sold," she whispered, "in case your wife returned."

Rance held his breath at a ping that stung near his heart. He wasn't ready to consider the option of Beth never returning, and never would be. Angered at the thought, he asked, "What do you know about my wife returning?"

"I don't. Buzz said she'd died in an accident and that you didn't believe it. That you waited for her to return until the day you died."

Beth would have known he'd wait for her forever. And ever.

"So, back to your ranch," she said. "Riley left it to Lou and Nate, along with money for the upkeep, but, I suspect, considering it's been over fifty years since you died, they've decided to sell it. Lou is interested in learning how much the antiques out here are worth." She shrugged. "I don't know about Nate. I haven't met him, and I only met Lou a short time ago when he unlocked the gate for me, but my first impression says money means a lot to him."

"Oh?" Despite the situation, and the ideas still floating around inside his head, he found himself as charmed by her as much now as he'd ever been. Beth had always laid a lot of faith in first impressions. She'd told him the day they'd met that he'd marry her. He'd laughed at the idea. That day. A week later, he knew she was right. That he would marry her. And had a few months later. In January. Beth hadn't been willing to wait any longer.

Drawing in a breath that caught in his lungs, he turned his focus back to this woman. "Why do you say that?"

"A vibe I got. He drives a brand-new Camaro and wears high-buck clothes. That tells me he knows what money is. And he likes it."

"Everyone knows what money is," he pointed out. "What's a vibe? And a Camaro?"

"A vibe is a feeling, like a gut feeling when you

know something despite what people say, and a Camaro is a car, like my Mustang, but it's a Chevy instead of a Ford."

He had his own gut feeling, and it said this was Beth. She just didn't know it and was making up a wild tale. He bit the inside of his cheek in an attempt to keep his heart from thudding right out of his chest as his gaze wandered over her from head to toe. Stopping briefly on that tight-fitting top. If he let his eyes linger too long, he'd regret it. "Is that what you're wearing? High-buck clothes?"

"Jeans and a tank-top?" She shook her head. "Not hardly. These are from the farm store."

"Webster doesn't carry things like that."

"Webster?" She frowned. "I've never heard of Webster's. These are from *Ted's Farm Store*. I like shopping there. Can't beat the quality or the price."

A tingle made the hair on his neck stand. Beth had said those exact words when he'd driven that set of mustangs up to Montana for her father to buy for her mother. Her father had seen one of Bill's shows and wanted a set of matching mustangs for his wife. It had been the best sale of his life. He'd gotten more than money out of those horses, he'd gotten a wife. Cautious, knowing she'd argue about him being a ghost again, he asked, "You have family in Billings?"

"No," she said. "I don't have family anywhere."

Her answer surprised him until it clicked that if she's forgotten him, she must have forgotten her family as well. And Webster. The shopkeeper was as charmed by her as everyone else. Including him from the moment he'd laid eyes on her. He was going to have to go slow with her this time around. Like a two-year-old filly right off the range. They needed time for things to become familiar and so would she. In fact, he'd even play along with her ridiculous tale for a bit, if that's what it took.

Having lost the pebbles of the tale she'd laid out, he asked, "Who is this Lou again?"

"Um, let's see," she said, tapping her chin, "he would be Cliff's great-grandson."

"Great-grandson."

She nodded. "Yes, great-grandson."

Cliff had two sons, Ralph and Randy, so it was safe to say that someday he'd have a grandson and then a great-grandson. "So this Lou, he wants to demolish my house?"

"Not Lou." Turning her head, she scanned the room slowly. When her eyes landed on him again, sorrow filled her face. "But Nate does." She shrugged one shoulder. "I guess Lou does, too. Nate changed his mind."

He lifted his hat off the bed and plunked it on his head.

"Where are you going?"

He grinned. Beth always knew he was leaving when he put his hat on. Unable not to, for it's what he'd always done, he winked at her. "To stop him." Whoever this Lou is. Sitting around was not his way. Doing was. He stood.

She leaped to her feet beside him. "You let go of the mirror! You promised you wouldn't."

He'd forgotten that, how she couldn't see or hear him when they both weren't touching the mirror, but he didn't take a hold of the handle right away. If this was Beth, as he knew it was, it didn't make any sense that she couldn't see him. He could see her with his eyes closed. Her vision anyway.

His gaze roamed over her again. Those blue pants, that tiny pink top that didn't have any sleeves, the golden skin of her arms, her neck. He snapped his gaze up to hers but couldn't keep it there. That shirt was so tight it molded the shape of her to precise perfection. Memories of exploring every curve and crevice of her body sent blood surging through his veins.

"Rance Livingston, you take a hold of this mirror this instant."

He wiped a hand over his grin, and then, wondering, he reached out to touch her. His fingers slid right through her arm. Disappointed, but not ready to give up, he tried her shoulder.

She didn't even flinch. Probably because he hadn't touched her. Couldn't. Damn, but this was the strangest thing.

"This instant. You hear me?"

Having to try just once more, he let his hand hover close, lowering it slowly over her shoulder.

A scowl formed on her face. "Rance?"

His fingers tingled, but inside, he knew the sensation was in his mind only. His hand hadn't touched her. It couldn't. Despite how real she appeared, there was nothing to touch. Nothing real about her.

"If you don't take a hold of this mirror, I'll—"

Grabbing the mirror handle, he asked, "You'll what?"

He laughed at how she jumped and again when she stomped a foot.

"Don't do that," she ordered.

"What?" Whether he could touch her or not,

whether she was real or not, he hadn't felt this alive in weeks, months, and could only credit it to her. Right down to the saucy little look she gave him. Ghost or not, there was no way this wasn't Beth. His Beth. She just didn't remember it. He'd have to change that.

"Don't disappear on me like that," she said.

That was a problem he'd have to solve. The mirror thing.

"And just how do you plan on stopping Lou or Nate? Or both of them?" she asked.

He wanted to rub his head again but knew it wouldn't help. He had no idea who these fellas were but was going to find out. Watching her nibble on her bottom lip wasn't helping him either. When Beth did that, she was thinking of something she wasn't sure how to say.

Could these Nate and Lou fellas have found her after the accident and held her hostage or something, telling her crazy things, like the wrong year and that they were related to Cliff? Maybe that Buzz person had been with them. That was enough to irritate him. Knowing she'd been alone with three men.

His mind gnawed on that like a dog did a bone, and seeing her chew on her lip made him want to know what she didn't want to tell him. "Spit it out."

Her eyes narrowed, which made her look enticingly cute instead of irritated. "Don't snap at me," she said. "You are the one who let go of the mirror."

"You're right, I did, and I apologize for that."

She nodded her chin. "Thank you. Apology accepted."

Damn it, this was Beth. She always made him apologize and then responded with those exact words.

44

Another sensation tickled his spine. There was now a hint of cunning in her glare. She'd always been shrewd when it came to getting what she wanted. Clever, too.

"What are you thinking?" he asked.

"Maybe you could start haunting this place in twenty-eighteen" she said quietly. "That might scare Lou and Nate away. Anyone else snooping around, too. Most people are afraid of ghosts."

He stopped shy of telling her he wasn't a ghost, but the notion that she was had made inroads in his mind. She wasn't completely his Beth; it was more like Beth was inside her and needed to be coaxed out. Was that because she was Beth's ghost? He'd need time to come to grips with that, and what could be done about it. What could be done about being married to a ghost? Letting her believe he agreed with her might be the route to take. At least for now.

"I'd need your help," he said. Whether he could touch her or not, his next step was figuring out a way to keep her from disappearing again.

A hint of the glimmer that used to live in Beth's eyes nonstop appeared for a brief instant. The glimmer quickly disappeared, but a smile remained on her lips. "Of course, I'll help."

In the midst of sinking deeper into bizarre thoughts of living with a ghost, and how that could possibly be, it was a moment before he recognized a sound drifting in through the window. No more impressed with the interruption than he'd been for the past several weeks, he grumbled, "Someone's here."

She frowned but didn't say a word as they walked to the window together. There, as they both once again looked out the opening, she said, "I don't see anyone."

"There's a wagon pulling up to the house," he explained.

"Who's in it?"

"Nan Dixon and another woman." Disgust rumbled across his chest. Nan meant well, but her relentless visits had long grown old. She'd said much the same thing to him as Cliff had, that if instead of Beth dying, he had, Beth would have been heart-broken and would need friends. He'd agreed with that. But hadn't agreed with the notion he needed friends showing up at all time of the day. Still didn't.

"Who is Nan Dixon? Wait, is she related to-to Cliff?"

He stepped back, bringing her with him. "Yes, she's Cliff's wife."

She stretched her neck, attempting to see out the window again. That too was Beth. His stomach clenched. He could handle a ghost, but Nan was as no-nonsense as a rock.

"You stay here, I'll be right back." A wallop of fear washed over him, making him wonder if she'd disappear when he let go of the mirror. No, it was the other way around. He could see her without the mirror, she just couldn't see him. That, and Nan shouting his name had him saying, "Stay away from the window."

He let loose of the mirror and watched how she glanced around, as if searching for him. Reluctantly, he turned and headed for the doorway. Then he raced down the steps and through the house, anxious to get rid of Nan as soon as possible.

Nan and her companion, a young woman with blonde curls poking out from beneath a calico bonnet, had both climbed out of the wagon and were walking toward the house. He let the screen door slam shut behind him in his hurry onto the porch.

"There you are. I knew you were nearby; your horse is still saddled in the corral." Nan grinned as her keen eyes landed on his face. "You look more like yourself today. There's color in your face. And I'm glad to see you're using the house." Her gaze went upward, to the second story. "Beth would like that."

He waited for the wave of anger that engulfed him every time someone mentioned what Beth would or wouldn't like. When nothing came, he followed Nan's gaze and glanced up, but the porch roof prevented him from seeing the upstairs window. Bounding down the four steps in a single stride, he asked, "What brings you out here today?" He shot another glance toward his bedroom window. The shut window. The curtains were closed, too.

He hoped that was because Beth had listened to his request to stay away from the window, but the eerie sensation rippling his spine said it wasn't. An urgency to get back inside filled him. "I've got a lot of work to do today, Nan. Tell Cliff I said h—"

"Rance Livingston," Nan snapped. "I've never seen you so rude."

He pulled his gaze off the window and turned. Nan looked as ruffled as a grouse that had just been rousted off her nest. He knew the feeling.

"I just introduced you to my niece, and you totally ignored—"

"Hello," he said, and flinched slightly. Interrupting her wouldn't set any better than not hearing her make the introduction. He'd been too busy thinking about Beth to hear anything. Still, he held out a hand toward the blonde woman.

"Hello, I'm Cindy Franklin," the woman took his hand delicately. "I'm very pleased to make your acquaintance. Uncle Cliff speaks so highly of you."

He nodded, pulled his hand out of hers and, after a brief glance over his shoulder—toward the upstairs window again—he turned his attention back to Nan. "As I was saying, I've got—"

"What? A cake in the oven?" she asked. "You've been staring at the house since you walked out the door." As straightforward as ever, Nan hitched up her skirt. "Let's go inside then, so you can see to whatever it is."

"No," he said so abruptly and fast Nan stopped dead in her tracks. He took her elbow. "There's nothing in the house. I need to get back to my horses. One's still saddled and standing in the sun."

"It moved to the shade of the barn," she stated dryly.

He pulled up a grin. "Smart horse."

Nan spun around. "Come along, Cindy."

"Thanks for stopping out," he said, prepared to walk Nan to the wagon.

"We aren't leaving," Nan said. "Not yet. We came out to conduct a bit of business and aren't leaving until we do so."

Getting rid of Nan when she didn't want to leave was like getting rid of small pox. He remembered that from the days she'd ventured out to help Beth put up wall paper and sew curtains. After a brief glance at the still closed window, he huffed out a sigh. "What sort of business?"

"Cindy will be staying with us for a while, and

therefore, we will need another horse." Nan was now marching beside him toward the barn. "One trained to pull. Cindy will use my old Sunday buggy when needed. As you know, with the boys at hand, I much prefer the wagon."

"One trained for riding, too," the niece said. "I so enjoy a ride in the countryside. Don't you, Mr. Livingston?"

He didn't answer. His gaze had gone over his shoulder to the upstairs window again. He sure wished that curtain was floating on the breeze.

"Cindy hails from down near Cheyenne," Nan said. "My sister's daughter. Cliff suggested and I agree a nice, gentle horse will be best."

He didn't miss the cool edge of Nan's voice. Or the heavy sigh that came from the niece. He let his gaze slip from the house as they neared the barn.

"One that can pull my buggy," Nan said firmly. "One of the boys will accompany Cindy on all of her outings."

Nan didn't pawn her sons off on anyone, and that meant she would be sending them with her niece to keep the girl out of trouble. Which was information he didn't need. Women were a lot like horses. One look told him which ones would be more trouble than they were worth. He'd already gotten that sense from the younger woman. The two of them looked a bit alike, with blonde hair and blue eyes, but the low-cut neckline of Cindy's dress said more than words ever could.

"Most of the horses are spoken for," he said, pointing to the full corral. "But I can spare one." Buffalo Bill's order didn't need to be filled for a few weeks, but even if that hadn't been the case, the horse he was thinking of wouldn't work for Bill's shows. It was too old and slow.

"I want that one."

They'd neared the corral, and he followed the general direction of Cindy's pointing finger. The blood around his heart warmed as his gaze landed on a liver and white paint. It was a little mustang mare with more spirit than horses twice her size. Just like Beth. The two of them had made a fitting pair, as he'd known they would when he'd given that horse to his new wife as her welcome-to-your-new-home gift. Beth had named her Esmeralda, and he'd laughed, saying that was a hell of a name for a horse. Esmeralda it was though, and there was a saddle he was making just for her in the barn. The tree was done, and the leather stretched, but he was still working on the tooling. Had been. He hadn't worked on the saddle in over two months.

Unable to stop himself, he glanced once more at his bedroom window. Still shut. The curtains still closed. This time he grinned, recalling how she'd called her automobile a mustang. Horseless carriages, as some referred to them, were becoming more and more popular out east, but he wasn't about to place any bets they'd make it this far west. Too much trouble, that's what he'd heard about them, and as unreliable as coyotes.

"Mr. Livingston, did you hear me?"

He turned to Cindy and ignored the way she batted her eyelashes. She could do headstands for all he cared. Since the moment he'd met Beth, every other woman had dulled in comparison, and they forever would. She'd sent his spirit into a whirlwind back then and had done so again today.

"That horse isn't for sale." Esmeralda had missed Beth as much as he had and would be happy to see her home. Almost as happy as him. With that thought, he waved at the barn door. "The one I'll sell you is in here."

"In the barn? I don't want some old nag."

"Cindy," Nan snapped.

If he'd had a mind to care, he may have wondered what was behind the niece staying with Nan and Cliff. It certainly smelled like trouble, but he had his own quandary to contend with right now. That closed window was eating at him like a festered sliver. "Horse isn't an old nag." He opened the barn door.

"Horse? It doesn't have a real name?" Cindy asked with a bit of arsenic in her tone.

Because the back door leading into the corral was open, he waited until both women entered and then closed the barn door behind them. "Horse is her name. She's never needed another one."

Just as he'd known she'd be, the big brown mare was standing in a stall. She was smart. It was hot outside. Grabbing a rope hanging amongst many on the wall, he gestured for the women to stand back. Patting Horse on her rump, he walked along her side while loosening the slipknot in the rope and then slid it over her neck. The animal backed out of the stall with little more than a pat on her shoulder and followed him back to where the women stood.

"I'll settle up with Cliff next time I see him," he told Nan while gesturing toward the barn door." In truth, Horse would be no more than a loan. The niece wouldn't be staying long. Nan wouldn't put up with any shenanigans, and the spiteful blonde was full of them. It didn't take her opening her mouth again for him to know that.

"She's brown," the niece snipped. "A dull brown horse."

"Horse is a good animal," he said, purely in defense of the horse. He couldn't care less how the girl felt. "She'll do anything you ask. If you treat her fairly." He added the last bit with a touch of warning.

"She'll be treated fairly," Nan said. "I personally guarantee that."

He shut the barn door once they'd all excited and then led Horse to the wagon. There he tied the lead rope to the tailgate.

"Good seeing you, Nan," he said, taking extra time with the knot. The niece was standing next to the wagon, obviously awaiting assistance in climbing aboard. He wasn't about to play gentleman to the likes of her. Not when Beth was inside his house. He was beyond itching to get back in there himself.

Nan didn't miss much, and having already climbed aboard the wagon, ordered, "Climb up, Cindy. Rance is busy, and we've taken up enough of his time."

He tipped his hat in farewell. "Tell Cliff I said hello."

"I will, and don't worry about Horse," she said, gathering up the reins. "She'll be well-cared for."

"I don't have a worry one about that." He slapped the animal on the rump when the matching pair pulling the wagon stepped forward.

He waited, though it practically killed him, until the wagon had turned about and rolled beneath the long board nailed to the tall posts marking the entrance to the yard before he made a mad dash for the house.

His feet slid to a stop, so did his heart, even before the screen door had slammed shut behind him. He didn't need to go upstairs. The overwhelming emptiness inside him said Beth wasn't there.

Not even her ghost.

Not upstairs.

Not downstairs.

Not anywhere.

Chapter Five

Mere seconds after Rance faded into thin air right before her eyes, Liz heard gravel crunching. She moved to peer out the window and half expected to see a wagon. That, of course, was crazy. The double-cab Dodge pick-up was much more feasible, and more disappointing. She couldn't be certain but had a good idea the man climbing out the driver's door must be Lou's cousin, Nate.

Of course, I'll help. Had she really said that? She'd helped people in the past—she'd worked in customer service for seven years—but when Rance had asked, or his ghost had asked, she'd felt something. Inside. Had answered without a thought. And had meant it. She would help him.

She pulled the window down and closed the curtains. Nate probably wasn't any more likable than Lou—who had been about as appealing as day old pizza stuck to the bottom of the box. Some men had a lot to learn about sex appeal. Especially those who thought they owned it but didn't. She'd spent seven years fending off a boss who had acted as if he'd been made for women to love. He'd been wrong. Not only did she not believe in love, men who tried to play off other's emotions disgusted her to the core. She had no doubt she could put both Lou Dixon and his cousin Nate firmly in their place if they tried barking up that tree.

She replaced the mirror on the dresser, glass side down after a final check showed nothing but her image, and then put the century old copy of the *Ladies Home Journal* magazine she'd been reading back on the table beside the bed. With a sigh, she picked up the now empty crate and crossed the room.

Sex appeal was so overrated. Respect was where attraction began. Self-respect. A man who honored himself and treated others in the same manner. That was far more important than sex appeal any day. How the hell did she know all that? She turned and scanned the room one last time. Guess how didn't matter. She did know and must have never realized it before.

Rance had self-respect. Even as a ghost that came through.

A shiver had Liz pausing on the stair steps and glancing around. "Rance?"

There was no hum in the air, no feeling that someone was watching her. Actually, the house had that long-lost empty feeling. She had felt it when she'd first walked through the door.

Had she really seen a ghost? Talked to one? Or had her passion for antiques finally gotten the best of her?

No. She'd seen Rance. Some form of him. And seeing it had opened something inside her. An intuition of sorts, one that somehow had broadened her perception. Was that even possible? Could seeing a ghost bring out a person's thoughts about love and men? A person who had never even cared enough about such things to question them?

Liz shook her head slightly, just to clear her thoughts and hopefully get her mind back on track as she continued to the ground floor.

The crate was once again beside the old stove in the kitchen—an exact duplicate of the stove that had caught her attention the first time she'd walked into the antique store and met Vivi Anne—when the screen door was pulled open as wide as it could go. She stopped herself from saying that would ruin the spring as she turned about to meet Cousin Nate. It wasn't her door, so why should she care about the spring?

He strolled through the doorway, and Liz held her breath against the ire tightening her neck muscles as the door bounced against the frame to bang, not once, but twice. Everything old, even screen doors and their springs, should be appreciated and treasured. That was simply respect. Everything old had a story to tell. Such reasoning might make her an odd duck in today's disposable world, but she didn't mind. It was who she was and had long ago come to grips with that.

As Nate stopped just inside the door, she glanced around, half hoping to be able to detect a hum. There wasn't one, but that didn't stop her from silently telling Rance this would be a good time to start haunting the twenty-first century. The way Nate eyed the room told her he didn't appreciate a thing about this house or the stories it could tell.

He had on a black T-shirt and black jeans, which had to have come from the same store where Lou shopped. Expensive and a size too small if you asked her. A black cowboy hat covered a good portion of his face, and his boots had silver toe tips that were as shiny as the chrome wheels on the big truck he'd parked outside the door.

Letting out a sigh, for Rance was certainly nowhere around, she took a step forward. She wasn't afraid of Nate but did get an immediate dislike. Much like she had with Lou. Much like she had with most every man she'd ever met.

"So what did you find, sweetheart?" he asked, without any sort of introduction. "Enough jing to make me sing?"

His laugh included a wink that increased her disgust. Both he and his cousin could be considered handsome by some, but that was all she'd give either of them.

"I'm Liz Baxter," she said, letting her expression tell him she wasn't impressed. "I assume you are Nate." She almost said Dixon but wasn't sure if that was his last name or not. It was Lou's, and Buzz had said they were cousins, but that didn't mean Nate had the same last name.

"Sure am. Nate Dixon."

His grin flashed bleached teeth. The kind that came from a dentist office, not a blue box from the drug store.

"And I know who you are. Lou called me, said you were out here. Thought I'd stop by, see what you found and what it's worth."

She drew in a breath to calm her irritation. "There are a lot of quality antiques here," she said honestly. "But I haven't had time to place a value on any of them."

He pulled a cell phone out of the back pocket of his jeans—which was amazing considering how tight they were—and glanced at the display.

"You've been here an hour and a half," he said, replacing the phone. "What have you been doing all that time if not putting a value on things?"

"I was doing a walk through." That had been her plan, until she'd espied the old magazine and encountered a ghost. Of course the stove had been the first thing to gander her attention, and then the items on the dresser. That's when she'd returned to the kitchen for the crate, to gather a few things to research back at her motel room this evening.

That wouldn't be happening now. A sense of gut-wrenching betrayal soured her insides at the thought of removing anything from the house.

Waving a hand at the area in general, she said, "I'll need a lot more time, several days at least."

"Days?" He lifted a brow. "We don't have that kind of time." Leaning one hand on the door frame, he tapped a toe. "I have a pretty full agenda right now, darling. This place is just one of my projects."

She was no man's sweetheart or darling and would appreciate telling him so, yet she would have to step gingerly. He could easily call in someone else to appraise things. Someone who might not take to Rance as easily as she had. Or vise-versa.

Speaking of ghosts, she thought. *Come out, come out, wherever you are.*

Still no hum. No goose bumps prickling her arms. No thudding of her heart.

Liz sighed. "Well, this project as you call it, is going to take me days. Whether you have the time or not."

His lifted brow was saying she could convince him, with certain offerings, something she had no intention of ever doing. He sincerely thought he had the upper hand. Delusional fool. She'd fended off far better men over the years. Those in cowboy hats as well as those in suits and ties. And she'd spent the last seven years managing the customer service department of a cell phone company that didn't give a rat's ass about its customers, yet she'd had to pretend that Cell One had.

Wrapping her brain around how she could use that, she said, "I believe you have several very valuable items here. Unique, one of a kind items, but I need time to examine them, research them, and find a buyer for them."

"I thought you were the buyer." He walked toward the old wooden kitchen table and chair set.

They were elaborately carved and the buffet along the far wall matched the table and chairs, adding value to the set. Everything in the house looked so untouched, practically unused. She flinched inwardly when he pulled a chair out and set one foot in the center of the seat.

"I, or Vivi Anne, the dealer I work for, may buy some items, but in all honesty, you have more here than we can afford." Liz was not only looking for a way to buy time, stroking his already overly inflated ego was necessary. She was being honest, too. Every item in this house would be considered an antique. Added up, she and Vivi Anne didn't have that kind of money to spend on inventory.

Nate drummed four fingers on his knee. "I don't need the money that bad, you know. Neither does Lou. We just thought we'd help Buzz out by letting him broker a deal for a few things. He doesn't get paid much working at that tourist trap he loves so much, and his health isn't the best."

Plying on her sense of benevolence would get him

nowhere, but she wasn't in the mood to tell him that. Never would be in a mood to tell him anything about herself.

"It's my understanding that you've wanted to tear the place down for some time, while Lou wanted it preserved," she said.

He chuckled. "If he says so."

Although she had no desire to defend either cousin, she said, "Lou didn't, Buzz did."

His bellow of laughter echoed off the walls. "That's because Lou's afraid of this old place. Swears he saw Rance watching him out the window one time. We used to have to mow the place when we were younger. I told him I saw old Rance once. Just to keep him scared." He laughed again as he glanced around. "Had some fun times out here as a teenager." He snapped his fingers. "But never could get a girl to venture inside with me."

His actions disgusted her as much as his words. A girl would have to have the scruples of a self-imposed socialite with their own TV reality show to go anywhere with him.

"Lou wanted to sell the entire place to Buzz. The house that is, have it moved into town as part of the tourist trap, but Buzz said it was too valuable. That the non-profit that runs his place couldn't afford it. I suspect it's because of old Rance's connection to Buffalo Bill. The town still thrives on that connection. Old Bill made the entire world believe America was full of cowboys." He laughed. "People still believe that's all Wyoming is made of."

The big museum in downtown Cody that she'd driven past, the one that brought in tourists by the thousands, proved people enjoyed the legend of Buffalo Bill Cody. She had a poster from one of his shows. Had been drawn to it, and because it fit in her budget and apartment better than the stove, she'd bought it from Vivi Anne at the grand opening of *Here for Now*. Still not willing to fall into whatever kind of trap Nate was attempting to set, she shrugged. And called his bluff. "Well, if you want top dollar for the things here, I'll need more time. If you don't need the money, pack everything up and give it to Buzz. It'll help his non-profit, and it'll be off your hands."

Nate frowned, but she was sure the brim of his hat hid the dollar signs dancing in his eyes.

"Top dollar?"

"There are some unique things here." She hadn't seen anything that was as valuable as she was making things sound, but he didn't need to know that. Not right now.

"How much time?" he asked.

Appreciating how he was considering the bait she dangled in front of him, she took a moment to think. During her tour down the center of town earlier today, she'd counted numerous antique and pawn shops. Considering what Buzz had said about the place being haunted, she wondered if the cousins had contacted other shop owners, but no one had been interested because the items were from Rance's place. The local haunted house. That was plausible, but in reality, not that many people believed in ghosts, or were afraid of them. However, being connected to a local legend could add to the value of the items.

Either way, she said, "I can't say how long it will take for sure. Finding the right buyer in order to get you the maximum price may take weeks, but in the end, it would be worth it." In the end, she might be able to buy enough time to save the place from being burned down. It certainly wouldn't hurt either of these cousins to just let Rance go on waiting for his wife. Then again, at the rate he was aging, that could take centuries.

She paused as that thought took hold. Centuries. The place wouldn't be left alone that long. That was for sure. She might save it from being burned down next week, but what about next year, or the year after? These cousins wouldn't indefinitely put off demolishing the buildings or selling the property.

Her own mind made her pause. What was she thinking? She wasn't here to save anything from being burned down or to preserve the place so Rance could go on living in it. Ghosts don't need their own houses? Do they?

"Why are you in such a hurry to get rid of everything?"

Nate shrugged his bulky shoulders. "Don't need any of it, and this here is a prime piece of property. The fact it's ten miles from town makes it even more attractive to some." Leaning forward, he set both hands on his knee. "Tourists, coming to see Buffalo Bill's Museum or heading on in to Yellow Stone, is how money comes into Cody. I have a buyer interested in this place. Thinking about a resort. A big hotel with a golf course in the summer and snowmobile trails in the winter." He waggled a brow. "Could be a gold mine for the right person."

"Why don't you build it yourself then?" she asked, already knowing he didn't have enough ambition for that. He was a wait on me kind of person.

"I don't have the time." He dropped his foot to the floor. "I've got other irons in the fire."

I'm sure you do, she said to herself. From the moment she'd seen Lou, and now Nate, she knew the kind of men they were. They type who liked talking about themselves but didn't like getting their hands dirty. She doubted either of them worked. Had a real job. They'd lived off family money from the day they'd been born and would continue to until they died. Buzz had told her about that. How they both had inherited plenty.

Having no family whatsoever, that rubbed her wrong. Even if she'd had a family, her thoughts would still be along the same lines. She'd been called old-fashioned her entire life because she believed differently than most. She didn't own a credit card—believed if she couldn't buy it with cash; she didn't need it, and also believed everyone should be responsible for themselves. Dependency was a fault. And a sign of weakness.

Despite what she assumed both Lou and Nate thought, their money and looks didn't make them as desirable as they thought they were. Not like Rance. Ghost or not, he was a real man. A self-made man. Reliable. Honest. Trustworthy. And handsome. Besides his thickly lashed dark eyes and black hair that was just enough on the long side, he had a ruggedness about him that was adorable. And sweet. Perhaps debonair even. Bottom line, Rance was eye-candy.

Serious eye-candy. A candy connoisseur's dream. A chocolate bar, dipped in a chocolate fountain, covered with caramel—Sheesh, what had gotten in to her? She barely had a sweet tooth, let alone an obsession. Leave it to her. The first time she'd ever been drawn to a man, he was a ghost.

Or was he?

Maybe this was all a dream.

"Texas, Florida, New York."

No, it wasn't a dream. Nate was still talking and giving her a headache. People didn't have headaches in their dreams. She had no idea what Nate was talking about, so faking it, she pulled up a smile. "I see."

"Takes up all my time," he continued. "Had to sell off the other family places, too. There's only so much lawn a man can mow." He shifted as he pretended to re-tuck the bottom of his shirt into his jeans. "Or pay to have mowed."

She waited until his preening was over. "In my opinion, you don't want to move too quickly here."

He tilted his head back and stared as if waiting for more.

"It would be in your best interest, moneywise, to let me catalog everything," she explained. "It might take a bit of time, but it will be worth it in the end."

He remained silent while his eyes roamed the room. "Doesn't this place give you the creeps?" he asked. "Being so neat and clean without being lived in for decades?"

She walked over to the stove and rested both hands on the smooth cast-iron top. "No. Does it you?"

He huffed out a fake laugh. "No. I started some of those rumors."

"About it being haunted?"

He glanced around before answering and rocked on his heels. "Yes."

Liar. "According to Buzz, that rumor is older than

you." She gave him a solid once over gaze. "Rance died in the nineteen sixties."

His brief grimace said he didn't appreciate her discounting him. Lifting his chin, he gave her a mocking grin. "Folks have said the place was haunted before Rance died. That his wife haunted it. That's why he lived in the old log cabin rather than the house. Right up until his death. He died in that cabin. In an old iron cot. Just never woke up one day." Eyeing her straightly, he asked, "Does that creep you out?"

It did him. She pinched back a smile. Maybe Rance had been haunting the place, he just didn't know it. Could it work that way? She had no idea but suspected it could work however the ghost wants it to. "No, it doesn't creep me out." It might have if her first ghost encounter had been different. However, Rance made her want to have a second close encounter. And a third.

"I guess it shouldn't, being an antique dealer and all." Nate pushed the chair in. "I gotta go. I just wanted to make sure you were all right. That old Rance hadn't scared the life out of you."

"He didn't." She bit her tongue, hoping he hadn't heard.

Nate's frown said he had.

"Meaning I haven't seen anything except antiques." She grinned and shrugged.

He nodded. "Some nice ones."

"Yes, some nice ones."

He glanced around again. "All right, then. You ready?"

"Ready?" She shook her head. "I've barely started. There's still plenty of daylight." The house had no electricity, but there was plenty of daylight left. "I'll stay until dark."

"Sorry, doll. I've got plans for the evening and don't have time to come out and lock the gate after you leave."

Once again, she ignored how he threw pet names around. "I'll lock it."

"No. You can keep the key to the house, but Lou or I will let you in and out of the gate." He waved a hand toward the door. "We have to protect our assets."

She clamped her back teeth together and didn't bother pulling them apart. Being accused of theft, no matter how subtle, infuriated her. The only thing holding her back from spouting out just what Nate could do with his attitude was Rance. She couldn't chance losing the opportunity to see him again.

With little choice, she followed Nate to the door. "I'll need the gate opened early in the morning. So I can get in a full day."

"Lock the door behind you." He shoved open the screen door.

She grabbed the knob of the inside door, but before pulling it all the way shut, she twisted. "I'll be back tomorrow."

She waited for a response to her whisper, but there was no hum. Disappointment washed over her as she stepped out of the house.

After locking the door, she shoved the single key back into a front pocket on her jeans and then gently closed the screen door. Turning, she hissed in a breath of air.

"What are you doing?"

Nate pushed off her passenger door, where he'd been looking inside her car. "Just checking things out.

You have a pretty sweet ride for a girl who peddles antiques."

Seething, she stomped down the porch steps with every intention of telling him she knew he was looking to see if she'd taken anything out of the house. It wasn't the need to defend herself as much as it was the principle of it all. A noise had her pausing once her feet hit the gravel.

"Look at that," she whispered. The land beyond the barn was a kaleidoscope of rolling hills, and on the top of one a short distance away was a horse. It was too far away to see the exact color, but her skin goose-bumped as the horse tossed its head and nickered again. The animal looked majestic, regal, standing there, overlooking the house and barns.

"You own horses?" she asked Nate.

"No, there are still a few wild ones around this area. That must be one of them. That's why we keep the gate shut." His gaze went back to her car. "And locked."

Not even the joy of seeing the horse eased her frustration at him. Glancing toward the horse again, she sighed. It was gone, and not a single sign in any direction to prove it had been there. Just like Rance.

She pulled the car keys from her other pocket and hit the trunk button, wishing the spring-loaded catch had more tension. If it had a bit more oomph, the trunk lid would have smacked Nate. "I assumed you would want to check the trunk. Make sure I wasn't trying to drive away with any of your assets."

He flashed her a snide grin before glancing into the open trunk. Walking past her, he flicked her beneath the chin. "I trust you more than that, doll." He winked again. "I'll follow you."

Closing her trunk with one hand, she wiped her chin with the other. Jerk. She had half a mind to head back to Billings right now. Her gaze shot to the house, and then the hill. A ghost and a phantom horse wouldn't let her leave. Not yet. The horse had been real. Nate had seen it, too. The ghost, well, that she had to see again. Had to.

She'd climbed in her car and buckled her seat belt. Nate's truck roared to life the same time she started her car. Shifting into drive, she steered the Mustang around to drive beneath the long faded old board stretched between two poles. The truck was tight on her rear bumper. She really didn't like him. He was a fake. Give her a ghost any day.

Plucking her cell phone out of the cup holder in the center console, she used her thumb to swipe the call tab, but stopped before tapping on Vivi Anne's name. What would she say? *I saw a ghost, but he doesn't think he's a ghost. He thinks he's alive and living in nineteen-o-one. Rance Livingston was an old man when he died, could his ghost be young? Was that even possible? And what about him thinking she was Beth? That had been strange, and sad.*

Hefting out a sigh, she set the phone down. She had to think about all this before calling Vivi Anne— who would want to know more about the antiques than the ghost anyway. Rance's antiques. No one had the right to sell them without his permission. Not while he was still alive.

But he wasn't alive. He was a ghost.

"Oh, Good Lord! This is crazy. Just crazy."

Nate's engine roared behind her, so close all she

could see was the grill of his truck in her review mirror. If she didn't care about her car, she would slam on the brakes, just to teach him a lesson in tailgating. What was with her? Why was she getting so worked up? So involved in something that really shouldn't matter to her one way or the other? That was as out of the ordinary as seeing ghost. It was almost as if there was a part of her she'd never known before. Like it had been buried inside her waiting for a chance to come out.

That was a strange way to think about things. Maybe seeing a ghost did that to people. Made them think of all sorts of things they'd never really noticed before—including things about themselves.

She kept her car in the center of the dirt road, giving Nate no room to pass, and kept her speed at one that wouldn't jostle the little Mustang about too much. After slowing considerably to amble over the bumpy cattle guard at the gate, she stopped long enough to make sure the road was clear before pulling onto the highway.

Nate had climbed out of his truck to lock the gate. She didn't waste a second look in her review mirror. Having to put up with him while she figured this all out was going to be about as fun as getting gum off the bottom of a shoe. Or dog shit.

Once in town, she drove straight to the old west town to talk to Buzz. The parking lot was full and Buzz, leaning heavily on his cane, was elbow deep in a conversation with a young couple in the gift shop. He paused long enough to hand her a little blue "admit one" ticket and waved her toward the door.

She smiled and waved back before exiting the gift shop to work her way through the dozen or more cabins connected by a rippling wooden boardwalk. There was plenty to see, each building unique in its own right, along with the few graves and more old buckboard wagons than a person could imagine surviving the number of years they had.

Usually antiques, anything old and full of history, intrigued her, but today, her thoughts were on Rance. A ghost. As she ran a hand over the top of a long bar in a saloon building, she wondered if he'd ever visited this place. A sign on the wall said it had been in a building downtown until the 1920s, when prohibition hit.

She touched every mirror she encountered, looking and listening. No other ghosts appeared. Not that she'd expected any to, but still had to check. To confirm in some way she wasn't losing her mind.

After making her way through the entire compound, she reentered the gift shop. Buzz was now conversing with another couple, mainly about Jeremiah Liver-eating Johnston and his burial here. Liz laid the seven dollars she'd taken out of her purse on the counter to pay for her admittance and then took a seat in a chair behind the glass counter. She hoped Buzz wouldn't think she was infringing on his territory, but she wanted to talk to him and was willing to wait as long as it took.

His grin said he didn't mind, and when a man and woman entered, looking to buy tickets, she sold them two, silently handing the money over to Buzz.

When his conversation ended a short time later, he eased around to lean against a built-in desk as well as his cane. "Didn't you meet up with Lou?"

"Yes, he let me in the gate and gave me the house key, and Nate came to the house a little over an hour later." Trying to cover up her disgust, she shrugged. "He has plans this evening and wanted the gate locked."

"You could have locked it," Buzz said.

"He wants to be the gate keeper." She crossed her arms. "Afraid I'll try to smuggle out the goods."

Buzz shook his head as if disgusted. "That doesn't surprise me." Then he grinned. "What did you think of the place?"

"It's amazing!" A need to elaborate sprang forth. "It's full of antiques. I barely knew where to start." She hadn't started, not really. "You said Rance Livingston was old when he died, right?"

"Yep, in his eighties, or ninety would be my guess. Why?"

She had to decide where to start. "The place looks like it had never been lived in."

"It hadn't. They'd just finished building it when his wife died in that train accident. After that happened, Rance lived in an old cabin behind the house, leastwise that's how the story goes. The stuff I sent up to Vivi Anne, the old saddle and tack, that all came out of the barn."

"I didn't get a chance to visit the out buildings." She knew the saddle. It was in the back room of *Here for Now*. She'd admired the hand tooling that was only half done. The saddle was in pristine condition and had been the reason she'd agreed to come down to Cody to look at the other items.

Another couple entered, looking to buy tickets, and another set behind them. Guessing it would be like this until closing time, she stood. "I'm going to get checked into my motel. I'll see you later."

"Okay." He gave a parting nod while, hitting a key

to open the old-fashioned cash register in order to give change from the twenty-dollar bill one of the new customers had given him.

Her motel was just down the road, back toward town. The kind where you parked right outside your door. Vivi Anne had suggested it. Liz grinned. That was part of the reason she didn't go across the road to a multi-level chain motel. This old motel was nostalgic, and she liked that. She'd always enjoyed old and unique far more than new and modern.

The man inside the lobby was as friendly, and probably as old as Buzz. It took him three tries before he managed to write her name on the right line of the carbon papered slip. Afterward he laid a diamond-shaped key chain on top of the receipt he still had to hand over. "Number ten. It has the newest TV."

"Thank you," she replied. "I appreciate that." She didn't care about the TV at all, but he thought he was doing her a favor, and that much she did appreciate.

"Ten's around the side, toward the back." He nodded toward the door. "More quiet than some closer to the road. And we have coffee here in the lobby starting at seven in the morning. Wife brews a fresh pot every half hour up until nine."

"Good to know." She reached over to slide the receipt and key out from beneath his hand.

"We got the internet, too. Right over there, next to the coffee table."

She glanced in the direction he gestured. A big boxed-in computer screen and single key board sat on a small desk. Both had to have been put there before the millennium. "Okay." Once again, she attempted to gather her receipt and key.

"Got some amenities back here behind the counter. Toothbrushes and combs, that sort of thing, if you've forgotten yours, and the lobby's open from seven to eleven." He leaned closer. "Just ring the bell if the door is locked. The wife or I will hear it. We live right back there."

He'd taken his hand off her key to point over his shoulder, and she took advantage of that. Snatching the key and receipt, she nodded. "Got it, just ring the bell."

A tinge of guilt struck when she pushed open the door. He'd just been being friendly and she was escaping as if he was a mass-murderer. "See you for that coffee." She waved while stepping out of the door.

"There'll be cream and sugar, too."

"I'll probably need it," she whispered while closing the door. She only drank coffee that Vivi Anne delivered to the shop, and that was always heavily sweetened.

She drove around the side of the building and parked in front of door number ten. Then climbed out of the car and went to examine the room. It smelled clean, and the bed seemed comfortable. The water faucets all worked. "Good enough." She walked back to the door she'd left open and laughed at the TV the size and shape of the computer monitor back in the lobby. If that was the newest one, she'd bet the ones in the other rooms didn't even have a remote.

It truly didn't matter. Neither did the orange painted walls. She'd never been one to fret over accommodations. Some may attribute that to her foster home upbringing. She didn't. It was just her. The latest and greatest never interested her much. Not in homes, furnishings, clothes, or just about anything else.

She walked to her car and after opening the driver's door unlatched the seat to lean it forward and grab her bag and suitcase off the backseat. Odd that Nate hadn't scrounged through them.

Shaking her head at such thoughts, she told herself to stop. Just stop when it came to Nate. He was simply who he was, just like every other person in the world. That had always been her attitude in the past, and it had served her well.

Emotionless.

That was her.

Besides, Nate was not the issue. Rance was. She had to learn all she could about him and his life. Back in her room, she stretched out on the bed and swiped her phone out of sleep mode. Ten minutes later, she was still waiting for the internet. Cell One wasn't known for its service. Then again, there might not be an internet signal strong enough for the hotspot to pick up.

What felt like an hour later, and four frozen screens and three error displays, she gave up. Leaving the phone on the bed, she picked the room key off the end table.

The old man ambled through the door behind the check-in counter as she closed the front door.

"Just me." She gestured toward the computer. "Thought I'd use the internet."

"Go ahead. Just use your room number to log on. It's on a timer." He shrugged. "We can't have one customer on it for hours. If no one's waiting, just go ahead and log in again, and it'll give you another fifteen minutes."

"Got it." Hers was the only car in the parking lot, so a line for the computer probably wasn't going to happen. Settled in the chair, she followed the instructions taped to the top of the screen. It reminded her of elementary school when the computer lab was a new and fascinating thing rather than an everyday necessity.

Tapping her fingertips on the desk top, she decided patience certainly was not her friend today.

Finally, a search engine appeared, and she typed in a few key words related to ghosts. Scanning the links, she quickly disregarded most of them, a few others proved worthless as well. Just as one hinted at being closer to what she wanted, the screen went black.

Drawing a deep breath, she read the instructions for when a time-out happens and logged in again. When the home page appeared, she clicked history, only to feel cheated that it was empty. A few misguided clicks happened before she found the website she wanted again, and then she was barely a paragraph past where she'd been before when the screen went black again.

"Seriously?

"Having trouble?"

"No." She leaned back in order to see the check-in desk around the corner. Maybe she should have gone modern instead of nostalgic. "Just didn't know fifteen minutes go by so quickly."

"Anything I can help with?"

She started to say no but stood instead. "Actually." She walked across the small lobby. "Do you know anything about a haunted farm house around here?"

He grinned. "*The Rocking L*? It's a ranch, not a farm. Rance Livingston's place."

"That's it." Encouraging him to go on, she leaned an elbow on the counter.

"You one of those ghost hunters? The wife watches those shows on TV." He leaned closer. "I'm a western man myself. Give me John Wayne, and I'm a happy camper."

"North to Alaska," she said.

"You know the Duke?"

"I've seen a show or two." Or ten or twenty. Norman Walker, her foster dad, had been a fan of the Duke, and by default all the kids in the Walker's home knew John Wayne. "And, no, I'm not a ghost hunter. I'm an antique dealer."

The man's friendliness turned colder than a Popsicle. "Did Lou Dixon call you?"

"No, Buzz did." Liz crossed her fingers that was the right answer. Too bad she didn't know Buzz's last name. Lightyear came to mind, but she knew that wasn't it.

To her surprise and relief, the man grinned. "You that friend of his up Montana way?"

She kept her fingers crossed. "No, but I work for her."

He held a hand over the counter. "Les Burrows."

She shook his hand firmly. "Liz Baxter. It's nice to meet you Mr. Burrows."

"Call me Les. Buzz and I are good friends. Play cards together every chance we get. There's more time for that come winter than the summer."

"I'm sure there is." Not wanting to stray too far off subject, she asked, "Have you ever been out to the *Rocky L*?"

"No, not too many have. Riley was as protective of the old place as Rance had been in his days. Waiting for his wife to return. That's how the story goes. He never believed she'd died and spent every day of his life waiting for her to return."

Liz squeezed her hands together, trying to contain how they'd started to shake.

Glancing around as if to make sure no one was listening, Les lowered his voice. "Half the town wishes old Rance was haunting the place, just to scare the bejeebers out of Lou and Nate. Would do those boys good."

Liz giggled, for neither Nate nor Lou were boys, but remained on task. "Nate says he might have a buyer for the *Rocking L*."

"Does he now? Guess that don't surprise me none. Those boys sold off their daddy's places fast enough, and Riley's." Les shook his head as if disgusted. "Nate built himself a big house on the edge of town in one of those developments. Even got himself a swimming pool. They're expensive, you know. If not, we'd have one here, might draw a few more customers from across the street. And Lou, well, he's living in those fancy apartments over on the north part of town. Had to with the divorce and all. Bet he's wishing he hadn't sold Riley's place now. Then he'd have a house to live in."

"Is that so?"

"Yep. Things would be different right now if old Rance had remarried, had some legitimate kids." Les sighed. "He'd have left a legacy rather than gossip and ghost stories. Ask me, the *Rocking L* might still be up and running if that had happened. Rance trained horses for Buffalo Bill's Wild West shows and everywhere Bill performed, people wanted to buy horses just like the ones in his shows. Rance sold horses worldwide at one point."

Two words kept repeating over and over in her head. *Legitimate kids.*

"So, you're here to buy antiques." Les frowned. "From the *Rocking L.*"

Not exactly sure how her answer would be taken, but needing to keep him talking until she could get back to Rance having kids of any kind, she took the long route. "Buzz called my boss to come look at things. She and Buzz have been friends for years. She has an antique store up in Billings. *Here for Now.* It specializes in local antiques, the tri-state area." Okay now she was babbling. Though her mind wanted to know why he'd said that line about kids, another part of her wouldn't let a question form.

"Buzz knows folks from all over. He'd want to see Rance's stuff goes to a good home if'n it has to be sold. Town folks don't want to see that happen. To see it sold."

"Why?"

The caution that filled his eyes seemed to have locked his lips. That also amped up her curiosity considerably. A suspicion told her whatever was at the bottom of selling Rance's property involved others. "Les." She used his name to make a closer connection. "I really need to know all there is to know about the *Rocking L* and Rance. Maybe I could then convince Lou and Nate to reconsider…" She wasn't sure she could convince either of them of anything, but she did want to know.

"Not to burn the place down?" Les shook his head. "That's the talk around town right now. Some folks claim the house should be moved to Buzz's old village, given its history and all. That's what makes Cody survive. Our history. People believe this is an old west town, and that's what they come to see. Not some fancy-dancy resort with golf courses and water fountains."

Her heartbeat kicked up a notch, as if it had just shifted from first gear to second, and thoughts were striking her faster than she could process them. Of course Les wouldn't want another hotel. "Maybe if we sold enough antiques that could be part of the deal. Having the house moved to Buzz's place."

Les let out a low whistle. "Now that would be a tourist attraction. A haunted house from the turn of the century. That could boost old Buzz's visitor numbers, and mine." He winked. "Folks visiting his place need a somewhere to sleep. He refers them here all the time."

Although she felt like jumping up and down, she contained the urge and gave him a single nod.

"Come on around." Les waved a hand toward the opening on the end of the check-in counter. "My wife grew up with Riley. They were sweethearts at one time, and Edith loves telling people about that." He winked again. "But I'm the one she married."

Chapter Six

Rance sat on the bed, staring out the open window, watching daylight fade and the hill cast shadows that gave way to the settling dusk. Darkness would soon consume the horizon, and him. A heavy sigh left his chest. He should go to the cabin, but tonight, the first in over two months, he didn't want to leave the house. The connection was back. The one he'd longed to feel again.

He'd gone through all the scenarios. Everything from thinking he'd lost his mind, to half-ass believing he was asleep down in his cabin, locked in a dream and unable to wake.

He reached over and picked up the book he'd set down on the bed beside him. At one point this afternoon he'd retrieved it from the small bookcase in the spare room down the hall. He'd heard the tale before then, but last Christmas, while courting Beth, the two of them had read the novel together. Then, he'd joked and teased her about Ebenezer Scrooge and the three ghosts who'd visited. Today, he'd hurriedly scanned the pages to get to the ghost from Christmas yet to come. That ghost was just a year into the future. His was more than a century.

It all seemed as impossible as it did real. He turned the book over and ran a hand over the top. The story was impossible, yet the book itself was real. He could touch it, feel it, hold it.

If only he could do those things to Beth again.

His throat started to swell again, stealing his very breath as it did more often than not. God, he missed her. Missed her with as much intensity as he'd loved her, and it wasn't right. There was no outlet for his pain, not like there'd been for his love.

Seeing her, that ghostly, perfect vision, bottled up his pain worse than ever. Even with shorter, *bleached-striped* hair and using words he knew she'd never used before, he'd known the moment he'd seen her, inside where it counted, that it was Beth. His Beth.

He'd seen her doing that before. Sitting there on the bed, reading. The house was full of all sorts of things to read. Books. Magazines.

Drawing in a deep breath that rattled inside him, he glanced around the room. The entire house was full of things she'd brought with her.

She'd arrived at their new home with wagons full of furniture, cookware, linens, and all sorts of other household goods. Just a few things she'd been collecting over the years, she'd said. He'd laughed and insisted she must have robbed a mercantile at some point in her life.

She'd laughed, too, and said he'd appreciate everything she'd brought.

He closed his eyes while acknowledging she'd been right. She'd been right about so many things.

A chill rippled his spine. Was she right again?

Opening the book, he flipped through the pages and questioned if she'd appeared to tell him he had to change. If he didn't, he wouldn't like the outcome. Maybe it was her way of saying that others had been right, that she wouldn't want him to keep mourning her so deeply.

He set the book down and walked to the window. He didn't buy that. Beth wasn't that kind. If she'd come with a message, she'd have blurted it out. She'd have been kind about it, and caring, but she'd have made her point before disappearing.

The house knew it, too. Her presence was as much a part of it as the wood and the nails holding it together. During those few minutes today, it had come back to life as completely as he had. Without her, it was an empty shell. Just like him.

Sighing, he turned away from the window and crossed the room, stopping next to the dresser. Rather than picking up the picture, he grasped the mirror. His reflection appeared, but that wasn't what he wanted to see. He didn't know much about ghosts, but one that needed a mirror had to be the stranger than all the others.

Or, more special. Beth had always been more special than all others.

He set down the mirror in order to rub his nose and blinked his eyes, but he couldn't stop the sting, or the tears from forming. "Why?" His voice shook and echoed against the hollowness of the house. "Why Beth? Damn it, why?"

He picked up the picture. "You were so beautiful, so full of life, and so sassy, and so special." His whisper was hoarse. "So uniquely special." He shook his head, recalling a very poignant moment. "I hadn't even held your hand, hadn't even touched you, when you told me I loved you." Regardless of the tears in his eyes, a smile formed. "Do you remember that? You told me that I loved you," he repeated with emphasis. "And I did. I loved you more than I could ever have imagined. I still do."

He shook his head, in as much wonderment now as he'd been several months ago when the event had taken place. "I asked how that could be, how I could love you when I hadn't even gotten up the nerve to hold your hand."

An odd sense of peace entered him as he ran a fingertip over her image.

"You told me that I had touched you. That I'd touched your heart." He swallowed at the memories warming his insides. "Then you curled your fingers around mine, and said, 'Once you touch a person's heart, touching their hands is easy.' Remember that?"

There was no answer. No softly whispered words.

He set the picture back on the dresser and once again glanced at the mirror. "Are you still here and I can't see you? Are you listening to me ramble on like some love-struck fool? Enjoying all this?"

He picked the mirror up. "Well, I am some love-struck fool." Looking directly into the mirror, he announced, "I think I'll go to the cabin now."

To say he felt like a babbling idiot would be true, still, he was willing to try whatever it took. Threatening to leave might make her reappear. It was a long shot, but he didn't have much else.

"I think I'll go to the cabin and get some sleep." He jiggled the mirror.

The house was so quiet he could have heard a mouse, if he'd had one. Which he didn't. He was alone. Completely alone.

"This clearly is not working." Why had it earlier?

Where had she gone?

He set the mirror on the dresser and returned to the bed, picked up the book again. Maybe he was dreaming. That's how the book ended. Everything had been a dream.

Frustrated, he headed for the door. Down the hall, he replaced the book to the shelf, guided only by the murky light of dusk that could make a man believe there were things hiding in the dimness.

Ghostly things.

He left the room, but rather than heading for the stairway, he gave into the nagging inside him and walked back to his bedroom. Their bedroom. Staring at the bed, he let several thoughts float around in his head, snagging amongst themselves now and again. Then he nodded. There was still a tingle in the air. Faint, but it was still there. Had Beth, or her ghost, been here all this time—since the day of the accident—but he'd never noticed because he'd been too busy wallowing in grief?

He'd dismissed it at the time, but that dreadful morning, before Cliff had arrived to tell him about the accident, he'd thought he'd heard Beth call for him. Yell, actually, like she'd needed him.

"I'm here. Hear that, Beth? I'm here. And will remain. I'll be right here, waiting for you. Whatever it is you need, I'm here."

With that, he hung his hat on the hook near the door and made his way to the chair in the corner, where he removed his boots and shirt. The rest of his clothes followed.

Although the bed was a homecoming in its own right, sleep didn't come immediately, but when it did, it was peaceful and undisrupted.

He awakened surprised by the sunlight that filled the room. Somewhat taken aback by the odd familiarity that surrounded him, he closed his eyes for a moment.

That same familiarity was what had his eyes snapping open a second later and him leaping off the bed.

"Beth! Beth!"

In two steps he was at the dresser but stopped shy of grabbing the mirror. He didn't need it to see her. At least shouldn't.

He closed his eyes. His heart swelled at the tingle that was back. As strong, if not stronger, than it had been yesterday.

He knew before opening his eyes what he'd see, and he held onto the excitement it caused as long as possible. Like a kid would opening a wrapped present, even while knowing what was inside. It was part of the fun. The anticipation. The thrill.

His entire body was tingling by the time he lifted his lids.

She was in the doorway, and his heart banged the inside of his chest like a blacksmith hammering steel on an anvil. He watched her sneak into the room, on tiptoes as if not to wake him. Wiping at his grin, he reached for the mirror again but stopped once more. The same reaction she'd caused in him every morning of their married days was the reason. Ghost or not, he didn't need her seeing that.

He crossed the room, still watching her tiptoe toward the bed. What he wouldn't give to grab her by the waist and toss her upon the covers still rumpled from his sleep and twisted from his fast exit. The bedding would become more tousled once he was done with her. The mattress might even end up on the floor the way his need throbbed with an ache that was indeed real.

Hell, was he really thinking about doing *that* with a ghost? Grabbing his pants, he deduced, he was thinking about doing *that* with his wife. The one who stood at the foot of his bed.

Once dressed, he walked back over to the dresser. She was beside the bed now, staring at it with a certain longing in her eyes.

He muffled a groan.

"Rance?" she whispered.

Now behind her, he reached around her shoulder and held the mirror before her face.

She jumped slightly, and he laughed—for a moment. He'd tried to catch her with his other hand, but once again, it went right through her.

Damn. This was so crazy. So exasperating.

Her smile, though, when he caught both of their reflections in the mirror, almost made up for his disappointment. Almost.

She twisted around, holding onto the mirror. "I didn't want to wake you. Did I?"

"No, you didn't."

A little frown tugged at her brows. "Did you sleep here last night?"

"Why?"

She shrugged. "Just curious. The bed's still made and…" She shook her head slightly. "Rumor has it you slept in the cabin out back after your wife died."

He wasn't sure how to answer that, but in the end, went with the truth. "That's not a rumor."

The tenderness of her gaze encrusted his heart,

filling it with a warmth he hadn't felt since the day he'd learned of the train accident.

"I felt you in the house the moment I entered it," she said quietly.

"I felt you, too."

She closed her eyes and blew out a breath. "So you didn't sleep here."

He smiled. Without being able to touch her, his expressions were all he had to comfort her. "The bed's not made."

She glanced at the bed, and her sigh was heavy. "It is in my time."

He might have hidden his stiffy under his britches, but it was still front and center, and in his mind. Standing beside her, talking about beds, made or unmade, was not helping. He swore he could smell her too. She always smelled so good. Fresh and clean. Like the sheets of their bed she hung in the sunshine each Saturday. God, he loved climbing into bed with her on those nights. Actually, he loved climbing into bed with her every night.

Close to losing whatever control he had, he abruptly said, "Let's go downstairs. I haven't had my coffee yet."

She nodded but stopped after talking a single step. "What if I can't see you down there?"

"We'll take the mirror."

"What if it doesn't work down there?"

Down there? Everything of his 'down there' worked just fine. Of course she wasn't thinking along the same lines as him. Or with the same body parts. She couldn't possibly know what his thoughts were focused on. "Then we'll come back up here."

She nodded again, and this time they made it all the way out of the bedroom before she spoke. "Was it yesterday, in your time, when we met?"

Biting his lip to keep from saying no, it had been last year when he'd delivered horses to her father; he waited until they started down the steps. "Yes. Was it yesterday in your time?"

"Yes." A hint of smile crossed her lips. "That's good to know, that time, at least hours and days, is the same for both of us." She frowned. "Is it July? In your world, is it July?"

He contemplated the days since he'd last checked a calendar. "Yes. Tuesday, the twenty-third."

"It's Wednesday the twenty-third for me."

"At least the dates are the same."

They crossed through the center room of the house, where the little blue sofa and matching chair sat, the set she'd had her mother ship down from Billings as soon as the house was finished, along with the white tatted doilies hanging over the backs. They'd coupled on that little sofa. More than once. On the floor too, while building the house.

One particular afternoon while she'd been hanging up the flowered wallpaper, they hadn't been able to keep their hands off each other. The flowers she'd plastered all over the walls had all but come to life that day. It had been as if he and Beth had been rolling in a field of daisies loving each other instead of on the floor inside a half-finished house. He wouldn't admit it to many, but he'd grown to love that flowery wallpaper that day.

He swallowed a groan. He had a one thought mind today, and memories were not helping matters. They entered the kitchen. "Have a seat. I'm going to make some coffee."

"But—"

He waited for her to say more. Not for long. The tension was too much. "But what?"

"You'll have to let go of the mirror."

The touch of panic that flashed in her eyes was understandable. If it was the other way around, if he could only see her when she was holding the mirror, he'd glue the damn thing to her hand. And his.

"You can't see me at all without it?"

She shook her head sadly. "Not at all."

"I'll be right here. I promise."

"I have some things to tell you." She pinched her lips together briefly. "Things you need to know, and, and it'll be harder if I can't see you."

A knot as cold as a rock pulled from the bottom of a well formed in his stomach. She was not a ghost from his future, coming to tell him things he didn't want to hear. He couldn't believe that. Did not believe that.

"What do you need to tell me?"

"It's complicated."

"This is all complicated, Beth."

She grabbed the table with her free hand as if a great wave of dizziness had overtaken her. He tried to touch her, but his hands were useless. If she fell, there was nothing he could do to stop it. He cursed under his breath when he pulled out a chair, and it only moved in his world. Right through her.

"Sit down," he said softly.

She nodded and grasped the back of a chair that appeared as soon as she touched it, then as she pulled it away from the table as he had, the two chairs, the one he'd pulled out and the one she did, merged into one. Slowly, she lowered onto the seat.

Even as odd as that was, his concern remained on her. He knelt beside her, never releasing his hold on the mirror. "Are you all right?"

"Yes, just dizzy," she whispered. "It's not bad, though." She took several deep breaths before lifting her head and sighing heavily. Her eyes grew as sad as a lost soul. "My name is Liz. Elizabeth. I got dizzy yesterday, too, when you called me Beth."

"You did?"

"Yes, when we were both looking out the window."

He remembered that. She'd gone as white as a sheet. He hadn't known why, but he had called her Beth then, and now. Not calling her Beth would be difficult, strange, but a mere name was the least of their worries. His anyway. Yet, *Liz* didn't want to form on his lips. "How about Elizabeth? Do you get dizzy when I say that?"

"Say it again."

"Elizabeth."

Like an early morning sunrise, her smile rose and brightened her entire face. "No."

If the result was a smile like that, he'd call her whatever she wanted. Testing the name one more time, he repeated, "Elizabeth."

A spark flashed in her blue eyes. "That seems to work."

"Works for me." When Beth had first introduced herself to him, she said her name was Elizabeth, but that he could call her Beth. He'd never forget that day, how she'd perched herself on the top board of her father's corral while he'd demonstrated how well-trained the set of horses he'd driven north to Billings were. Buffalo Bill had arranged the sale, after Conrad, Beth's father, had seen one of Bill's shows and wanted a pair of the matching white mustangs for his wife, Millie.

Call her Beth, or Elizabeth, the woman sitting before him with her sparkling blue eyes and pink cheeks had his heart beating as hard as it had that day and memories of how much they'd loved each other in the months following had need flaring in his britches.

Attempting to squelch that need, he went back to their earlier conversation. "Now, what do you have to tell me?"

Her face scrunched. "It's complicated."

She had the most adorable expressions, and he loved every one of them, and remaining this close to her while remembering some particular expressions wasn't squelching his desires in any way. "You said that." He rose from his crouched stance beside her chair and leaned against the table. "I'm listening."

After licking her lips, slowly, enticingly enough to make him quell a groan, she smiled consolingly.

He frowned.

"It's not bad. Just complicated. I believe I mentioned my friend Vivi Anne. She owns an antique shop, *Here for Now*, the one I work for, and…"

This was Beth, the need to explain everything, even the tiniest detail, especially when she was arguing a case. "And…" he coaxed.

"She also, well, she knows things, or understands things that others don't, or can't."

"All right." He wasn't overly concerned about her

friend but would listen. Always had.

"I talked to her last night, and she said that neither of us is a ghost."

His spine tingled. "You or her?"

Her grin was adorable. "Me or you," she clarified.

That wasn't necessarily news to him. He'd known he wasn't a ghost. The jury was still out on her.

Growing serious again, she sighed. "She says time isn't like one long rope, it's more like several pieces laid side by side. While you're living on one string, I'm living on another, a hundred years later, and somehow, we've found a way for those two timelines to bump into each other, intercept."

He scratched his forehead. That didn't sound like Beth. She was too sensible, too down to earth to make up impossible theories. Then again, she'd said her friend had said all this, and that was like Beth. If a person was lucky enough to be her friend, she'd believe in them, no matter what, and stand by them through thick and thin.

That's how it had been for the two of them, right from the beginning. Her straightforwardness had been as original as her, and endearing, and by the time he'd left Billings two days after meeting her, she'd told him if he wasn't already in love with her, he soon would be. He'd laughed at her, but her words had stuck. Especially after he'd returned home and hadn't been able to get her out of his mind.

For the next two months, he'd spent more time traveling to Billings to see her than training horses—and that had never happened before. However, he knew a thoroughbred when he saw one. Beth was a thoroughbred. Absolute perfection in every way. She was the one who'd asked him to marry her. Said if he didn't, he was going to go broke coming to see her. She'd been right, but he'd insisted he had to build a house first, that he couldn't expect her to live in his little cabin.

There too, Beth had been unrelenting, saying she'd help him build a house, that way it would be exactly what she wanted. Six weeks later they'd been married. A warm January day six short months ago—Beth wouldn't even wait for spring. And in the weeks that followed, she'd pounded nails right beside him, building their house to the perfection she'd envisioned.

A vision she'd made him believe in too.

"Imagine two worlds, each existing in their own time, at the same time." She held up two fingers on one hand. "I'm living in twenty-eighteen, you in nineteen-o-one, and somehow, we've managed to interconnect." She then crossed the two fingers she held up.

New inventions, different ideas, strange happenings—none of those things ever disturbed him, but her seriousness, and an elusive belief tingling inside his head, had him questioning this one. In a way he'd never questioned things before. As if he might need to take her theory under consideration. Then again, if it meant she'd eventually remember being his wife, he'd believe in ghosts, goblins, trolls, unicorns, and...

"Two worlds existing at the same time," he said aloud.

She nodded. "Vivi Anne says there are numerous case studies of such things. It's what's made scientists believe in time travel."

"Time travel?"

She nodded again. "Time has no boundaries, no

beginnings or endings. It doesn't measure itself in minutes or hours, or days or years. People do that."

"Can I make that coffee now?" Her not seeing his reaction to all this might be a good thing. He'd never not believed her, but time travel?

"You won't leave?"

"I won't leave."

"All right. Make your coffee."

He let go of the mirror and gave his body a good shake, like a dog does after jumping out of a pond. A good case of the willies had set in. He also rubbed his head with both hands and then scratched his tingling scalp.

"Are you still there?"

He touched the mirror briefly. "Yes. I'm going to the stove now."

"I have more to say."

I'm sure you do. He grinned. When attempting to prove a point, Beth could corner a fly and keep it there until it saw things her way. "Talk while I make coffee." Taking his hand off the mirror, he walked around the table. Coffee would help.

Coffee.

Would.

Help.

If he could find it.

He'd opened three cupboards. It had been a couple of months since he'd eaten in the house, but he'd never taken any supplies out of here. In the fourth cupboard he hit the mother lode. The bag of ground coffee beans and the coffee pot he'd washed and put away the morning before Cliff had arrived. Oddly enough, for the first time, that memory didn't fill him with pain.

Carrying both the coffee and the pot, he went to the sink and started pumping. The well needed to prime itself, and the pipes needed a minute to rinse out before he used the crystal-clear water that started flowing to fill the pot. After adding coffee, he went to build a small fire in the stove.

"I'm assuming you're listening, so I'm going to start. This is a long story, so touch the mirror when you have a question."

He heard her but didn't turn around. Not because she couldn't see him. Rather, because, he'd never used her stove.

"I met this woman at my motel in Cody last night."

He spun around. A hotel in Cody? Ghosts didn't need hotel rooms.

"She was friends with Riley Dixon. Cliff's grandson. It gets complicated, and I hope I got things straight. Cliff was married to Nan, and they had two sons. Ralph and Randy."

He went ahead and built a fire. The stove wasn't doing anyone any good sitting unused.

"They also had a third son."

He let out a humph at that. Cliff wasn't getting any younger. He'd be a ripe old age by the time another baby grew to adulthood.

"He wasn't really their son, but he was raised as their son. His name was Robert. Ralph never had any children, but Randy had a son, and his name was Riley. I guess they all had a thing for the letter R. Anyway, Robert had two sons, Clayton and Leonard. Yes, finally names that don't being with R's. That got confusing." She looked toward the stove. "Are you following this?"

Hurrying across the room, he touched the mirror.

"Yes." He knew Ralph and Randy, and the rest, well, he wasn't sure it mattered.

She smiled up at him.

His heart took a serious tumble.

"Well, everything was fine, until Leonard's wife, his third or fourth one, Edith, that's the woman I met last night, wasn't sure considering Leonard was married several times. Anyway, Leonard's wife and Rosie, who was Clayton's wife, got into a fight. Leonard's wife claimed Rosie got pregnant only because she was also pregnant. She and Leonard were Lou's parents and Rosie and Clayton were Nate's."

He nodded as if he agreed, whereas in truth, he had no idea who she was talking about. He was racking his brain to remember if he knew an Edith who worked at one of the hotels. It sure didn't ring a bell. Buffalo Bill was building a new hotel, named after his daughter Irma, but that hadn't opened yet, so no Edith could be working there. Then again, if he had an open mind, a very open mind, he didn't know an Edith working at any hotel because she didn't work there until twenty-eighteen. Which meant said Edith wasn't born yet.

A shiver raced over him. If Edith wasn't born yet, neither was Beth. This Beth. Another shiver had him squeezing his temples. He needed to get his head around this. Somehow. Maybe his first thoughts yesterday had been right, that she'd hit her head during the accident and when she awoke, unable to remember much, she created this story to confuse him as to why she hadn't returned to him right away.

Beth wouldn't do that. There'd be no need to.

Another shiver made his spine quiver. Maybe this wasn't his Beth. What if she was telling the truth and—

"Where'd you go?"

He laid a hand on the mirror. "I'm here, but I have to check the coffee."

"Are you using that stove?"

"Yes." He moved away from the table but didn't go far. The idea this wasn't Beth, his Beth, was too impossible to believe. Almost as unbelievable as living in two worlds, time traveling, and ghosts. He had no experience in believing in such things, other than in reading books. Books that Beth had brought here after they got married. She had all kinds of books. He couldn't remember one about time traveling, or two worlds, but he did know that one about ghosts.

A hiss and sizzle had him turning about and moving to the stove, where he grabbed the handle of the bubbling-over coffee pot, only to let it go again before using the tail of his shirt to protect his hand as he took a hold of the handle again and moved it to the side.

"So this wife of Leonard's..."

He started for the cupboard in search of a cup as Beth started talking again, but his feet stalled mid-step. She'd stood up, was now pacing back and forth near the table. Regardless of everything going on in his head, he grinned. He'd never had any experience in loving until he'd met her. That had been unbelievable too.

Everything had been so perfect right from the start. A late onset of winter had allowed him to set the house foundation before the ground had frozen, and the men he'd hired from town had framed it up and set the walls before the first snow had flown. He'd helped, but not much during that time, having been up in Billings for weeks on end, courting Beth. By the time they'd married, the outside of the house had been completed, leaving him and Beth to work on the inside during the colder winter days.

He'd moved the stove from the little cabin into the house, for both heat and cooking, before the wedding. It had been fine for the cabin, but too small to heat the entire home, which had meant they did a lot of cuddling in their bed upstairs. Those days and nights had been so full of joy and love. And hopes and dreams and promises.

He'd promised her a new stove, and the timing to provide it had been perfect too.

In the few months he and Beth had courted, and been married, he'd come to appreciate her family, and loved them in parental sense, and was thankful they, in turn, had accepted him so fully. Had accepted how Beth moved away from them to be with him in Cody. He'd worried about that at first.

His mother had died giving birth to him, and her family had blamed his father, blamed him for being a half-breed and for moving her away from them. Their bitterness had turned into a battle of wills, which his father had lost. He'd been only a few months old when his father had left him with his mother's parents, who'd raised him, and tried to force their hatred upon him.

He'd never wanted that kind of misery imposed on anyone, or to see families separated. When Beth had said she'd like to go visit her mother, he'd readily agreed. It was a short trip, little over a hundred miles. He'd traveled it numerous times himself and figured she'd be safe. It also had provided him the opportunity to surprise her with her new stove.

"Janice." Her pacing brought her closer. "Leonard's wife's name was Janice, I don't think I mentioned that, and she was a real piece of cake, Edith's words, not mine."

She stepped closer to him, and sweat popped out on his forehead. He'd seen her earlier but hadn't *noticed* her. As in what she was wearing. Blue pants again, this time they were rolled up at the cuffs, showing a good section of her ankles and shins, and her feet were covered with clunky white shoes with laces. The pants fit her as tightly as the ones yesterday, like a second skin, but it was once again her shirt that had his blood beating against his skin.

The shirt was white, and rather than sleeves, narrow strips barely covered the tops of her shoulders. Loose-fitting, and short, the bottom of her shirt stopped above the waistband of her britches. The thin, white material billowed and bounced as she walked, giving him a glimpse of her flat stomach and belly button.

His mouth went dry. He remembered that belly button. Remembered tickling it. Beth was extremely ticklish. His fingers curled into his palm as more memories assaulted him. He'd done more than tickle that belly. He'd kissed it. Every inch of skin surrounding it. Every inch of her.

Another groan built in his throat, and this time he couldn't stop it from emitting.

"Janice, you see, was mad when Riley inherited your place and told everyone about it. She claimed if anyone should inherit your place, it should be her and Leonard." The tiny hum that she'd barely heard stopped Liz right there.

She sighed heavily. Telling Rance all this seemed like a good idea this morning, but actually telling him and thinking about telling him weren't settling the same way inside her. Essentially, it made her feel rotten. She'd never felt that way before. This way. It wasn't as if she considered herself cold-hearted, she just never allowed herself to care enough to get involved. '*Where there's caring, there's hurt.*' Vivi Anne had said that last night, along with time having no boundaries, only moments that were either acted upon or not. That all could be true. Especially the caring part.

It was all so confusing. And strange.

Of course, talking to thin air didn't help, especially when she could feel him. A distinct vibration had come alive inside her as soon as she'd stepped in the house. Similar to the one she experienced when looking at him in the mirror. Was her intuition getting stronger?

"Are you still listening?" Scanning the room, her attention fell on the stove. Focusing on it, she moved closer. Yesterday, the stove had looked brand new. She'd swear her life on it. Today, now, it looked…used. Still in very good condition, but not untouched like yesterday.

As she laid a hand on the top of the stove, a hum sounded, and the mirror appeared before her face. She grasped the handle with her free hand.

"Hot."

She'd obviously caught the very end of what he was saying.

"I said, don't touch that. It's hot."

"No, it's not." Her stomach gurgled again at the solid differences between his *time* and hers. "Not in my time."

"Well, it is in mine. Don't touch it."

"Why?"

"Because I'm afraid you'll get burned."

He had the most expressive eyes. Dark, dark, brown with the tiniest bits of gold when she looked close enough, long enough. There was more about his eyes. Something unique and powerful. She'd never encountered it before. Yet, deep down it felt as if she had. As if his eyes were familiar, and that at one time she'd been able to read them. Know what he was thinking.

That idea wasn't frightening, but it made her heartbeat increase. In fact, it did something to her entire insides. It had her core temperature rising in a very unique way. A womanly way.

"Is it warm in your time? Here in the kitchen," she clarified. "Is it warm?"

"Yes, there's a fire in the stove."

She lifted her hand off the stove. The little buzz in her head said the heat in the room wasn't the reason she felt flushed. "Maybe we should open the door."

He stared at her in length. So long a tiny quiver rippled her shoulders. There were other reactions inside her too, things she understood. Leave it to her to be attracted—seriously attracted—to a man she could never have.

She fully understood his meaning when he said, "We both know opening the door won't help."

They stood facing one another. Each touching the mirror that hung between them. The air, whether it was separated by a century or not, was so charged Franklin could have discovered electricity all over again. She bit her bottom lip to keep it from quivering and drew in a breath so shaky her lungs rattled. She'd heard of this, seen actors pretending to be drawn to one another so uncontrollably they couldn't stop themselves. But she

Lauri Robinson

wasn't an actor, and even if she was, he wasn't real. Not real enough to kiss.

Her heart landed in her throat as he leaned forward. Liz closed her eyes and held her breath as the charged vibration between them grew stronger, and stronger.

Tingles of anticipation washed over her.

But there was nothing more. No pressure. No meeting of lips. No kiss.

A wave of regret, of disappointment, of why me, why now, was so great she wobbled and grabbed the stove to hold her upright.

As her equilibrium returned, he whispered, "Let go of the stove, Elizabeth. Hold your hand up."

Drawing a fortifying breath, she did so, copying how he held his up. She watched, as did he, as they both slowly brought their palms closer. Her fingers trembled. It may have been her imagination, but it was as if a halo, a faint golden light, formed around their hands as their fingertips grew so close they should be touching. Yet weren't. Or were they? Her fingers vibrated, and heat spread up her arm.

Their eyes met, and the smile on his face was about the most wonderful, and dangerous thing that could have ever happened to her. The heat generating at her hand, running up her arm, hit her heart, where it pooled and then spread out into a radiance that went deeper and deeper inside her.

"Can you feel that?"

Convinced there was something there, she nodded. "Yes, can you?"

"Yes. It's as powerful as ever."

"What is?"

"Our love."

Chapter Seven

Liz was once again at the table, sitting down, and had gathered her nerves together as much as humanly possible. Rance was sitting there, too, holding the mirror with one hand while drinking coffee with the other.

She hadn't verbally denied what he'd said—love— but she couldn't believe it. There had been something there, between their hands, around their hands. A gentler version had settled in the air, but it couldn't be love. Her hand still vibrated, still tingled with heat, even though it had been several minutes since she'd dropped it to her side and moved to the table. The lingering effects on her heart were still there, too. But that could be fear or confusion. A person couldn't just suddenly feel…Love. That was impossible.

He wanted there to be something there, something more than a simple connection, but she couldn't lie to him. Couldn't pretend to feel love. She didn't want to disappointment him either. Which is why she'd let go of the mirror. He had been disappointed though. She'd seen it on his face before he'd let go of the mirror and disappeared. And that caused an unusual sense of anguish.

Emotions weren't her thing. Few things evoked any kind of a reaction inside her. She attributed that to her past. Being raised in a foster home. Though the

Walkers had been good people and she'd mourned their deaths when that had happened, she'd never really felt as if she *belonged* with them. She figured without a family of her own, a place she'd truly belonged, she'd never learned to love, or care a whole lot about most things, most people. It seemed to make sense and provided a solid reason as to why she didn't believe in love. Why she'd never wanted to feel deeply toward another person—nor have someone feel that way about her.

Until now.

But she couldn't *belong* with him. In his time. And he certainly couldn't belong in hers.

He took sip of coffee. She couldn't see the cup, except in the mirror. Another oddity. All of it, her compassion for him, the comprehension of their physical separation, the years of time separating them—even though they sat at the same table—should impress the impossibility of all that, and the importance of what she needed to tell him.

It didn't.

In part.

She still had to tell him, and would, but she certainly didn't want to. The outcome left a bitter taste in her mouth and turned her stomach queasy. She'd never claimed life wasn't fair. Hadn't cared enough to. But she did now, and this wasn't fair. It just wasn't fair. None of it. He and his wife should have lived a long and happy life together.

How could meeting someone—in this case a ghost—make someone question all they'd ever known about themselves?

"So." He broke the heavy silence surrounding

them. "This wife of Leonard's, why did she think I should will everything to her?"

Liz traced a finger along the image of his jaw in the mirror, glancing up when she knew he was watching her. Leaning back, she drew a breath. It had changed her. He'd changed her because none of this had seemed so difficult, so heart-wrenching last night. She exhaled. "Because she insisted Robert, the third son Nan and Cliff raised, was actually the child of their niece. A woman named Cindy."

"Cindy? Cindy Franklin from Cheyenne?"

"Yes." Regret weighed heavy inside her. "You know her." It wasn't a question. The future proved he knew her, but a girl could have hope, and she was a girl.

"Yes, I know her."

So much for hope.

She couldn't swallow past the thick lump in her throat. Why was this happening to her? She'd taken the job at the antique shop because she'd been laid off and didn't have anything better to do. No, that wasn't exactly true. She'd hoped Vivi Anne's *special powers* would help her discover her own past. Fill the void that had lived inside her for as long as she could remember. Her life, not knowing who she was, had left her searching around all sorts of corners.

"I met her yesterday. The wagon I heard when we were upstairs, when you disappeared, that was Nan. She'd brought her niece out to get a horse."

"I didn't disappear." Her instant justification was futile, for it certainly didn't matter.

"You did in my time." He met her gaze in the mirror. "I got rid of them as soon as possible, but the house was empty when I came back in. You were gone."

"Nate arrived right after you left." Frustration filled her. "I had no choice but to leave. He doesn't want me out here without his knowledge." Her gaze went to the stove. The now used-looking stove. It had been brand new yesterday. Brand spanking new.

"Why?"

She shrugged, still staring at the stove, questioning if it had changed or if that too was in her head. "He's afraid I'll steal something."

He muttered something under his breath. "It's my house, my things, if I say you can take something, you can."

A definite pain stung her chest. "No, it's not your house. Not in twenty-eighteen." Last night, while talking with Edith and Les, several things had crisscrossed her mind. Everything from having the old house moved into town, to finding a way for it to stay right where it was, but lived in by generations of his off-spring. That second idea was the one she'd gone with last night. The one that now twisted her insides into a knot so tight her stomach burned.

Maybe Edith's coffee was the cause of that. It had been rather strong, and she hadn't bothered to eat any breakfast. She'd started calling Lou to open the gate shortly after waking up. And had continued to call him every five minutes until he'd finally answered at quarter after seven. That's when she'd told him, in answer to his grumbles, that no one else in town would help him when it came selling off things from the *Rocking L* and he'd better be at the gate in fifteen minutes.

She'd never been so passionate about something

before, and had amazed herself with the threats she'd made, but she'd never taken this kind of a stake in anything before. Surprisingly, that didn't scare her. Not in the least.

It had taken Lou thirty minutes to arrive at the gate. She'd informed him that would not happen tomorrow. Then, because she'd been on a roll, she'd said she'd call him this evening, when she was ready to leave, and that he was to inform Nate of that. She truly didn't care whether either of them had other plans or not. Today, she would not be leaving until she said it was time.

On her way out of town she'd stopped at a convenience store and purchased a box of granola bars, a bag of dried fruit, and a few bottles of water so she wouldn't need to leave for nourishment. She questioned running out to her car to get something right now. It might help her stomach.

However, the pained looked on Rance's face quelled that thought. The desire to lay a consoling hand on his arm had her squeezing the mirror handle harder. Even though she'd felt a connection when they'd held up their hands up earlier, actually touching him, lying a consoling hand on his arm, was impossible. No matter how badly she wanted to do just that.

She glanced at the mirror and frowned. Just like the stove, the sterling silver around the glass had lost some of its luster. It now had an aged patina about it.

"It is my place, my ranch, in nineteen-o-one," he said, sounding somewhat hollow.

Reminded of what she'd learned last night, she nodded. "Yes, it is, and there is a way to make sure it still is yours in twenty-eighteen."

"I'll be dead in twenty-eighteen."

She bit her lip until it hurt. "But your decedents won't be."

A shine flashed in his eyes briefly before he closed them. When he opened them again the pain she noted was so strong her heart clenched. For a second she feared it had stopped beating right then and there and might never start up again.

"I don't have any decedents, not immediate ones."

Her heart was still working because each beat stung. "Yes, you do," she said so softly she barely heard herself.

He frowned, and bitterness filled his glare.

"The baby that Nan and Cliff raised, Robert, who was really their niece's son…" She had to let the burning air out of her lungs. "Was also your son."

"Like hell!"

His shout had made the windows rattle. He'd disappeared, too, but the hum banging against her ear drums said he was still at the table—or nearby at least. In her mind, she'd imagined him jumping to his feet.

With patience and a compassion that was new to her, she waited until the vibrations died down. "I can't see you when you're not touching the mirror."

His imaged flashed twice before it formed completely. "Maybe I don't want you to see me." He stood beside the table. "Maybe I don't want to see you."

She didn't take his anger to heart. It was understandable. She was experiencing her own misgivings about the gossip Edith had shared. However, Edith had also said Janice's tale of Rance being Leonard's grandfather had held credibility. Cliff and Nan had been his best friends, and quite possibly had invited Cindy to stay with them for the sole purpose of trying to make him get over the death of his wife. No one, not Cliff, Nan, or Cindy, ever breathed a word of who was Robert's real father. By the time Janice was putting the puzzle pieces together, he and anyone else who might have known, had already died, so there'd been no one around to disclaim her tale. That left plenty of people believing it was true. That he was Leonard's grandfather. Lou's great-grandfather. And Nate's.

Others may have believed it easy enough, but she didn't. Having met him and Lou and Nate. They were nothing alike. But considering all, stranger things had happened. Were happening.

"You said you met Nan's niece yesterday." She focused on the topic at hand rather than taking a route that would lead nowhere. Her own musings only caused more confusion.

"So? That doesn't mean—" He snapped his lips shut and his nostrils flared as he took a deep breath. "That woman, Cindy Franklin from Cheyenne, is more trouble than she's worth. I'll tell you that right now. And if she gets herself pregnant while visiting Nan and Cliff, I have nothing to do with it."

"But what if you do?" The thought was as pungent as the words, but she had to say them. "Think about it, Rance. If you have a child with Cindy and the two of you raise him instead of giving him to Nan and Cliff, everything will be different. It's the domino theory. Everything's connected, and one small change…" Wow, this was tough. Her insides were literally aching.

Stubbornly, he shook his head.

Her next statement would be no easier than the first, but had to come out. "Maybe Cindy, if you give her a chance, could make you forget your wife, make you stop waiting for Beth to return, and—"

He disappeared.

"Rance, don't do that now." None of this was easier for her to say than for him to listen to, and it wasn't going to get any better. She had to say it. The rumors about him living his entire life in the cabin were true. He'd said so himself this morning. She couldn't let that happen.

There was no hum, but he was nearby. Everything but her ears and eyes said so.

"Beth isn't coming back." Her eyes burnt and she pressed her free hand to the sting in her nose. "Not ever. She died in that train accident, and you can't waste over half a century believing she didn't."

The anger in his eyes when he reappeared sent a shiver over her.

"I…" he growled, "can believe anything I damn well please."

He disappeared again, and emptiness surrounded her.

He was gone.

The room became so blurry she closed her eyes. Moisture dripped from beneath her lashes, scalding her skin. She hadn't cried in a long time but knew that once tears started to fall, it was impossible to stop them.

She laid her head on the table and let them flow. All the strange and powerful emotions racking her insides needed an avenue of escape.

Time eluded her. No matter what century it might be, clocks clicked away second after second. She may have cried for ten minutes or two hours. All she knew was when she lifted her head, her cheeks felt as dry and brittle as cornflakes. Her insides were back to being empty, too. As emptied and hollow as they'd always been.

Her gaze first caught the mirror, and then the stove. Both looked brand new again.

Brand-spanking-new.

Rance stomped his way across the yard, toward the barn where he planned on—Aw hell, he didn't know what he planned on doing. He wanted to throttle something, rip it apart with his bare hands. Do something to channel all this pain, all this anger, out of his system.

What else could a man do when his very own wife sat beside him at a table and told him she was never coming back? Told him he should forget all about her and have a baby with someone else. A baby the two of them would have had if she…

He spun around, back toward the house, but mid-turn, he caught movement out the corner of his eye. A rider coming up the road had him cursing aloud.

In no mood for company, as soon as Cliff rode close enough to hear, Rance shouted. "What the hell do you want?"

Cliff brought his horse to a complete stop. Both the man and animal eyed him wearily. Never one to be guided by good judgment, Cliff dismounted.

"Came out to settle up for the horse." Cliff rubbed a thoughtful hand over his black mustache. "But—"

"There's no settling up to be done. Just return it when you're done with it. Or keep it, I don't care."

"What's happened?"

My wife just told me to forget she ever existed, he wanted to shout, but knew how crazy that sounded. Even to him. "Nothing." Changing his mind, he waved a hand at Cliff. "Other than your wife brought some silly young girl out here." Stepping closer, he waggled a finger. "You keep that niece of yours away from my property, you hear?"

"I hear you." Cliff removed his hat and wiped the sweat from his brow with his forearm. "Wasn't my idea to bring her here, to Cody. She got herself in a nip of trouble down in Cheyenne and her mother is hoping Nan will straighten her out."

"It's going to take a hell of a lot more than Nan." If anything Beth said was true, and for some only-God-knows-why-reason, he believed, at least parts, of what she'd said, Cliff and Nan were in for loads of trouble with Nan's niece. "You should send her right back to her folks. Deliver her yourself to make sure she gets there. And stays."

Cliff nodded. "I'll admit that I have the same misgivings, but I can't argue with Nan."

"Why the hell not?" He was still spitting-mad over arguing with Beth.

"Because it does me about as much good as arguing with you." Cliff folded his arms and leaned a shoulder against his horse. "So, how much do I owe you for Horse?"

His spine, the very top where it met his neck, was burning and tight. He rubbed at the spot. "You don't." He turned to look at the house. He'd never argued with Beth, either. There'd never been a reason to. Although, she looked awfully cute all flushed and huffy, trying to get her point across. A time or two he'd pretended to be mad, just to watch her ire grow. He'd never really been mad at her, but there had been couple of times he'd been afraid she'd get hurt. Those had been the only times they'd ever really argued—when she'd had something set in her mind that he'd thought she might get hurt doing.

Turning back to Cliff, he shook his head. "Just return Horse when you're done with her."

"Good enough." Cliff nodded. "And I'll tell Nan your place is off limits to Cindy."

"More than my place should be off limits," he warned.

"I agree, but a man has to keep his wife happy."

Nodding, his gaze returned to the house. "You're right about that."

An eerie sensation had him turning back toward Cliff, whose brows were raised.

"I-uh-I left a pot of coffee on the stove." He waved toward the house. "I best go check on it."

Cliff nodded. "Nan said you were living in the house again."

"Yeah, well…" He rubbed the back of his neck again. That's when he realized he'd forgotten to put on his hat. Cliff was sure to notice that. Being a lawman, nothing got past him, and the glint in his eyes said he was thinking hard. "I gotta go check on that coffee." Cliff could also smell a lie a mile away and was sniffing like a hound dog. "Thanks for riding out, and, um, I'll catch up with you in a couple of days."

Without waiting for Cliff to say more, or because he knew his friend was about to, he took off for the house, forcing his feet to walk when they wanted to run like a Comanche on the war path. That would only give Cliff more to investigate. Which, as a lawman, he was sure to do.

At the porch steps he paused to turn around. Cliff

stood beside his horse. Rance, tapping a toe inside his boot, held his own stance until his friend stuck a foot in a stirrup and swung into the saddle. He waved and cursed the time it took Cliff to rein his horse around and mosey under the *Rocking L* sign. Only when he was sure the man wasn't going to turn around did he spin about and shoot into the house.

The mirror was still on the table, but Beth was nowhere to be seen. She was here, though, the quickening beneath his beating heart told him so. He grabbed the mirror and hurried into the center parlor. The room was empty, but he smiled as his gaze briefly paused on the front porch. It was completely screened in—Beth's idea. She'd said it was their house and they could put the front door wherever they wanted to. Therefore, they'd build the house so the front faced the rolling hills of the western pasture, so they could sit out there in the evenings, watching the sun set together. They had, too, more than once.

Turning, he made his way down the short hall to the back parlor where Beth had sat at her treadle sewing machine making curtains, pillows, and all sorts of other things after they'd completed the house. He checked the washroom too, before going back to front parlor. Beside the door that led to the porch was the staircase to the second floor. Four bedrooms, the perfect number, Beth had said. The door to the first one was opened, not the one they'd shared. A smaller one that held little more than a rocking chair and bookcase. The room he'd visited last night.

She was sitting in a chair with a book on her lap.

Of a mind not to be noticed, not yet, he angled himself so he could see her, but the mirror was behind the wall beside him. Sunlight shone through the parted curtains, basking upon her, and though she looked whole, perfect, there was also a thin transparency to her.

He shook his head, unable to completely define all that he knew to be true and what sat before his eyes. He couldn't make out the title of the book on her lap but wondered if it was the one he'd searched out last night. That story might be closer to the truth than he'd wanted to believe. Beth would want him to know his ways were harmful, to him and others, and would want him to change. As determined now as she'd ever been, she wouldn't stop until she found a way to convince him, either.

Gently, yet as brilliant as the sun peeking over the hills in the morning, a tentative smile rose upon her lips.

"You're back," she whispered.

He checked to make sure the mirror was still behind the wall beside the doorway.

"I can't see you, but I can feel you."

He felt her too, in ways he couldn't describe.

"Come in," she said just as softly as before. "Please." Removing her feet from the squat footstool, she kept her gaze on the door. "Please. We need to talk."

He might stand over six-feet tall and weigh a hundred and seventy pounds, but his brawn and muscles were of little use when it came to her. She had the ability to bring him to his knees from the moment they'd met. Remembering that might make all this easier.

He entered the room, watching the way she closely

followed the mirror in his hand. She reached out and grasped the edge. "Sit down on the stool."

It was like sitting on a milking stool, but he did so, knees bent and poking in the air, and arm stretched out because he'd never let go of the mirror.

"I'm sorry," she whispered, "for what I had to tell you earlier. But it's the truth. I can't lie to you."

The unshed tears in her eyes stabbed at his chest. Beth had never lied to him. Not once. She wouldn't now, either. It would take more than a century to change that.

She shook her head. "I wish I could, but I can't."

The book he'd searched out last night was on top of the bookshelf, where he'd left it last night. "Are you my ghost of Christmases yet to come?"

"What?"

He nodded toward the bookcase, wondering if she'd be able to see it if he picked it up. She hadn't seen the coffee cup this morning, leaving him no solid understanding of what she could or couldn't see. The mirror was the only thing he knew worked for sure. "*A Christmas Carol.*"

Her gaze settled on the bookcase. "Ebenezer Scrooge. You have no idea how many versions of that story are out there. I have no idea. Walt Disney even has a version or two."

He had no idea who Walt Disney was, or how many books anyone had written like that one.

Sighing, she turned her gaze back to him. "I don't know. Maybe."

"Maybe?"

"I'm as confused by all this as you are. But I know I'm not a ghost. I'm not dead. I'm a real living person,

and even though I'm not living in your time, I feel…"
She closed her eyes and licked her lips. "It's hard to
explain, but when I'm with you, in the same room as
you, I feel things I've never felt before. Real things.
Things I couldn't imagine." Her lids fluttered open. "I
also have a sense of purpose, of…I don't know how to
describe it, but deep inside I don't want this place
burned down this weekend, or next weekend, or next
month, or next year. I don't want your things sold. I
don't want…"

Her gaze had landed on the mirror, and her fingers
were trembling as she ran them over the silver.

"What is it?" he asked.

"The mirror, it's new again."

"It doesn't look any different to me." Realizing that
wouldn't ease the disquiet he sensed, he twisted the
mirror slightly. "It's not very old. It was a wedding
gift."

"From you?"

He nodded.

"When?"

He purposefully chose to not focus on the fact she
didn't remember their wedding date. "January."

"Of this year." There was sadness in her quiet tone.
"Six months. You were just starting your lives
together."

He nodded again but had to speak. "Whether it was
six months or sixty years, I couldn't have loved—" He
stopped before saying *you*, and swallowed. "Her more."

"I believe that. And I believe she loved you just as
much."

"I believe that, too."

"Then you have to believe, she'd have never

117

wanted you to mourn her for the rest of your life." She wiped away a single tear sliding down the side of her cheek. "Beth would never have wanted that."

He'd heard that so many times, in so many ways, by so many people, he'd thought he'd grown deaf to it, but this time, it resounded in his ears and in his heart. There was no anger flaring inside him, either, just a dull, steady ache.

"That's not what you would have wanted for her, either. Is it?"

He shook his head.

"That's just easier to accept, isn't it?"

He nodded. Beth's happiness had been foremost in his mind since seeing her sitting on the corral at her father's house.

"I think that's why this happened. Why our paths crossed, even though we are a century apart. Something happened that wasn't supposed to have happened, and now the universe is trying to fix it."

Beth wasn't supposed to have died, that's what wasn't supposed to have happened. She wasn't supposed to have been on that train. He bit his lips together to keep his thoughts to himself.

"I know it sounds crazy, but all of this is crazy. And I know there are much larger, much more disastrous events that have taken place the last one hundred years, but I guess the fallout of all those things, were meant to be."

"She wasn't supposed to be on that train." The words were out before he could stop them and that goaded him. Admitting that was the same as admitting she was dead, something he'd refused to do.

"What?"

The air in his lungs burned as he let it out. "She wasn't supposed to come home until the next day but had sent a message that she was coming home a day early. Webster delivered it to me the same time he delivered the stove."

"Beth never saw the new stove downstairs, did she?"

"No."

She wiped at another tear sitting on her cheek, and he profoundly sensed this wasn't all about him, or Beth, at least not the Beth he'd known.

"What aren't you telling me?"

"It doesn't matter," she said.

"Yes, it does. It matters a great deal to me." When she shook her head, he forced himself not to call her Beth. "Tell me, Elizabeth; tell me what happened in your life to bring you here?"

"I don't think it's connected."

"I still want to know." He'd give his very life to be able to touch her right now, to make the intimate connection he felt in his heart real.

She laid a hand on her chest and closed her eyes. When her lids fluttered open, she shook her head, not in disagreement, but as if she couldn't believe something. "It is amazing," she whispered. "The things I feel when I'm talking to you."

"I know. I wish I could touch you, show you, exactly what I'm feeling." Because that was impossible, he locked his gaze with hers. "I can't, but I want you to look into my eyes so you'll know just how much you mean to me. Ghost or not, Elizabeth or Beth, I want to help you. I'm here to help you."

Lost in an upheaval of finding a way to make her

understand, he almost missed the slip of tongue he'd made and watched closely to see if she grew dizzy. There was no sign of it, at least not in her eyes, and he refused to even blink, not wanting to lose the connection holding them together.

It was several moments before she broke the connection by blinking, and then smiled. "I'm the one who's here to help you."

"What's wrong with helping each other?" he asked, with a hint of teasing. Beth had always responded to that.

It worked; at least it had her shaking her head as if exasperated. "All right." She frowned slightly. "I guess it could be connected, in a small sort of way."

"What?"

"When I was five, my parents died in a car accident. I don't remember it, I don't remember them, only what people have told me."

Once again, he'd give anything to touch her. For perhaps the first time, he seriously considered this may not be his Beth. Her parents were alive and well up in Billings. They sent messages regularly, asking how he was getting along. He sent a message in return each time, saying fine, he was fine, even though he wasn't.

Knowing how close she'd been to her parents, how much family meant to her, he whispered, "Aw, honey, I'm sorry."

"Thank you, but like I said, I don't remember them, so I don't miss them. However, I've always wondered about them." Her grin was a bit sheepish. "And tried everything I could think of to find out more about them. I joined an online heritage site but didn't even get a single leaf."

He bit his lips together to keep from asking what leaves had to do with any of this.

"I tried being hypnotized, which was a complete failure as well. So was the fortune teller at a kiosk in the mall. She wouldn't even take my money, saying she couldn't read me, that there was nothing to read. I even called a few internet hotlines, only to be given vague answers like *'your parents are at peace'* and several *'there's a tall dark stranger in your future.'* Which is complete garbage. Every dead person is at peace, and people walk past tall dark strangers every day."

It wasn't easy, but he kept a straight face at her gibberish.

"That's why I was so drawn to Vivi Anne. She claims she's not a psychic, but she is different. Not just her personality, which is a mixture of a child of the sixties and an eccentric elderly cat-lady. Vivi Anne is intuitive. Some of the things she knows, she senses, boggle a person's mind. I was hoping she could tell me something more about myself."

"Vivi Anne is your friend, the one who owns the antique store?"

"Yes."

"Has she told you anything about your parents?"

"No." She sighed as a thoughtful expression crossed her face. "But I don't know if she'd tell me even if she knew something."

"Why not?"

"Because she isn't like that. She'd want me to discover it myself." Her expression softened. "And I think that's why I'm here. In a way, I can relate to Robert. Maybe his life, his son's life, his grandson's life, would all be different if he'd known his real father."

He refused to allow himself to be provoked into anger. "I'm not his father, but if it will help you, if it's what you want, I'll help you discover who is."

Her eyes softened and he detected a fair amount of sadness in them.

"You may not want to believe it right now, but given time, your pain will fade, and falling in love with someone else won't seem so impossible."

Needing to be the sensible one, not the righteous one, he went for details. "All right, when was, or is, Robert born?"

She frowned, and grimaced, and shook her head. "I'm not sure. I didn't ask."

He doubted he'd love Beth any less five years from now but chose to push her logic. "If it's five years from now, it might be plausible." Not willing to give in too much, he shook his head. "But Nan's niece, the one I met yesterday, isn't going to wait five years to get pregnant."

She frowned, but then one brow lifted. "Maybe she sweeps you off your feet."

"I weigh a hundred and seventy pounds. Nothing sweeps me off my feet."

She pinched her lips together, but then, a rather insolent smile formed. "The right woman can sweep a man twice her size off his feet."

"I know," he said.

"You do?"

He nodded and leaned closer to whisper. "Because I know how much you weigh."

Chapter Eight

Liz couldn't say she was any closer to convincing Rance he was Robert's father, nor was she any closer to wanting that to be true, but at least, she had a starting point. Something tangible to work from. Her theory had depth. If he and this Cindy girl got married, his future would change drastically. So would Robert's and possibly Leonard's and then Lou's and Nate's. That one little incident could make all the difference in the world. He would never forget Beth. Liz knew that just by looking at him, but it could lighten the pain he harbored in his heart.

She'd seen it. As unbelievable as that was, it had happened. Upstairs, when he'd told her to look into his eyes to see how much she meant to him, she had, and she'd seen it. Love. Strong, undeniable and unstoppable love. So powerful she'd felt it in her heart as surely as if he'd reached out and touched her.

If someone had told her that was possible, she'd have questioned their stability. And hers. However, that had been before she'd been thrust into a dimension that allowed her to meet and converse with a man in the previous century. A man she wished lived in the here and now. He was so genuine, so authentic. There was nothing phony or bogus about him. He said what he believed and he believed what he said. If men like him still existed, she may have found the ability to believe in love. The way he did. Men like him might still exist somewhere and she'd just never encountered them. In fact, evolution would be a sad thing if they didn't.

She'd seen something else when she'd looked into his eyes. Sincerity. That had been why she'd told him about her parents, the car crash, and her search to find out more about them. About herself. He'd also offered to help. Of course he thought discovering who Robert's father was would help her, and that was fine. He was the type who'd much rather help someone else rather than themselves.

She spent a good portion of the day taking all that into consideration.

The day, as it was, would forever remain with her as one of the strangest, yet most wonderful of her life. Finding Rance had changed her. Not only in opening her mind to ghosts and other such possibilities, but to herself. Maybe she'd thought she didn't care about others because she'd never wanted to. At least not like she wanted to care about him.

After his comment about knowing how much she weighed, the room upstairs had become as charged as the kitchen had this morning. Sparks practically filled the air. Not willing her mind to go down the kissing line again, she'd suggested they come back down stairs.

He'd agreed, and as he put it, said the animals still needed to eat. He'd invited her outside, but even with both of them holding onto the mirror, once she stepped outside of the house, he disappeared. In the end, he went outside alone to complete his chores and afterward led her through the house pointing out various items for her to catalog in her notebook.

The details he pointed out gave her a greater

connection with specific antiques. As if she'd needed that. She hadn't. She'd already felt connected to so many things. It had always been that way for her, and the reason she enjoyed visiting antique stores. All she'd had to do was close her eyes and she could see herself living amongst all sorts of old and wonderful things— even if they were mere castaways from other people's lives.

Here, in his house, those inner impressions were stronger and more powerful than she'd ever encountered before.

Some things, like the stove and mirror, had grown tarnished again, while other things remained new, as perfect as the day they'd been in his time.

It was all so strange. There didn't seem to be a rhyme or reason to any one piece of logic. Except for the fact she cared about each and every item he showed her. She cared about him, too.

"Can we take a break?"

Looking up from where she was making notes about a stack of playbills from what she knew to be one of Buffalo Bill's first shows, she caught Rance's image in the mirror, and his grimace. "Getting tired?" They'd made their way through several of the downstairs rooms and were in the front parlor, looking through a side cabinet full of miscellaneous paperwork.

"Hungry."

She laughed.

He frowned. "What's funny about that?"

She shook her head and shrugged. It was hard to explain, and uncanny, how comfortable she'd become around him. "I just didn't expect a ghost to worry about food."

"I'm not a ghost."

"I know, but my mind still wants to categorize you that way." Mainly because she kept telling herself that.

"Why?"

To protect myself. Not able to admit that, she shrugged. "It's easier to believe, I guess." That and the fact that even though she could see him, he was a rather ghostly image. When the light hit him just right, she could see right through him.

"Not for me."

It was pretty hard for her to believe, too. This was all so flipping crazy. And just kept getting crazier. Yet, she'd never felt so, well, whole as she did while with him. She closed her notebook and stuck the pen in the wire binding. "Okay. Let's eat."

"I can fry some eggs, but not sure you'll be able to eat them. In your time I mean," he said as they walked toward the kitchen.

Enticed by the half-grin, half-scowl on his face, she laughed again. "One-hundred-year-old eggs? No thank you. I have some things in my car. I'll go get my lunch while you cook yours."

They stood next to the table but looked at each other as if waiting for the other to let go of the mirror. After several moments, they both laughed.

"On the count of three," he said.

"All right. You count."

"Are you going to let go, or am I?" he asked. "I don't want the mirror to fall."

She laughed again. Letting go of a mirror shouldn't be this arduous. "You let go, and I'll set the mirror on the table."

"All right. One. Two. Three."

He let go and disappeared.

She held her breath and stance for a second, just to make sure she could still sense him. Satisfied by his presence, she set the mirror on the table. "I'll be right back."

The kitchen looked completely empty when she returned with her food as well as the bag that held her camera and pricing book, but the hum told her it wasn't. She grinned and sincerely wished she could see him.

She took a chair at the table and knowing it would take him time to get the stove going, she took out the pricing book. A hum next to her ear had her touching the mirror. He appeared in the glass, behind her and gestured toward the book with his chin.

"What's that?"

"It's called a three-ring binder. Viva Anne put it together from several books and magazines that set values on common antiques."

"That lamp on the top of the page, it looks like the one in the parlor," he said.

"Yes, it does, and the one you have is in excellent shape."

"Is that the price?"

The shock in his tone had her glancing at the mirror, and smiling at the surprise on his face. "That is the approximate value of the one pictured. Yours is a duplex, meaning it has two wicks, so it's worth is closer to the bottom price." She pointed at the number. "Two-hundred and seventy-five dollars."

"That lamp isn't worth that much. I know. I bought it, and believe me, I would never have paid anywhere close to that much. I'd have sat in the dark first."

"That's what its worth in twenty-eighteen." She

stopped shy of saying that was the reason why Nate and Lou wanted to sell everything, it was getting harder and harder to stomach that idea. "How are your eggs coming?"

"Stove's heating up. Turn the page, what else is in that book?"

She flipped through several pages until finding a table like the one in the parlor that the lamp sat on. "Your table with claw feet will easily appraise at seven-hundred-fifty." Scrolling one finger to the page on the other side, she stopped to point at another picture. "And the dresser in your bedroom is a lot like this one, but larger, so it'll appraise out at more."

"More than one-thousand-five-hundred?"

"Yes." Flipping a few more pages, she stopped on a page with kitchen items. "Here's your ice box."

He whistled. "Fourteen-hundred?"

"Yes." She closed the book as a sickening feeling rose in her stomach. "Your stove should be hot."

His image disappeared from the mirror, and she let out a long breath. The thought of Lou and Nate benefitting from all of Rance's personal possessions had never pleased her, but now the idea of selling his items hurt. It was odd, but she'd known about some of the items even before he mentioned when or where he'd acquired them. That could have been easy enough to decipher considering he'd clammed up every time an item had been one that Beth had brought with her from Montana upon their marriage. Other items hadn't surprised her either, the Native American ones.

He had been born in the eighteen-seventies when the west had been really wild. An era they made movies about. It was so easy to imagine him during that time, and she hadn't been the least bit surprised when he'd said his father had been half Shoshone and had lived the nomadic life of a plainsman. Nor that his mother had been a white woman.

Once again, a hum drew her attention and she touched the mirror. He was already seated at the table. She lifted the mirror and angled it enough to see a plate of scrambled eggs.

"Those look good." She laid the mirror flat again but adjusted the angle so she could see the reflection of his face.

"They are. What are you eating?"

She plucked things out of her bag with her free hand. "These are called granola bars, and this is dried fruit, and this, a bottle of water."

"Water? There's water—" He shook his head. "What's it in?"

Letting go of the mirror long enough to open the bottle, she took a several swallows before setting down the cap and touching the mirror again. She drank enough that she could squeeze the bottle without any water flowing out, and did so. "It's called plastic. Practically everything is made out of it in some shape or form. Even my car."

"Your car?"

"Yes. Much harder plastic than this bottle, but plastic nonetheless." She picked up the granola bar and bit the corner to tear open the package using only one hand. "Even this wrapper has plastic in it."

"What is that?"

His reflection was staring at the granola bar, and his grimace said it looked utterly appalling to him.

She grinned and took a bite.

He flinched and looked as if he was about to gag.

She had to swallow fast, twice, to keep from choking as a laugh bubbled up her throat. A drink of water helped wash down the granola. "It's not that bad."

"I won't even say what that looks like, but I've cleaned up plenty of it."

"Are you saying my lunch looks like horse shit?"

"Guess you've cleaned up some too."

She laughed at his quick wit. "Actually, I haven't, but I've always had a faint memory about horses." That was true, for as long as she could remember, she had an inkling there were horses in her past. The Walkers never had any animals, but her memories had been before then. Like when she was really, really little. "It's not really a memory, more like a feeling deep in my stomach."

"It's probably the food."

She tried not to laugh again, but failed. "How are your eggs?"

"Good." He made a show of poking a fork full of scrambled eggs into his mouth. "Mmmm. Too bad you can't taste them."

More than willing to play along, she took bite of her granola bar and closed her eyes as she chewed, pretending it was the most delicious thing she'd ever eaten. After swallowing, she opened her eyes. "I know mine is better, it has chocolate chips."

He lifted a brow. "What are chocolate chips?"

She leaned in his direction. "Oh, you have no idea what you're missing."

"Yes, I do," he said.

He wasn't referring to chocolate, and that sent a

rush of heat throughout her system. How could she possibly have the hots for someone who was over a hundred years older than her, still mourning the loss of his wife, and a ghost? Time warp or not, he was not alive and well in twenty-eighteen.

"So, what else do you have to eat?"

She picked up a small bag. "Dried tropical fruit."

"Is that the only kind of food you have in your time? Dried stuff?" He nodded toward the binder. "Is it because everything is so expensive?"

"No, we have lots of other foods. We still have eggs and bacon. The world loves bacon. They even put it on ice cream."

"They do?"

"Yes, if I had my computer I'd show you pictures, or if I had better cell service."

"What's a computer and cell service?"

That started an in-depth conversation about *modern* things. Of which he thought she was fibbing most of the time. Some of the things she told him about made him laugh, others, like the wars and diseases made him thoughtful and forlorn, and he seriously didn't believe her when she said men had walked on the moon.

He'd told her things too, surprising details she hadn't thought about until he started talking. Like all the horses he trained for Buffalo Bill Cody, and the man's Wild West Shows. The performances were a phenomenon in his era, worldwide.

She asked questions about his family, but it was as if she knew the answers, in part at least, before he answered. As strange as it was, and it was strange, her knowledge hadn't come from Edith last night or her years of studying American History. She intuitively knew things about him. They just popped into her head moments before he said them. His father's father had been white, a trapper, who lived each winter with his father's mother's tribe.

Liz searched her mind as he talked but found no explanation for knowing the things she did. Perhaps, because of his way of life, she knew he'd been raised white. But that didn't explain how she knew other things, things he skirted around but didn't completely say. Like how he'd lived with his mother's parents near Laramie. His mother's parents had never believed their daughter could have fallen in love with a heathen, as they called all Indians, and when she died after giving birth to him, they'd sent the army out to retrieve their grandchild. She questioned if it might be because, like her, he had no memory of his real parents. If that somehow gave them an internal connection. She didn't ask that aloud. Mainly because, bottom line, it didn't matter.

"When I left my grandparents' house," he continued, "I came out here to meet my grandmother's brother. He told me that my father had given me to the army to take back to my grandparents when I was little in order to save the lives of many in their tribe."

Her breath lodged in her throat at the idea of him as a baby being taken away from his father and put into the hands of virtual strangers. She'd been there herself, and knew how frightening it was. "Did they welcome you when you arrived?"

He nodded. "Yes. My father had died shortly after the army took me away, and most of his people had been confined to reservations, but they knew who I was, and were happy to see me. I didn't stay with them long before I came here to Cody and started training horses with Hiah. He lives north of Cody on his own land. He never went to the reservation because he'd married a white woman."

She wished she could meet that uncle but understood the impossibility of that. She did, however, take note of the hint of Native American heritage in Rance. The fine sculpture of his cheek bones, the darkness of his eyes, how his glorious tan might not be all from the sun. That had her wondering if he'd have the often-teased farmer's tan when he took off his shirt.

Of course she'd wonder that. Her mind kept bugging her about all sorts of things pertaining to his body. Which was utterly ridiculous.

Liz was trying to get her wandering mind back in order when a noise startled her.

"What is it?" Rance asked. "You jumped."

"Someone's here."

The both stood and moved to the door, with the mirror between them. The let down and utter disgust that washed over her as Lou strut around his sportscar was like none other. She should be glad it wasn't Nate, but in truth, she didn't want to see either cousin.

"Who is it?" Rance asked.

"Lou. He said he'd come get me before dark." She took a step back so Lou couldn't see them through the screen door. "Let go of the mirror. We don't want him to see you."

Rance's grin was a bit evil as he disappeared. Feeling him still standing next to her, she whispered, "Don't do anything foolish."

A hum vibrated her ear, and she almost told him to grab the mirror, would have if the door hadn't open right then.

"Hello."

"It's not dark yet," she said.

"It's after six." Lou stepped inside. "I tried calling, but cell phones don't always work that well out here."

She had no idea if her phone worked out here or not, she'd left it in her car and hadn't thought about it all day, other than when explaining it to Rance. She was surprised it was so late. Had no idea they'd been sitting at the table talking for so many hours.

Lou let the screen door shut slowly behind him and gestured toward her left hand. "What's that?"

Her heart skipped a beat before she realized he was referring to the mirror. She held it up. "Just a mirror."

She didn't want to, but considering what could happen if she didn't, she relinquished her hold when Lou grasped the mirror.

He gave it a couple twists and turns. "I sure hope you found more than this."

She balled her hand in to a fist to keep from snatching the mirror back. However, the hum that vibrated her ear made her smile inwardly.

Lou glanced around cautiously and swallowed visibly. "You hear something?"

"No." She pinched her lips tighter to keep a smile at bay.

Somewhat sheepishly, he handed her the mirror. "I know you said you'd call when you were ready, but I really was worried about you being out here all day by yourself, and tried calling."

She considered saying she wasn't ready to leave yet, but it would soon be dark, and she wasn't certain she should stay alone with Rance after dark. Leaving

134

would be best, give her a more clear perspective. She already cared far more about him than she should. "I didn't hear my phone. I left it in the car." Not about to put much credence behind his concern, she held up the mirror. "I'll go put this away upstairs. I was documenting things." Waving at the table, and her empty wrappers and water bottle still sitting there from when they'd eaten, which seemed like just a short time ago, she added, "Then I'll gather my stuff and meet you outside."

When Lou glanced around again, she got a feeling he was considering following her up stairs. She tensed, but upon closer inspection, pinched her lips together again in order to hide another outward smile. He was nervous. Like the place gave him the willies. It was a luxury, knowing what she did and he didn't, and too good to not use. "It might just have been the wind, but there was a lot of creaking in the house today."

His attempt to look unaffected was classic, and comical. "I do have plans this evening, so if you could hurry up."

"Sure, go ahead and wait outside." She gestured toward the door while holding back a giggle. "It'll get stuffy in here when I start closing the windows."

His hurried exit was almost comical, but she waited until he'd crossed the porch before she left the room. Rance appeared at her side when she was half way up the stairs. She'd known he was there, and hadn't needed to whisper for him to take the mirror.

"Did he go outside?"

"Yes. You can't see him?"

"No. Couldn't hear him either," he answered. "Just you. What did he say when he took the mirror?"

"You saw that, but not him?"

"I saw the mirror disappear and then reappear. What did he say?"

"That he hopes I found more antiques than just the mirror." Walking next to him was so natural, the mirror hung at her side as they climbed the steps and talked. "I heard a hum, like you said something when he took it."

"I did. I asked where the mirror had gone and told you to get it back."

That sounds exactly like something he'd say. It was amazing how well she already knew him.

"What did he say when you told him about the creaking?"

No longer needing to hide her joy. She giggled. "He told me to hurry up."

"Scared of ghosts, is he?"

She laughed again, especially at the hint of pride in his tone. "It appears so."

"But you're not."

"Of course not, No one's afraid of Casper."

"Casper? Wyoming?"

She laughed, and then again at his frown. She really shouldn't be having this much fun but couldn't help it. Simply couldn't help it. "No. Casper was a ghost. A friendly ghost and a children's cartoon character."

"Oh. So you think I'm a cartoon character?"

His grin was about the sexiest one she'd ever seen. For a flash of a second—or longer—she found herself extremely jealous of Beth. As ridiculous as that was.

"No." She drew in a deep breath to contain the mixture of emotions that she couldn't explain, and really didn't want to, or need to. Fact is, she was happy.

Something she hadn't been for some time. "But you are a character."

They'd reached the top floor and were walking along the hallway, toward the bedroom. "So you have to leave."

It was a statement not a question, and the sadness of his tone made her stomach tighten. The happiness inside her started to fade. "Yes." She stopped shy of saying she had to, it was Lou's house. It wasn't. Not to Rance. "I'll be back tomorrow."

"I'm going to miss you."

Heat flushed her face. He'd made blood rush to other areas of her body more than once today. She couldn't react to that, nor could she tell him she'd miss him too. Her goal was for him to live his life in his time, not for…She shook her head to erase thoughts of things that could never be as they walked into bedroom. This caring for others was intense, leastwise when it came to caring about him. "I'll be back in the morning." She stopped near the dresser. "As early as possible."

"I'll be here all day."

Her mind and body were on two very different wave lengths. A crazy, wonderful, swirl was overtaking her body. Drawing a deep breath, she held the air in her lungs, hoping it would slow her internal reactions. It wasn't working. Not with the way he was looking at her—with a look that said he wanted to kiss her. She wanted that too. Even though she knew it was impossible. Crazy. He wasn't real, but a phantom from another era.

Her mind knew all that.

Her body was a different story. It had never wanted something so badly. Had never ached so profoundly.

Sexually.

She closed her eyes, trying to get her body in sync with her mind. With reality. Which proved impossible when a second later the most amazing thing happened.

Rance kissed her. As unfeasible as it was, heat covered her mouth along with a mystic pressure, like she'd experienced with her fingers this morning, in the kitchen when they'd held their hands up together.

The pressure on her mouth grew, became more intense. So did the swirl of sensations inside her. They became so strong, so specifically concentrated, her toes curled inside her shoes.

She was losing it. Totally losing it.

Yet at the same time, she refused to open her eyes in order to prove it wasn't happening. Couldn't. It was too magnificent. And she couldn't, wouldn't, deny herself just how amazing the impossible connection felt. If this is how he kissed, he had to be a fantastic lover.

She was kissing a ghost. And thinking about having sex with him.

Sex with a ghost.

Shut the back door and lock her in. She was nuts.

Between her swirling libido and her thoughts, she grew dizzy.

A dizzy, sex -craving, nut.

Dizzy.

She couldn't become dizzy.

She couldn't do this.

She tore open her eyes, only to close them again. He was close, but not close enough to kiss. That was more startling than if they'd been nose to nose. She'd been fantasying him kissing her?

No, he'd kissed her.

She'd swear it.

The way she was struggling to catch her breath proved it.

Didn't it?

His smile was mischievous, and all-knowing.

She stumbled. "I-I gotta go."

"Wait."

She was still holding the mirror. They both were. The mirror wasn't as heavy when they were both holding it. Another fantasy no doubt. He was a ghost. His touch couldn't lighten whatever she held. Yet, it seemed as if that was so. He looked so real, too. As valid and true as the mirror in her hand.

Real enough to kiss. Real enough to love.

She tried to get her disorganized thoughts back in line. She had to have at least a thread of rationality left somewhere. There was. "Lou's waiting."

Rance was still looking at her, but his expression had turned soft, as if he completely understood all the absurd thoughts dancing around in her head.

"Today was fun. Nice." He shook his head as if he wasn't able to say what he really wanted to. "I-I just want you to know how much I enjoyed your company. I guess I've been a little lonely, lately."

Her heart took a tumble. "I'll be back. I promise."

"I'll be here."

"Promise?"

He nodded and disappeared.

A wave of panic assaulted her but disappeared as fast as Rance had. He was still near. She could feel him. That allowed her to take a deep, calming breath, and another. She wasn't nuts. Was just having an encounter with a ghost. A nice ghost who was fun to talk to, extremely handsome, and made her feel whole. Complete. Wonderful.

She laid the mirror on the dresser and then crossed the room to close the window. As she turned, the mirror floated in the air near the door.

"You can't—" Flustered, she crossed the room and touched the mirror. "Put the mirror back. Lou might see it floating around."

"I will, but first, come with me."

"Where? Lou's waiting."

"It'll only take a moment."

Lou could wait. Rance was far more important. "All right."

He led her down the hallway, into the room with the small bookcase. "That box on the top shelf, can you see it?"

"Yes."

"Take that with you. Don't open now. Just take it with you."

A shiver rippled over her skin. Not of fear, but anticipation. "Why?"

"Just take it with you, and bring it back tomorrow."

It was small, no larger than a hardcover book, and looked like an old cigar box. She picked it up and turned toward the door. The mirror and Rance were gone. The desire to open the box was strong, but she told herself to wait.

And was glad because a moment later, his presence was as strong as when she could see him. He walked down the steps beside her and stood near as she gathered her trash off the table. She put the wrappers, her notebook, and the box in the bag with her extra water bottles, snacks, and the camera and pricing book, and then walked to the door. There, she whispered, "I'll see you tomorrow."

There was no hum, but still she smiled, convinced he'd heard. A wave of contentment, of knowledge that held no doubts, washed over her. He'd be here tomorrow, and so would she.

She stepped over the threshold and pulled the inside door shut, locking it before closing the screen door.

"Ready?" Lou asked.

"I guess," she said, while silently admitting she may never be ready to leave Rance's house.

Lou grinned. "You really like this place, don't you?"

"Yes, I do."

"I do, too." He shrugged. "It gives me the willies at times, but it also has, well, for lack of a better word, charm. It's charming how Rance loved his wife so much he waited his entire life for her to return. Left money in his will for this place to stay just as it is until Beth returned."

His smile, the sincerity in his voice struck her in an invisible and vulnerable way.

As a shiver rippled her spine, the idea he could be Rance's great-grandson gave birth in her brain. Her mind was still ping-ponging that information, until one ball landed in a hole. "When was your grandfather born?"

"My grandfather?" He shrugged. "I don't know."

"You must have some idea," she insisted.

"Why?" He glanced toward the house and back at her. "Wondering if the rumors are true? That Rance was my granddaddy's father?"

She shrugged, yet that possibility was gathering momentum. If he and Rance had to be related, she'd much prefer a fourth cousin twice removed or some other distant relative, but even that could mean Rance had children. With someone other than her.

Hopeless. That's what she was. Not only wanting to have sex with a ghost, she wanted to have his children.

Lou leaned closer. "Want to know what I think about that?"

She shivered, but then realized Lou couldn't know what she was thinking. She'd give anything to be able to say no she didn't want to know what he thought about Rance being his great grandfather, but she did want to know. Every last detail. "Yes."

"Then have dinner with me tonight."

"I thought you had plans."

"I do, but that doesn't mean they can't include you."

Her stomach flipped. Lou had the same brown eyes and dark hair as Rance. He wasn't as handsome. Well, to some, Lou might be considered very handsome, just not her. Back in school, when all the other girls where ogling over one guy or another, she'd never understood why. She'd always found something that *wasn't right* about them. About every man she'd ever met. Up until Rance.

She closed her eyes for a moment, once again searching for a coherent thought.

"You have to be hungry. You've been out here all day."

Opening her eyes, she glanced toward the house.

Why was that? Why did Rance seem to have every quality she'd deemed as *must haves* at one time in her life? Why was he able to make her feel things, to recognized things, that no one else ever had?

"I'll let you in on all the family secrets," Lou coaxed.

Her gaze had gone to the second floor, and she wondered if Rance could see them. Most likely not, unless something had changed, yet she had the distinct feeling he was there, watching her. The curtains were parted, and she distinctively recalled pulling them together when she'd closed the window.

"Personally, I think my mother came up with that story, about Rance being Robert's real father."

She snapped her head around. "You do?"

"Yep," Lou said.

"Why would she have done that?"

"To cover up the fact half the town wondered if I belonged to Leonard." Lou lifted a brow. "While Daddy had been out prowling for wife number four, Mommy hadn't been sitting at home twiddling her thumbs. She knew she was on her way out and figured if she could finagle a way for me to inherit Rance's place, she wouldn't end up empty-handed like wife number one and two had."

Her gaze had gone to the house again. Rance would never condone jumping from wife to wife as Leonard evidently had. He loved Beth too much for that. Or maybe, that's why it happened. Maybe because he'd loved Beth so much and never saw her again, he became a woman hater and instilled that trait in his grandson.

"What about Robert?" She turned to Lou. "Was he

married several times?"

He shrugged. "Have dinner with me and I'll tell you."

A lump formed in her stomach. Having dinner with him seemed wrong. He was the enemy. She sighed at her own thoughts. Lou was no more the enemy than anyone else, and having dinner with him wasn't going to hurt anyone. Not her. Not Rance. In fact, it might help. She needed to know more. Furthermore, of the two, her gut instinct said she preferred Lou over Nate ten-fold.

"All right."

Lou grinned and spun around. "I'll pick you up at your motel."

"No." She pulled open the driver's door of her car. "Just tell me where. I'll meet you."

Already climbing in his car, Lou laughed. "I'll pick you up in an hour, Liz."

She climbed in and pulled her door shut. Numerous thoughts congealed together as she started the engine. Whether she wanted to believe Lou or his father, or his grandfather were related to Rance wasn't the point. The truth was. She wanted to know the truth. Rance deserved to know the truth. That had to be why her and his times had merged. It wasn't for her like or judge. Just find a way to help him. Everything happens for a reason, and that had to be why she was here.

Holding that thought first and foremost, she steered her car around. As Nate had been, Lou was practically attached to her back bumper. He'd arrived before dark for a reason. The house scared him. Maybe he had seen Rance before. The ghost that is. Or maybe he'd heard him tonight, when Rance had told her to get the mirror back.

She considered all those possibilities, and more as she drove past the gate and onto the highway. And purposefully refused to think about how fun the day had been. Although it had been probably the best day of her life so far.

Entering town, she considered stopping to see Buzz, just to gather a bit more information, but drove straight to the motel. Lou would be there within an hour, just like he'd said which didn't leave her much time. Certainly not enough to visit Buzz, he liked to chat, and not enough time to use the internet in fifteen-minute increments, either.

In her motel room, she pulled her phone from her purse and plopped down on the bed.

Vivi Anne answered on the second ring. "My computer's up and running, and on my lap. I have a full glass of wine beside me and the phone on speaker."

Liz laughed. "How'd you know—never mind. I need a birth date."

"Name."

"Robert Dixon. Cody, Wyoming. My guess is nineteen-o-two." She dug in the bag to pull out the spiral notebook she'd used out at Rance's house and flipped it open to a new page.

As she reached back into the bag for her pen, the lid on the box opened. She hadn't forgotten about it but hadn't planned on opening it until after talking to Vivi Anne. Perhaps because she didn't want to share what was inside. Even though she didn't know.

"They didn't have birth certificates then," Vivi Anne said, "but all births had to be registered at the nearest courthouse."

She pulled out the pen and set it down. Still holding the phone to her ear, knowing Vivi Anne was making small talk while typing, she used her other hand to carefully ease the box out of the bag without spilling the contents.

The top was flipped all the way open, and her breath snagged in her lungs. It held pictures. The brown sepia type ones. Of Rance and Beth's wedding. She glanced at a couple of the pictures, but when she picked up one that was just of Beth, her hands trembled so hard she dropped the photo, and the phone.

Picking up the photo, she glanced from it to the mirror over the dresser at the end of the bed, and back to the picture. "Holy Hannah," she whispered.

It was a moment before a sound entered her head. A squawk came from her phone, and she picked it up. "I'll call you back." Clicking off, she tossed aside the phone and shot off the bed. In the bathroom, with the florescent light flickering overhead, she held the picture next to her face and stared into the mirror. Though grainy, the picture held an uncanny resemblance. Too uncanny of a resemblance.

"No wonder he thinks I'm Beth. I would too."

It was amazing. She'd never seen a picture of someone who looked like her, or one that she looked like. Whichever way, this was unbelievable and remarkable at the same time.

How could that be? It's said everyone has a twin, but this…this is crazy. And it had to be more than a coincidence.

Didn't it?

Her phone rang. She considered answering it. Vivi Anne would wonder why she'd cut the call short.

Other questions bounced around, things Vivi Anne may have answers to, or opinions, but suddenly she wanted to hold off asking them. The more disconnected she could make herself, the better off she'd be. She'd been telling herself that for years. To stay disconnected. To not care. Why? She'd never questioned herself before, but suddenly it was there.

Glancing at the picture again, she backed away from the mirror. "This is crazy. Crazy as in bat-shit crazy. Looney bin time." She took a deep breath and held it to a count of three before letting it out. "Okay. No. I'm not losing it. This is all—Oh shit. It's crazy."

Looking at the picture again, she huffed out air. "I just need to keep it together. Stay sane."

Glancing back at the picture, she rubbed a hand against her forehead.

Sane? In that case, she was toast.

Toast.

She believed a ghost, or a specter from another century, had kissed her. The desires that had sprung into life at his house had done something to her. During the drive to town, she'd started to feel guilty, almost as if accepting Lou's invitation to dinner made her feel as if she was cheating on Rance. If that didn't make her as fruity as huckleberry pie, nothing ever would.

Other than believing she looked just like his wife.

The jangle of her phone made her jump so fast the picture fell from her hand. Scrambling, she caught it before it landed in the toilet. Dropping onto the floor, she leaned her head against the wall.

Pictures didn't lie, did they?

Suddenly, everything she'd known about herself felt as if it was twisted into a knot. She needed help.

Serious help.

She jumped to her feet and exited the bathroom to snatch her phone off the bed. Swiping the green button, she said, "You aren't going to believe this."

"What?" Vivi Anne asked. "Before you answer, are you okay? I was ready to call the police. You sounded scared."

"Shocked." Drawing in another deep breath, she repeated, "I sounded shocked. I was shocked."

"By what?"

"A picture of Rance's wife. Beth. You aren't going to believe this, but I look just like her. Or she looks just like me." Liz closed her eyes briefly, in preparation. She wasn't sure what she was preparing for, other than Vivi Anne's answer.

"I got that date for you," Vivi Anne said. "It's April, nineteen-o-two."

"I just told you I look like a dead person, and you give me a date?"

"Yes, of Robert Dixon's birth," Vivi Anne replied. "It was filed on April fifteenth, but that doesn't mean that's the exact date of his birth, but it does mean his mother would have gotten pregnant around July of nineteen-o-one."

Still trying to get her mind to go in one direction, which it apparently didn't want to; Liz plopped down on the bed and pressed a hand to her forehead. "How do you know that?"

"Reverse due date calculator. There's an app for everything on the internet."

"So any day now," Liz muttered to herself. Any day now Rance would get Cindy pregnant. The idea of him getting anyone pregnant, no matter what century, was disturbing. Massively. To the point her stomach felt as if she'd eaten at the wrong place. Bile was burning the back of her throat. She grabbed one of her water bottles.

"You still there?" Vivi Anne asked.

"Yes." She took another long gulp. Trying to make sense of so many things at once was impossible. "Some rather strange things happened today."

"The picture?"

"Yes." Picking up the picture, she stared at the uncanny likeness. "Other things too. The stove in Rance's kitchen. The one I told you about that is identical to the one in the store, well, sometimes today it looked new, other times it looked old. Still in good shape, like it had been taken care of, but used. Definitely used. And the mirror. It looked well-used, too."

"You know what that means, don't you?" Vivi Anne asked.

Refusing to take a gander, she answered, "No."

"It means something's changed."

"Nothing's changed," she disagreed.

"Because it hasn't happened yet," Vivi Anne interrupted. "But you've planted a seed, and it's growing. The pendulum is swinging back and forth."

Her stomach clenched. She knew what seed she'd planted. "Rance and Cindy get married and raise Robert rather than giving him to the Dixon's."

"That could be it. We won't know until the deed is done, but that's the logical one."

It didn't sound logical. Or rather she didn't want it to. She wanted the illogical, but that was also the impossible.

"All time is connected," Vivi Anne said. "One little event puts a series of reactions into place."

"I know all about the domino theory," she said. There was also the chaos theory—where one random act set pandemonium in order. That was exactly how this all felt, and it was so confusing, and unbelievable.

"Some things aren't for us to understand," Vivi Anne said quietly, as if reading her mind and trying to calm her down.

"I know that, too," Liz said. "I'm just not as accepting as you are. Not as open minded." There was more to it than that, but Vivi Anne would never admit to it. Years ago, Vivi Anne had a vision of the crash her husband Otto had died in prior to it happening and claimed that had been the catalyst that led her to 'listen' more intuitively. Liz believed people experienced premonitions, and doubted few became psychic afterward, but Vivi Anne was different. Liz had felt a *connection* from the first time she'd set foot in *Here for Now*, and after knowing the other woman for several months, she considered Vivi Anne the best friend she'd ever had. The one and only person she'd ever felt a connection with.

Up until she'd met Rance.

"You could be more open-minded," Vivi Anne said. "If you wanted to be."

If it helped Rance, she was willing try anything. Because despite all else, in the core of her being, he was the only thing that seemed to matter. Even if that meant convincing him to have sex with another woman, she'd do it. The idea was painful, and sickening, yet there really wasn't a choice. "How? How do I become more open-minded?" Before I go insane.

"Start by asking yourself why the idea is so hard for you to believe," Vivi Anne said. "When you have that answer, ask yourself why again. And again. And again. Until you get to the very heart of the matter."

Flustered because she wanted a tangible answer, Liz asked, "How will that help?"

"Because that's where the answer lies—"

A bleep interrupted Vivi Anne's answer. Pulling the phone from her ear, Liz glared the battery icon flashing.

Putting the phone back to the side of her face she heard Vivi Anne say, "…beneath your heart. You just have to find it."

"Exactly what am I suppose to ask myself? And how will that help? That doesn't make sense to me."

"It will. The answer to the future is always in the past."

"I don't have a past and—" Before she'd completed the sentence, the phone went dead. She hadn't plugged it in last night, so was surprised the battery had lasted as long as it had. Her thoughts drifted to Rance, and how he'd had a hard time understanding how cell phones worked. He didn't have a phone, but said he'd seen them, even used one, however, talking to someone without seeing them had been too strange for him.

He should be in her shoes.

Actually, he sort of was.

Smiling at her own wit, or the craziness going on, she crossed the room to where her suitcase sat on a little metal stand. He'd had the same reaction to other things, and they'd laughed together over his comments. It had been such a fun, wonderful day. She'd never met anyone like him. He was so easy to like. And that made it easy to want to help him. He didn't deserve to be alone, lonely, waiting for Beth to return, for the next sixty some years.

That was easy to believe—him waiting for Beth—so why didn't she want it to happen? Why didn't she want him to be Robert's father? He could be happy then, couldn't he? Truly happy and he did deserve that. His happiness was what she wanted.

Lost in thought, she unzipped the outer pocket on the top of her suitcase and dug for her phone's charging cord. As she pulled it out, something fell onto the floor. After checking the detachable plug-in was still attached to the cord, she bent down to look beneath the stand to see what had fallen out. A warmth filled her chest at the shimmering gold band lying on the carpet. "I'll be." She picked up the ring. "I thought I'd lost you."

Briefly, she thought about the last time she'd seen the ring. It had been her mother's wedding ring. That's what Gladys had said when giving it to on her thirteenth birthday. Gladys had said she'd waited until Liz was old enough to appreciate it, and not lose it. Which was the exact reason why she'd never asked Gladys if she'd left it behind when she'd moved from their house to her apartment. She hadn't wanted Gladys to know she had indeed lost the ring.

Frowning, she glanced at the suitcase. She'd received that suitcase, an entire set of luggage, as a graduation gift from Gladys and Norman. She'd used the other cases a few times over the years, but never this one, and couldn't remember ever putting anything, especially this ring, in the outside pocket. She must have though. Years ago. Maybe the day she moved out.

She held the ring up to the light and twirled it between her fingers. It was a simple gold band, with no markings other than the stamp claiming it was 22ct gold. Hoping that little mark had meant more, she'd taken it to a jeweler when she'd been sixteen, only to be told nothing more than it was old and worth about two-hundred dollars.

She'd stopped wearing it then. Two-hundred dollars had seemed like a lot, and she hadn't wanted to lose it. Although she'd learned nothing more about her parents from the ring, having something that valuable had scared her, and she'd asked Gladys to keep it in her jewelry box. Gladys must have given it back to her the day she'd moved out.

That had been the same day Norman had tried to give her the trunk.

Her stomach clenched at the same time the room started to spin. The bed seemed a mile away rather than a few steps, and by the time she made it to the edge, her legs were stiff from forcing them to move and sweat beaded her temples. She sat and tucked her head between her legs, to stop her head from spinning.

Slowly, gradually, her equilibrium returned, but an odd intensity lingered. Her mouth had gone dry and she reached behind her for the bottle of water she'd left on the bed. A long drink eased the burning in her throat, and several deep breaths made her feel more normal.

It was ridiculous. How the mere thought of an old trunk was enough to bring on a panic attack, but it did, and seeing it was worse. Norman had felt so bad the day he'd tried to give it to her.

That had been last time she'd seen the trunk. Had no idea what happened to it after Norman and Gladys both died last year, him from a heart attack, her from cancer a few months later.

She'd been moving out of the Walker's home and into her own place following graduation. The one-bedroom apartment she still lived in. Norman had carried the trunk down from the attic, and upon seeing it sitting next to the stairway she'd grown light-headed by the force of panic that had gripped her.

That had happened once before, when she'd been ten and heard a couple of women in church talking about how she'd been draped over a trunk in the river when the rescuers had arrived at the scene of the accident that had killed her parents. She'd asked Gladys about it that day, and Gladys had confirmed that was true and told her the trunk was in the attic. They'd gone up there together, and upon seeing the trunk in the corner, a cold darkness had surrounded her and sent her heart into a raging panic. Intense pain had stolen her breath away so fast and hard she'd collapsed on the floor in the attic. Gladys had rushed her downstairs, and they'd never spoken of the trunk again, until the day Norman had carried it downstairs.

That day, before the pain had overtaken her, she'd bolted out the door. Norman had found her in her car, crying, and apologized, said he hadn't known how she'd reacted to the trunk before. He'd just thought she'd like to have it.

She'd told him she didn't want it.

She still didn't. Many nights she'd dreamt about that trunk and had woken up in a complete panic, calmed only by the fact it was nowhere near her.

Like now.

Glancing at the ring in her hand, she wondered

why it never made her feel that. In fact, it was about as opposite as could be. The way the ring glistened in the light made her smile.

Liz slid the ring on her left ring finger. It fit better now than when Gladys had given it to her and would most likely be safer on her finger than in her suitcase. She still didn't own a jewelry box. There was no reason. She had no jewelry. Had never even had her ears pierced.

She picked up her the phone, grabbed the charger off the floor, and carried them into the small bathroom, and the only available outlet. After connecting the phone, she pressed the power button and waited for it to power up in order to check the time, absently twirling the ring on her finger as she waited.

She didn't remember it feeling this nice. Comfortable—comforting actually. Glancing up, she shook her head at her own image in the mirror. "You are losing it. Rings don't feel nice nor are they comforting. They are rings. Period. Just like stupid old trunks are just stupid old trunks."

Her phone dinged, and she picked it up. Making sure the plug was firmly in the outlet, she clicked the text message icon.

Vivi Anne. What a surprise.

—What else happened today?—

Liz considered a reply before typing:

—Lou asked me out to dinner.—

—A date?—

—No. He's going to tell me about his family.—

—Going out to dinner is a date.—

Frowning, she responded:

—I don't date. No desire to. But I do want to know

about his family.—

—Lou is a man. You are a woman. That's a date. Dates are fun! You need some fun in your life. Don't think. Just enjoy it!—

She considered not responding, but her fingers were already clicking at the keys.

—Stop. I'm not here to find my long-lost love. I don't believe in it, so your abilities are not needed in that sense.—

—K. Have fun and call me tomorrow. Gotta run. I'm meeting with the man from Helena tonight.—

A touch of guilt crossed her stomach. So focused on Rance, she'd forgotten Vivi Anne was busy with other things. The antique store was popular and kept them both busy, which meant Vivi Anne was doing it all by herself right now.

She quickly typed, *I will. You have fun, too.*

The clock icon said Lou would be here shortly, so she washed her face, brushed her hair, and then retrieved a light-weight jacket out of her bag in case the restaurant had their air conditioning on high. She was interested to learn what he had to say about his family. Not having one of her own might be a part of her interest, but a much larger part had to do with Rance.

Maybe Vivi Anne had rubbed off on her more than she realized. Vivi Anne had numerous stories about how she'd helped people find lost loves. Could that be why she was here? To make Rance realize he could love again. Love Cindy.

Laying the jacket on the bed, she sat down and pulled the box of pictures onto her lap. There weren't many, less than a dozen, and most of them were of both Rance and Beth, and too grainy to make out their faces as clearly as she'd like.

The wedding had taken place in Billings. At Beth's parents' house. She didn't remember Rance telling her that, but he must have at some point today, because she knew it. Knew it had been a warm January day. And that they'd been as happy as they looked in the pictures.

Replacing all the pictures in the box, she closed the lid, wondering what Rance was doing right now. If he'd made himself more eggs for supper. He'd said he wasn't much of a cook. She'd said she wasn't either. That's why she ate granola bars.

She put the box back in the bag. Ghosts didn't eat. Not eggs or granola bars. Then again, he wasn't really a ghost.

This was all too much to get her head around. Ghosts who weren't really ghosts. Psychics who weren't really psychics. Matchmakers who weren't really matchmakers.

She really needed to talk with Lou. Learn more about his family, and hopefully Rance. Buzz had said Rance didn't believe Beth had died because they never found her body. At that thought, she walked into the bathroom and typed another text to Vivi Anne.

—Please look up a train accident near Billings in June of 1901. Passenger Beth Livingston.—

A knock sounded as she hit send. Rather than going to the door to answer it, she walked to the window and peeked out, staying concealed behind the curtain. Lou waved, indicating he either saw her or the curtain move. Of course he did. It was probably the exact thing every person did when someone knocked on their motel room door.

She walked to the door and pulled it open.

"I'm a touch early. Was afraid you might skip out on me."

She shook her head at Lou's grin. It was almost as charming as Rance's, which should goad her much more than it did at this moment. "That happen to you often, does it?"

"No," he answered, "but there's always a first."

The desire to laugh was as out of the ordinary for her as everything else that had happened since she'd pulled into town. Lou was obviously a charmer. That should have her sending him on his way. She didn't want to though. She wanted to have dinner with him. She wanted to know all there was to know about his family. "I just have to grab my jacket and purse."

"I'll wait right here." He waved at the stoop he stood on. "Wouldn't want to give Les and Edith anything to gossip about."

"*You're* afraid of gossip?"

"My reputation was ruined long ago," he said with a wink. "It's yours I'm worried about."

Her stomach hiccupped, with a mixture of excitement and anxiety. "Mine is stellar," she said, lifting up her jacket and purse. A fleeting thought of Vivi Anne had her glancing toward the bathroom. Her phone wasn't charged yet, so there was no sense in taking it.

"I believe it." Lou stepped aside so she could exit.

Chapter Nine

Sleep was not his friend. Every time Rance dozed off, dreams woke him. Nightmares actually. The kind that left his heart racing with dread.

After untangling himself from the covers, he swung his legs over the edge of the bed and sat there, rubbing his head with both hands. He should be dreaming about Beth, damn it. They'd spent the entire day together.

But that wasn't Beth, was it? Not the women he'd married. The wife he'd planned on growing old with.

He rubbed his head again. Why was this happening to him? *What* was happening to him?

He stood and walked to the window. The breeze that blew across his chest carried the scent of rain and the darkness of the night sky hung heavy, broken only by a fast flash of lightning far on the horizon.

He had dreamed of her. *His* Beth. The one he'd married and would love until the day he died. It had been her lips he'd been kissing, her body he'd been loving, but when, in his dreams, he'd opened his eyes, it was Nan's niece in his arms. He'd tried to get away, to escape, but she'd clung to him, insisting she was pregnant with his child.

That's when the dreams turned from horrific to horrendous.

His child.

The one he and Beth had hoped of having, and would have if not for that train accident. He should never have let her go.

It was impossible to think of Beth, the one he'd known, loved, and married, and not see the one who now filled his mind. The one who'd left today, promising to be back tomorrow.

Her hair was shorter, her words different, but they were one and the same. Just separated by a century. It made no sense, yet, in his heart, where rational thinking lost out to a devotion that held no understanding of time, his validation was as true and real as the heavens above and the earth below.

The jagged shards of lightning increased in number and in velocity, growing closer as he stood in front of the open window. The wind and lightning came at him like the demons of his dreams had, yet the flashes and the glow left behind to briefly mark the sky as the bolts disappeared reminded him of things that don't change.

A hundred years from now, lightning would still be the same. The earth would still be the earth, the sky the sky, trees, trees, rain, rain.

Hands braced on the windowsill as the storm arrived, he made no attempt to move, to close the window. Instead he welcomed the wind and soon the rain, cold droplets pelting his arms and chest.

Time may change some things, but not all things. It wouldn't change him. He might age, as all men did, as all living things did, grow old and feeble, but inside, he'd always be exactly who he was this minute. Who he'd been last year.

As determined as he was, he knew he was wrong, too.

He wasn't the same man he'd been last year. Beth had changed him. His ambitions, his goals, his life, had all changed because of her, and those things affected a man.

A jarring bolt of lightning hit so close the house rattled, drawing his full attention. Lightning is what had taken Beth from him. It had been storming the morning of the train accident. A bolt had hit the bridge causing it to collapse beneath the train.

That would not happen again.

Beth would not be taken from him again. Not in any time.

The storm raged on. A bright streak of lightning hit the ground, rattling the house.

Sticking his head out the window, he scanned for flames. Grateful there were none, he pulled the window closed and walked to the dresser. There he picked up the mirror. It was too dark to see his reflection, except for when flashes of lightning filled the room. Then, his image was there, staring back at him until the light faded.

Had she returned to change him again? Trying to convince him to forget the love he still harbored for her and start a future with another woman?

That would not be Beth.

Not even a hundred years could do that to her.

He set the mirror down, not willing to give the other thought screaming in his mind credence. The one about ghosts and timelines and dimensions.

A hundred years might not change her. But love would. The love they'd shared.

He raked his fingers through his hair and squeezed his temples. As much as he didn't want to admit it, what everyone had been telling him was true.

She wouldn't want him going on like he had been.

The storm raging outside held the same velocity as the one overtaking him from the inside. When the windows rattled and the house shook, he couldn't say if it was because of another lightning strike or the anger burning his throat as he let it out.

He didn't want to know, either.

"She is not dead," he growled. Spinning about, he paced the floor. How could he prove that? To himself and her. He already knew it, felt it, but how could he convince her?

How could he—

Another flash of lightning lit the sky as he walked past the window and what it exposed had him grabbing his pants. After pulling them on and his boots, he snatched up his shirt and headed for the hallway. Not stopping until he stood on the back porch, he shrugged on his shirt before running for the open barn door.

The old man was rain soaked and leading his horse into an empty stall.

"Hello, my nephew."

Other than his once broad shoulders were now stooped slightly from age, his uncle's appearance hadn't changed from what was depicted on the posters for the Wild West Shows.

"Here, let me," Rance said, crossing the barn to enter the stall. As he loosened the chinch strap of the traditional hammock-styled Shoshone saddle Hiah used both in the exhibitions he did for Buffalo Bill's show and for regular travel, he asked, "What are you doing out in the rain?"

"It was time," Hiah said.

He lifted the bone-framed saddle from the horse and carried it out of the stall. He wasn't surprised to see his uncle, except for the fact he didn't expect the old man to travel nearly twenty miles in a rain storm. He'd known Hiah would eventually arrive to show his respect for Beth's passing, and hadn't looked forward to the visit.

"We die and are born many times," Hiah said.

Those were the exact words he had not been looking forward to. Firmly embedded in the Shoshone ways of long ago, his uncle looked at death completely different than he did. Always had.

"Your Beth is no different."

Fully prepared to argue that point, he turned around, but something internal stopped his protest. Instead, he asked, "How? How does that happen? I don't understand how a person can be born or die more than once."

They exited the stall at the same time, standing face to face. Almost three-quarters of a century old, Hiah's face was wrinkled, his long hair varied shades of gray, but his eyes held a youthfulness of one much younger, as well as an intelligence of those far more educated.

The crevices near his eyes deepened as Hiah smiled and lifted a hand. "You must take what you see here," he said, while touching Rance's forehead. "And put it back here, beneath your heart." His hand went to Rance's chest. "This will help you find endurance and patience, once you have that, you will see the answer."

He didn't want patience or endurance. He wanted Beth. In the flesh. Not some ghostly form that was impossible to hold.

"Your love for your wife, and hers for you, was great," Hiah said. "She will come back to you, but you must see with your heart, not your eyes."

As a child, he'd never been allowed to learn the ways of the Shoshone, and years later, when he'd become reunited with the few family members left, he'd been too busy earning a living to devote much time or attention to such things. "See with my heart because she will look different to me?"

Hiah shrugged and then turned toward the open barn door. "I would drink some of your coffee."

The old man was wet, and probably chilled. Rance led the way to the house. Now no more than a mist, the storm had moved on as quickly as it had approached, leaving an aftermath of miniature rivers and lakes for them to cross. In the kitchen, he lit several lamps and after building a fire and putting a fresh pot of coffee on the stove, retrieved a couple of towels. His uncle had removed the blanket that had been draped over his shoulders. After hanging it over the back of a chair, he pushed it closer to the stove to dry. His mind was a jumbled mess of what to ask. Of what answers his uncle may or may not have.

"Will Beth know?" He sat down at the table. "Will she know when she is reborn?"

"She must find her spirit home." Hiah glanced around the room. "Then she will know."

His uncle's gaze settled on the screen door for so long, a tiny shiver rippled along Rance's spine.

"She has already been here," Hiah said.

His hands had never trembled, or his body, the way it did at that moment. Swallowing past the lump in his throat, he nodded. "Yes, she has."

"Then all is good."

"No," he disputed. "All is not good."

Hiah's smile was serene. "She will be back."

"But here isn't here." He wasn't sure how to explain it. "She's not here in my time."

"Tell me, my nephew. Do you have time in your heart or love?"

****

The plethora of emotions—some completely foreign and unnamable—battling for ground inside her had Liz calling Lou every degrading and unbecoming name she could think of. She even made up a few. He'd spent more time flirting last night—with her and their waitress—than telling her anything.

Robert had only been married once, but his wife had died long before Lou was born, he'd told her that much. He'd had no idea when his grandfather's birthday was, or anything of importance. All he knew about Cindy—his grandmother—was that she'd been Cliff and Nan's niece. He had talked a lot about Cliff and how he'd invested money in Buffalo Bill Cody's oil drilling company—which had gone broke. Lou said Buffalo Bill and Cliff had tried to get Rance to buy in and explore his land, but he had refused. That hadn't surprised her, neither had the fact that Lou had tested the ranch property for oil shortly after inheriting it and had come up empty.

"That was certainly four hours of my life I'll never get back." The motel door shut with a solid thud behind her. She'd wanted answers, and a part of her had wanted to like Lou. To form a connection where they could see things jointly. Things that would be in Rance's best interest.

That certainly hadn't happened.

Her call this morning went directly to the jerk's voicemail. That wasn't surprising either. She was ninety-nine percent sure he'd gone back to the restaurant in order to hook up with their waitress after he'd returned her to her motel. That flat out pissed her off. He seemed to have no interest in his family, in his history.

She had half a mind to call Nate but wouldn't get any further with him than she had Lou. They were both nothing but playboys.

Dialing Lou's number again, she waited for the end of the message. "I will be at the gate in fifteen minutes. If you aren't there, I'll climb over."

Determined to do just that, she threw her phone in her purse, tossed it and her other bag on the passenger seat, and started her car. It was barely after seven in the morning, but the information in Vivi Anne's text made getting out to see Rance urgent. She had to talk to him before he—before Cindy becomes pregnant.

That's what happens when you seek the truth, you discover it's more complicated than anticipated.

Lou was nowhere in sight when she turned off the paved road and onto the gravel driveway. She hadn't expected him to be, and waiting wasn't an option. The idea of climbing over the gate didn't thrill her. It was large and made of metal pipes, and on both sides, was the cattle guard—more large metal pipes built into the ground. Tall grass surrounded the posts near both ends, making an ideal place for snakes to hide.

She shook off a shiver, parked as near to the gate and off to the side of the gravel as possible, and drew in a breath of fortification. After stuffing her purse into her larger bag, she climbed out and locked her car doors. Looping the straps over her shoulder, she approached the gate. It might have been a good idea to contemplate her outfit before deciding to climb the gate.

The yellow tank top wasn't an issue, but the white capris and sandals weren't exactly attire for climbing through rusty pipes. Last night's rain left the metal wet and slippery, which caused a couple of smear marks that probably wouldn't wash out of the white material, but she made it over the gate. The rubber soles of her sandals slid on the wet metal of the cattle guard, and she had to use both arms—held out at her sides—to keep her balance as she cautiously and carefully stepped from pipe to pipe.

The cattle guard was longer on this side of the gate and the idea of kissing the gravel driveway when she finally stepped on solid ground crossed her mind. Briefly. There wasn't time for that. The narrow, more weeds than gravel driveway, lined by tall grass, was over a mile long, and uphill.

It wasn't long before she concluded sunscreen would have been a good idea. The blazing sun was drying out her shoulders faster than it was the puddles in the road. More bothersome than the heat and sun was how thoughts of Lou were what kept her marching forward. He had to be the lowest type of human-being that ever walked this earth. There couldn't be a caring, humane bone in his body. Not for his family. Not for his community. Not for any living, breathing creature. He was a fake. He hadn't been attempting to preserve Rance's property. That had been an excuse. She didn't doubt Nate was in on it too.

Gorgeous in its own right, nestled on the edge of the Big Horn Basin, the land surrounding her covered miles and miles of property that had been untouched for years and years. Heart Mountain looked especially spectacular this morning, and that fueled her indignation. Rance had settled on some of the best property in the area, even way back when. While the rest of those claiming land back then had to worry about water rights, many waiting until Buffalo Bill Cody had erected the damn named after him on the Shoshone River, Rance had acquired land where water was plentiful. A still highly sought after commodity.

The text message on her phone this morning from Vivi Anne made convincing him to preserve his legacy all the more imperative.

She topped a small hill. One that hadn't seemed so steep in her car, but the way the backs of her legs screamed proved the incline was more than what she was used to walking up. Her heart skipped a beat as buildings came into view. Here too, she saw more than on her previous trips. Or maybe, because she wasn't driving, she had the time to look. To appreciate the house, the barn, the other out-buildings. How they filled her with an uncanny sense of welcoming. She'd never had a place that she'd truly considered home, but instinctively knew, if she did, this is what a homecoming would feel like.

Leave it to her to find that in an abandon piece of property.

Not completely abandoned. Rance was there.

"A ghost. A haunted house is your dream house. You are beyond help."

She started walking forward again, but as she

neared the wide, faded board stretched between two tall poles, she had to smile.

The words *Rocking L* had been carved in the wood so long ago they were barely readable. But she knew they were there, and how much they meant to Rance. They'd meant that much to Beth, too.

After walking beneath the sign, she stopped and turned around to gaze up at it. The name had been carved on this side too, which also made her smile. He'd worked hard on that sign. Had built it to last for generations.

On impulse, she pulled out her phone and clicked a picture, and then took out a bottle of water and enjoyed a long, much needed, drink.

The night's rain may have turned the grass greener, plush beneath her sandals or maybe she'd been focused on other things and hadn't noticed it before. Either way, she enjoyed the soft comfort as she cut across the lawn rather than staying on the circle gravel driveway. On the porch, she dug the key out of her pocket and unlocked the door.

The mirror on the kitchen table made her heart quicken and a smile form. "Good morning," she said brightly.

As the mirror floated into the air, her happiness faltered. She was glutton for punishment. No one in their right mind purposefully inflicts pain upon themselves. Yet, that's what she was doing to herself. For some ridiculously stupid reason, she'd expected to see Rance the moment she stepped into the house. In the flesh.

Closing her eyes, she swallowed against the disappointment of how that could never, ever happen.

A steady hum had her lifting her lids and taking a hold of the mirror handle floating in front of her.

His smile weakened her knees more than the mile walk had. He was so flipping handsome. His dark hair was wet, as if recently washed and still had comb marks in it. He'd shaved, too, and his shirt still had fold marks in it.

"Good morning," he said. "Sleep well?"

Not at all the truth, but she went with, "Yes, you?"

"Nope." His gaze had turned deeper, intrusive, but kind. "And you didn't either."

Letting out a sigh, she shrugged. "You're right, I didn't."

"Missed me?"

His teasing tone and the hope in his voice made her grin and her heart pound. Her head refused to shake.

He grinned. "I missed you."

She sighed again. There was no sense putting it off, no sense torturing herself. "Have you had your coffee?"

"Yes, why?"

"Because we need to talk."

"All right," he said. "In a minute."

His smile never faltered as he leaned closer. So close she could no longer see his face. As his image become little more than a fuzzy blur, a powerful wave of bliss overtook her. An unexpected yet divine heat covered her lips and that made her lose coordination. She didn't go down. Didn't hit the floor and crack open her head or break an arm. God knows why.

Her upper arms tingled, and her sides and the small of her back, as if his hands roamed over all those places. It was all as real as it wasn't. She closed her eyes, planted her feet into the floor, and let her body, less her damnable brain, completely accept his ghostly kiss.

Chapter Ten

"Two kids?" Rance wanted to squeeze his temples. His head throbbed as if it had just been sliced open with a dull knife. "You want me to have two kids with Nan's niece?"

"And marry her," Beth said, as serious as when she'd told him a man had walked on the moon.

Something he still couldn't fathom. There was no way to get to the moon. There was no way he'd be having two kids with Nan's niece either.

"You two really should get married before she becomes pregnant. And yes, two kids. That way you'll be sure to have an heir. Hopefully several so Nate and Lou—"

That about did it. "I'm not going to marry Nan's niece, and I'm not going to have children with her. Not one. Not two. Not any."

"But you have to," she insisted.

"No, I don't."

"Yes, you do."

Arguing with her was useless, but the betrayal eating his insides wouldn't let him give in. He reached out to grab her by the upper arms, but his fingers just curled into his palms.

Damn it.

There was nothing to grasp onto. He'd felt her earlier, with his hands and his lips. "Damn it," he repeated, this time aloud. "I'm already married! To you!"

"I can't hear you when you aren't holding the mirror," she said sternly.

More flustered than he ever recalled being, he reached for the mirror she held by the handle, but something internal stopped him before he grabbed the side of the mirror. The rush of love that struck him was so great, so powerful, his chest tightened. Those skimpy little outfits she kept wearing were growing on him. He didn't like the idea of other men seeing so much skin, but he enjoyed the daylights out of it. Her skin was more golden now than it used to be, as if she spent more time in the sun, but he knew her flesh was as silky smooth as ever. Every inch of her.

A tiny smile curled her lips. "I know you're still here."

The bond the two of them had since meeting had been a spectacular thing, and visible to all. Others had told him so, with envy at times. He'd accepted it, exalted in it, and above all cherished the love that had immediately sprouted and grown between them. As he had her. He still cherished her. Grasping the edge of the mirror, he had to swallow against the swelling in his throat. "Why do you want me to marry someone else?"

She hesitated, her mouth opened, then closed as she lifted her chin. "It's not that I want you to marry Cindy. It's what has to happen."

"No—"

"It's the only way, Rance. The only way for you to change the future. Not just yours, but the future of your family, your legacy."

He was still flustered as hell but couldn't help

admire her diplomacy. She'd always been good at that. Negotiating. Making people listen. It wasn't what she said, but how. With all her heart. His irritation melted. Family, and them building their own together and a legacy to leave behind, had been her passion from the start. It had been his, too, still was, and he wasn't going to give it up.

Hiah didn't know why or how she'd come back as herself but in a different time. Rance didn't understand either, even when his uncle had said it wasn't for them to understand, but to believe. Hiah insisted if the two of them—him and Beth—worked together, believed together, they would be reunited.

He closed his eyes for a moment and told himself that he believed. Believed with all his heart and soul that would happen. Then, holding onto the mirror with one hand, he placed his other next to her cheek. A mystical warmth filled his palm as she tilted her head toward his hand. The connection was as real as any he'd ever felt, even while his eyes told him differently. That they weren't touching. His eyes hadn't believed they were touching earlier, when he'd kissed her, but his heart had. He'd felt her lips beneath his. Just as his hand felt her cheek pressed against his palm right now.

Not being able to offer a solution, he softly said, "We have no control over the future, or the past, just the present. The here and now."

"We aren't in the same here and now. We aren't in the same present. Right now, we are in two different worlds. The past and the future. Don't you see we've, you've, been given the opportunity to change the future? The one I'm in, the one you will soon be in. That has to be why this is happening."

He bit the inside of his cheek to combat the pain in his chest. If he could change something, it wouldn't be the future. It would be the past. The one that had stolen her from him. Stolen the future they'd dreamed of together. The legacy they'd been building together. He'd had it all at one time, the world in the palm of his hand, and then, in a split second, everything had been stripped away.

Given the opportunity, he'd make sure she never got on that train. Never let her travel to Billings. Never let her out of his sight.

The side of his face grew warm from her hand against his cheek, yet she wasn't really touching him.

"Just hear me out," she said softly. "Please?"

He sighed heavily, but nodded.

She closed her eyes and whispered, "Thank you."

He could've sworn he heard her intake of breath and a deep sigh before she opened her eyes.

"The answer to the future is always in the past," she said. "Vivi Anne told me that last night, and I didn't understand, but now I do. You will too, as soon as I explain everything. Let's sit down at the table." A coy smile overtook her lips, and a perceptive glint flashed in her eyes. "You may need a cup of coffee for this."

She'd always teased him about that. How he liked coffee. Strong and hot. She was right, too. He could use some. The pot was still on the stove. Not knowing when she'd arrive, he'd done the morning chores after Hiah had left, and had been pouring a cup out of the pot he'd made afterward when she'd walked through the door. "I'll have to let go of the mirror."

"I know. I'll wait until you're back at the table to start explaining."

"No, go ahead and start talking. It'll only take me a minute."

"Your coffee is already made, is it?"

"Yes." He stopped before offering her a cup. Even if it had been possible, she'd decline. She rarely drank coffee. When she did, she'd added so much cream and sugar it tasted like syrup. He'd never complained though, because it had made her lips, her kisses, that much sweeter.

He waited until she was seated at the table before letting go of the mirror.

"Well, Nate is claiming the people interested in buying this property are planning to build a resort here, but my friend Vivi Anne has discovered that's not true. It's also not true that Lou was interested in having the place preserved."

He checked the temperature of the coffee he'd poured in his cup by taking a sip. It was lukewarm, but drinkable. He crossed the room, sat down and touched the mirror. "What is the truth?" Whatever happened to his property a hundred years from now wasn't on the top of his worry list. He'd be long dead. It was a worry to her, and that's why he was willing to listen. Then he would tell her about Hiah, and how the Shoshone believed in rebirth. How that had happened to her, but she was in the wrong century and that they would have to work together to bring her back to the right time.

He set his cup down. She would never believe that.

"It's not a resort developer who wants to buy this place. It's a company out of Texas looking to buy land for a radioactive waste site."

"A what?"

"A radioactive waste site," she repeated. "In my

time we have nuclear energy. Basically, electricity created through a process of splitting atoms. Once thought to be a solution to reusable energy, it's no longer looked upon so favorably because of the radioactive waste it creates. Nuclear power plants built years ago are no longer safe to use and everything about them, from the steel and concrete they are made out of, to tools and clothing worn by workers are contaminated and need to be disposed of. They do that by burying it, but the places set up for that are full, and more sites are needed because more and more plants are being shut down. There're agencies that oversee the disposal of all the waste and claim its safe, but the jury is still out on that. Bottom line is no town wants a nuclear dump near them."

He didn't comprehend everything she was saying but got the gist of it all. It also explained her involvement. When Buffalo Bill had asked about investing in drilling the oil wells, Beth had gotten on her high-horse, became a crusader for preserving the land and the wild horses that roamed the hills. He'd agreed with her, to Bill's disappointment, and would now, too, whether it directly affected him or not. That's what a man did, stood beside his wife through thick and thin. He just might be the only husband to stand beside his wife through centuries.

Wrapping his mind around all that was close to impossible. "How will marrying Nan's niece stop any of that?"

"Because you'll have legitimate heirs, children, grandchildren and great-grandchildren who'll love this land as much as you do." She waved her free hand. "Raised here, a part of all this, they'll understand the importance of preservation. Lou and Nate don't. They were raised to love themselves and money."

"How do you know that?"

"It's obvious." She nodded. "You'd agree if you could meet them. Since that's not possible, you'll just have to trust me. You'll have to trust me in other ways, too. That I know best."

He fought a smile. She always thought she knew best. He picked up his coffee cup and took a drink of the now cold brew. "Including this notion you have about me and Nan's niece."

"Yes, and her name is Cindy."

"I know her name." Frustration had him balling a hand into a fist. "And no matter what you think is best, I won't marry her."

"You have to."

Switching, in order to hold the mirror with his right hand, he held up his left, showing her the wedding band on his finger. It had taken some getting used, wearing a ring, but he hadn't taken it off since the day she'd slid it on his finger. And wouldn't. "I can't. I'm already married."

Her face paled as she stared at his hand, specifically the ring. She started to shake, too. He lowered his hand, slowly, wishing he could reach out and touch her. Comfort her. As he reached toward her, she snapped her head toward the door.

His fingers curled into a fist, as she pushed her chair back. He understood why even before she spoke.

"Someone's here."

A regret-filled sigh left his chest. "Yes, there is."

"You can hear the car?"

"No, I can hear a wagon." It was a buggy to be

exact. That's what it sounded like, and unfortunately, the sinking of his gut told him who was driving it. He had a pretty good idea who was in the car, too, either Nate or Lou. Two fellas he'd like—well, it didn't matter what he'd like to do to them. Getting his hands around their necks wasn't likely to happen.

Liz didn't know if she trusted her legs to hold her. They were trembling along with every other part of her. Inside and out. The car outside had to be Lou. The interruption annoyed her, that was a given. The timing couldn't have been worse. Her gaze went back to Rance's hand. She'd never noticed the ring before. That just hadn't been a place her eyes settled. She slipped her hand into her pocket. The hand that wore a ring identical to his. They were simple enough. Just gold bands, but the odds of his matching hers, couldn't be that great.

Could it?

To add to the craziness, a flash of a memory said she'd seen his ring before. Held it. Examined it. With excitement. Which was more than completely impossible. There was a small jewelry box upstairs, but it had only held a couple pairs of clip on earrings. No man's ring. Or woman's.

He'd pushed his chair back, now stood beside the table, with one hand still on the mirror. "You wait here," he said. "I'll be right back."

The slamming of a car door had her reaching out to grab his arm, but her hand found nothing, even though he hadn't move. "Who's out there? In your time, who's out there?"

"Stay here. We aren't done with our conversation."

He disappeared before she could protest, which

was okay because she didn't want Lou or possibly Nate, to hear her talking. The next moment, when the door opened, she questioned if she saw a very faint illusion of Rance walking out the open doorway at the same moment Lou walked in. Besides both having brown hair and eyes, the men were similar in size and shape. It was almost as if the two men merged into one, and then separated. One going out, the other coming in.

"What the—" Lou grabbed the doorframe and wobbled slightly. He also spun around to look behind him. When he turned back around, he was frowning.

"Hello." If things were different, she might have grinned at how dazed he looked. As if he'd seen a ghost. Or felt one. The fact Rance was a ghost didn't hold any humor today.

Her thoughts stalled for a moment. She'd never seen Rance before—not without him holding the mirror. Which was lying on the table. She pulled her hand off it but couldn't take her eyes off it. Couldn't. The patina of the silver was slowly changing from old and used, to old and unused. It only took a matter of seconds, but it had happened. She'd swear to it. Cautiously, she touched the edge and waited, but nothing happened. Nothing changed.

"Do you have an obsession with that mirror?"

Though he was speaking to her, Lou was looking at the doorway.

She ran a finger along the handle before she pushed the mirror into the center of the table. "Maybe, I've never seen one quite like it."

Moving closer, Lou scanned the room more intently before he grasped the back of the chair Rance had sat in moments ago. "Looks pretty ordinary to me."

"It's not." The mirror was far from ordinary. She wished she could climb into it. If that was possible, she'd know instead of wondering who'd arrived in Rance's time. That certainly wasn't possible. Regretfully, she pulled her eyes off the door. "What are you doing here?"

"Checking on you. What's so important you had to be out here at the crack of dawn?"

"I have a lot of work to do," she answered, standing up.

"It's not so important you need to scale a gate at sunrise."

"It was long past sunrise, and, yes, it's important."

"To whom?"

"You."

He shook his head.

She touched the mirror again. "You are the one who wanted the antiques appraised."

"No, I didn't. Neither does Nate. That all comes from Sandra, my ex-wife. Or soon to be. The divorce isn't final yet. That was Sandra's niece, Joni, who waited on us last night. The one I needed to be so nice to. Sandra wants to pull every last dime out of my pocket. My lawyer suggested we have the antiques appraised before her lawyer convinces a judge to order it. That's when I hauled some of the stuff into Buzz, and he suggested calling in you to have them appraised." Lou shook his head while glancing around. "There's nothing worth a pot of gold here, other than the land."

She hadn't heard about the soon to be ex-wife wanting money, but it certainly made sense. "You don't know that."

"Yes, I do. Nate and I have been coming out here for years. If there had been a national treasure out here, one of us would have already found and sold it."

She didn't doubt that. Walking away from the table, she stopped near the stove. Maybe he wasn't behind the nuclear deal. "Nate seemed interested in having the items here appraised."

"He's agreed because it'll satisfy Sandra." His lip curled. "He owes me that much for sleeping with her while we were still married. We wouldn't be in the predicament we're in if it wasn't for that."

She had no idea how to respond to that tidbit but did wonder how much more convoluted could things get. She also questioned just what predicament he referred to.

Lou patted the chair. "Once Sandra gets all she can out of the antiques, she'll agree to the sale. Both she and I need to sign off on it. What I want to know is what you're so interested in." He picked up the mirror and spun it around. "Besides this old thing."

"It's my job." She rung her hands together to hide the way her nerves started ticking beneath her skin as she moved closer to the table, and the mirror.

"I don't buy that." He eyed her closely. "What have you discovered about this place?"

Swallowing so her voice wouldn't squeak, she replied, "Nothing."

He pulled out the chair and sat. "Time to pony-up, darling."

Anger zipped up her spine. "If anyone needs to pony-up, it's you." Grabbing the mirror out of his hand, she carried it to the counter and set it down gently. She had half a mind to tell him about the plans for a nuclear waste dump that Vivi Anne had uncovered, but telling him might do more damage than good. Going with a gut feeling that came out of nowhere, she spun around. "Isn't it time you admit you're still in love with your wife and try to work it out?"

The snap of attention, the shock on his face said more than he did. "Who told you that?" He added a laugh, as if it wasn't true.

"No one had to tell me." Since when? When had she become an expert on love? And why was she, of all people, sticking her nose into other people's love lives? She'd never had one of her own, so it certainly hadn't come from experience. She knew less about love than an earthworm. They don't even need a mate to reproduce.

He laughed again. "Well, darling, you need to get your eyes checked, because if that's what you think you're seeing, you're as wrong as you could be."

No, she wasn't. She'd bet the price of the kitchen table and chair set. "Sandra asked you for the divorce. You were willing to work it out, even after the Nate debacle."

"Who have you been talking to?" He leaned across the table. "Joni?"

"No."

His eyes narrowed. "Nate?"

"No." She crossed the room, stopping near the table.

"Who?"

"I'm not at liberty to say," she flat out lied.

"Not at liberty. In other words, it's hearsay without an ounce of proof to back it up."

"I have proof." She lifted her chin, believing in her

sixth-sense. "It's in your eyes. In your voice. You still love your wife." That was the truth. She instinctively knew it.

He opened his mouth but closed it as he glanced around.

She knew something else, too. He'd never planned on telling her anything about his family. "You took me to that restaurant last night, knowing Joni would wait on us, and would tell Sandra you were out with another woman."

Abruptly, he pushed away from the table. "You better hurry up and finish your job. Saturday's right around the corner."

She'd struck a chord with that one, but so had he. "I already told Nate I need more time."

"Yeah, well, you don't have it." He walked to the door. "Nate or I will be back to see you leave before dark."

Jumping to her feet, she followed. "I need more time. There is so much here. I have to catalogue everything and—"

"Then you better work fast."

She tried to catch it, but the screen door banged shut before she'd reached it. That irritated her. She caught it before it bounced against the door frame a second time, and pushed it open, but she stopped before following Lou outside. Arguing with him would get her nowhere, but more than that, Rance might come in while she was outside.

She had no idea how long that may be, and the desire to get more information out of Lou was too strong to contain. "Nate said he has this place sold to a developer. To build a resort," she said from the doorway.

Lou stopped and spun around. "Nate didn't have this place sold." He pointed a thumb at his chest. "I did. I'm the realtor. Nate thinks because his dad got lucky in a few stocks, he's a high roller, and likes to act that way. Truth is he wouldn't know where to begin looking for a buyer for this place."

"Are you still selling it to the developer you found?"

Lou shook his head. "The deal I brokered wasn't enough money for Nate, and he convinced Sandra it wasn't enough money for her, either."

"So why the rush?"

He huffed out a sigh. "In order to finalize my divorce. Anything worth value will be sold, the buildings demolished, and the property spilt in half. Nate can do whatever he wants with his half. My half will be sold, so Sandra can get her half of the proceeds and we'll go our separate ways."

She wished her cell phone wasn't in her purse. She'd read the text from Vivi Anne so quickly this morning, she couldn't remember if it was Nate or Lou who was selling to Leeman and Holmes. She could remember that name, so why not which cousin was selling? Or maybe she just remembered Leeman and Holmes had made an offer and Vivi Anne hadn't said to whom.

"Is Nate selling his half?" she asked.

"I don't give a rat's ass what Nate does," he snarled. "I only talk to him when I have to. My guess is yes. He doesn't want this place anymore than I do."

"To a developer?" she asked. "That's what he told me. That they are going to build a resort out here."

Lou shook his head. "Not for the price Nate wants. It's too far from town. It would take too long for anyone to recoup their money. But, if Nate thinks he has a buyer willing to pay the price he thinks it's worth, more power to him. I just want out."

His lip curled as he glanced around. "This place has been a pain in my ass for as long as I can remember. Every summer we had to mow the grass, paint the house, pound nails in loose shingles, fix the corral. Uncle Riley always had a job for us to do out here, and our parents made us comply. My mother and Nate's mother fought over this place like two cats over catnip. That's what killed all four of them."

"It is?" Edith had mentioned both Lou's and Nate's parents had died in a plane crash but hadn't elaborated.

"Yes. Uncle Clayton and my dad wanted to have seismic tests done on the land to check for crude oil, but Uncle Riley refused. The four of them, my folks and Uncle Clayton and Aunt Rosie were flying to Cheyenne to see about having Riley declared incompetent when Uncle Clayton's plane went down. Nate and I were eighteen, had just graduated high school." He shook his head. "We had seismic tests done right after Riley died, didn't turn up nothing." His gaze went to the house, and resentment filled his eyes. "This place is cursed. Has been from the day old Rance built it."

Chapter Eleven

Rance's jaw was locked together so tight, his neck ached. A crick had formed in his neck from looking over one shoulder at the house, wondering if Beth was still in there. He told her to wait, and she better, but when he'd walked out of the house, he'd had the same feeling as when he'd seen her in the bedroom that first day. The one when she'd walked right through him. She'd been sitting at the table, so that sensation could have only come from someone else walking through him. Whoever had pulled up to the house in her time.

"Is she all right?"

His spine quivered at the sound of Cindy's voice. He turned her way and didn't bother holding the contempt out of his tone. "If Horse *was* limping, you should never have made her pull that buggy all the way out here." He'd checked the horse's other three legs and hooves, and found nothing, and knelt near the last hind one. "You should have had Ace Burchett take a look at her. His blacksmith shop is just down the block from the sheriff's office. Cliff would've pointed it out to you. Nan, too."

"Well, maybe I exaggerated a little bit," Cindy cooed.

Her voice was so high-pitched it made his ears sting, and her frilly pink dress was covered with so much lace it made his eyes hurt. So did the matching hat with a big feather flaying in the wind. The idea of having *anything* to do with this woman was beyond his imagination. He glanced toward the house again, wishing he could see through the screen door. Cindy was the exact opposite of Beth. Of all the things he loved. A sense of urgency had him completing his inspection of Horse's leg and hoof. He stood and patted the horse's hip. "She wasn't limping?"

She batted her lashes and shrugged one shoulder up to her cheek. "It was more like she was dragging her feet. I figured she was homesick and seeing you would help."

Horses don't drag their feet, but they did get homesick, he knew that well enough, and couldn't blame Horse for feeling that way. He would, too. "Nan know you're out here?"

Still batting her lashes, she turned toward the house. "Your home is so lovely."

His home was a lot of things, but he wasn't about to agree or disagree with her concerning a single one of them. Nor would he invite her in. Ever.

"Could I bother you for a glass of water?" she asked. "I'm dearly parched from the trip all the way out here."

Before he'd married Beth and they'd built the house, he'd drawn water from the well near the barn. Still used it to water the horses and to get a drink himself when working outside. Clicking his tongue, Rance led Horse toward the well, and after filling a bucket for the animal, he dropped the rope back down and brought up another bucketful. Lifting down the metal dipper he kept hooked on the overhang that kept leaves and other debris out of the well, he filled the dipper and handed it to Cindy.

She frowned. "I usually use a glass."

He shrugged and drank the water himself. She could travel back to town as thirsty as a camel for all he cared.

As he started to hook the dipper back on its nail, she said, "Oh, well, I guess I could use that this once."

He refilled the dipper and handed it to her.

"I do hope I don't dribble," she said with a giggle.

He found nothing funny about not knowing how to drink out of dipper. Turning around, he said, "Just hook it on the nail when you're done."

"Where are you going?"

Walking around Horse, he answered, "Just checking the rigging so you won't have any trouble on your way back to town."

"Oh, that is such a long drive," she said. "I was thinking I might rest a bit before returning."

"There are some shade trees about halfway to town. A good place to rest." His stomach tightened as the little grove of trees came to mind. He and Beth often stopped there, not necessarily to rest, on their way home from town. On their way to town sometimes, too. His gaze settled on the house again.

"Nan has told me so much about you," Cindy said. "I feel as if I know you."

"You don't."

"I could."

She'd walked around Horse and stood directly behind him. That grated on his nerves as much as not knowing who was in the house with Beth.

"If you'd let me, I could even become your friend."

"I have friends," he said, skirting around her and

making his way to the other side of Horse. "Don't need more."

"I felt that way at one time."

He didn't care how she felt at any time.

"You see, Rance, I too have lost someone very dear to me. His name was Eugene, and we were engaged to be married. It's been almost a year now. He worked for the railroad, and there was an accident. I didn't believe it when I first heard. Said there was no way he could have died."

The hair on his arms slowly rose, and it took all he had to hold off a shiver. It didn't help that she was dabbing at her eyes with a handkerchief, and sniffling, and looking sincerely sad.

"Then I saw his body," she said close to a whisper. "And I had no choice but to believe it. People tried to comfort me, my friends and family, but I didn't want comfort from them, I wanted Eugene. Wanted him to be alive so badly I dreamed about him. Dreamed about us getting married." She sniffled again and dabbed at her nose.

He scratched the back of his neck, where the muscles had grown tight. She wasn't looking at him, was gazing down the road and looking as forlorn as any person could.

"He died two weeks before our wedding. Two weeks. Oh, it was awful. So, so awful."

His gut tightened. He would have been in rough shape had Beth died two weeks before their wedding. Twisting he looked at the house. What was he thinking? He had been in rough shape when she'd died. Would still be if she hadn't returned. His throat closed up. He had to swallow twice to open it back up. Beth hadn't returned. Not completely.

"People kept saying Eugene wouldn't want me to be so sad," Cindy said. "And that made me so mad. They didn't know what Eugene would have wanted. At least that's how I felt. Oh, goodness, I felt that way for a long time. Months. For months and months, I was mad and alone. Alone, and lonely. I was bad company. So bad my friends no longer came around. I thought I didn't care, but then, Eugene came to me in a dream, and told me I couldn't mourn him forever. That I had to start living again. I told him that I didn't want to, but when he asked me to do it for him, I knew I had to."

She sniffled again and wiped at her eyes before tucking the handkerchief under the cuff of her sleeve. "That's when I knew exactly what Eugene would have wanted. For me to live. Because he loved me as much as I loved him. So I put a smile on my face and started living again. It wasn't easy. Especially at first. But each day it got a little easier and eventually I decided maybe it would get even easier if I got away, so that's when I decided to come and stay with Aunt Nan for a while."

The smile on her face appeared to be as genuine as the red rims her tears had left around her eyes.

"Well," she said, dipping her head slightly. "I've taken enough of your time for today. Thank you for checking over Horse, she's a good animal, gentle and well-trained, and thank you for the water."

A good splattering of guilt at making her drink from the dipper curdled the contents of his stomach. "I-I-uh-could get you a glass of water if you want one. From the house."

"No, but thank you. A sip from the dipper was all I needed."

She turned to walk toward the buggy, and he followed and helped her onto the seat.

"Have Ace check Horse when you get into town," he said. "Just to make sure there's not something up with one of her legs."

"All right, I'll do that. You be sure to stop by the house if you come into town. Cliff and Nan will be glad to see you."

He nodded.

"I'll be glad to see you, too, especially if you want to talk, need a friend who understands."

He wanted to shake his head, say that wouldn't happen, but the muscles in his neck and throat didn't want to cooperate. So, he merely took a step back and watched as she skillfully backed Horse up and steered the animal around the well and out of the yard. It wasn't until she was little more than a speck on the horizon that he pulled his gaze away, wondering if he'd been wrong about her. Had that nip of trouble Cliff referred to been how she'd behaved after Eugene died? He would have been in more than a nip of trouble if he hadn't had horses to train during those first few weeks after Beth's accident.

He spun around then and jogged toward the house. She'd better still be there.

The door had yet to close behind him when he knew she wasn't.

****

Liz approached the little cabin cautiously. She hadn't explored any of the out buildings but considering Rance hadn't returned to the house by the time Lou left, she figured now was a good time. She didn't believe the property was cursed any more than she believed it was haunted.

That was a bit of an oxymoron. Yet, not really, because Rance wasn't really a ghost. He was a time-traveler, as was she. There was a definite difference.

The door creaked as she pushed it open and dust motes floated in the sunlight that entered the room. Surprisingly, or maybe not, the cabin, which was made of thick square logs that resembled railroad ties, had more modern appliances than the house.

Actually, modern wasn't the correct term. They'd probably been purchased in the forties or fifties. A fridge that was as round as it was square and a narrow electric stove sat along one wall, as well as a small set of metal kitchen cabinets that housed a sink.

There was a small metal table with a red Formica top with two matching chairs in the center of the room, and beyond that, a rocking chair, old freestanding radio, and a small wood stove. A curtain was pulled to the side and hooked behind a large nail, showing the only other room was a bedroom. In there was a single size bed and dresser.

Her heart filled with sadness at the idea of Rance living here for decades, right up until he died. One picture hung on the walls, it was above the dresser, and she moved close enough to see it was of a magazine. *Horse World*. Though he was old, his dark hair gray, Rance was on the cover. June 1946.

She felt a hint of happiness at the idea his ranch had been successful despite all else, but that wasn't enough. He deserved far more than a picture on a magazine cover. Far more than this little cabin.

Because it was her job, she made mental notes of items that might be worth collecting, and then left the cabin. She should have brought her notebook. There were so many things swirling around inside her head, what to write down may be forgotten before she got to the house. Rance was on her mind. Who he'd met in his time, but so was Lou. He was clearly still in love with Sandra. Oddly, she felt a considerable amount of dislike for Lou's wife, or soon to be ex-wife. Not as much dislike as she held toward Cindy for soon becoming Rance's wife.

Was it even possible to be jealous of a woman who lived more than a century ago? Of course it is. To a time traveler.

"Oh good, grief." Looking skyward for no reason other than it seemed to make sense, she said, "Vivi Anne, I need you. This has become too much for me to handle."

Of course Vivi Anne couldn't just appear out of thin air, but was only a phone call away. She hurried to the house, however, the moment she entered the kitchen, all thoughts of Vivi Anne disappeared.

The hum made her heart dance, as did the floating mirror. Testing her abilities or hoping to confirm what she thought had happened before, she stared at the area around the mirror, searching for a faint image or outline of him.

Disappointed at not seeing anything and anxious to see him, she grasped the mirror handle.

"Where the hell have you been?"

Stung by his tone and the anger on his face, she snapped, "Well, hello to you, too."

"What's that supposed to mean?"

Seriously? She's doing all she can to help him, and he's the grumpy one? "What are you so mad about?"

His eyes narrowed. "I told you to wait here."

Spurred by his attitude, she copped one herself. "I am here." But won't be for long if he keeps this attitude up.

"You weren't a minute ago." He waved a hand. "I searched the house over."

"I was right outside." She could understand his frustration, but it wasn't her fault. "When you never returned to the house, I went outside."

"What for?"

She shrugged, not wanting to tell him what she'd found. "To explore."

"Explore what?"

Now flustered, she threw her hands in the air, or at least tried. Only one arm rose. His tight hold on the mirror prevented the other one from moving an inch. His hold and the fact she wasn't about to let go of the mirror. "What does that matter? It doesn't. But if you must know, I went to look at your cabin. I'm supposed to be inventorying antiques, you know."

"No, you're not."

"Yes, I am." Caught somewhere between delusions and reality—or what appeared to be delusions and reality—she truly didn't know which, commonsense prevailed. Sighing, she shook her head. "I'm not Beth. I'm not—" For some stupid reason her eyes stung. Swallowing and forcing her eyes not to water, she said, "I'm not your wife. I'm not her. I'm Liz Baxter. An antique dealer who lives in twenty-eighteen. Up until a few weeks ago, when I got laid-off from a cell phone company, I wasn't even an antiques dealer. Just someone who liked antiques." She had no idea why she'd felt the need to explain all that, other than she was trying to assure him she was not Beth. Couldn't possibly be Beth. "I want to help you if I can, but I'm not your wife. I'm not your Beth."

Try as she might, a tear or two escaped. She blinked, but more wanted to follow. "I'm trying to do all I can, but you're making it difficult. More difficult than it needs to be." She couldn't see through the blur of tears, which was probably best because he was getting angrier. She didn't need to see to know that, and the pain welling inside her was all for him. "I know you loved her. Loved her with all your heart. But Beth died in that train accident. She died. And once people are dead, there's no coming back. They're gone forever."

The increased weight of the mirror said he'd let go. A mixture of blame, remorse, and shame, flooded her system. "Rance don't—"

It could have been her imagination, or pure instincts. Either way, the slamming of the door told her he was gone.

She set the mirror on the table, sank into the nearest chair, and for the first time in her life, cried because of someone else's pain. Really, sincerely, cried for him. She wanted to help him. Truly did. But her hands were tied. There was only so much she could do. She didn't want to hurt him, but she couldn't lie to him, either.

Tears began falling for herself then too. Why was this happening to her? What had she done to deserve all this? She was just a common everyday person. She'd never loved anyone deeply, profoundly, but she'd never hated or intentionally hurt anyone either. If this was karma making its rounds, it had no ground to stand on, no past to work from.

She let her pity party continue for a short time, but then, because it wasn't like her to be so emotional, she dug into her bag and pulled out her notebook. After forcing herself to jot down the few things she remembered from the cabin, she stood, and with pen and paper in hand, began cataloguing every item she came across, and tagging the ones worth having packed up.

The work was good medicine, as was cursing Rance, which eventually turned into praise for how well things had been preserved. By the time she made her way back downstairs, she felt more like herself. The Liz Baxter she'd always known. Her thinking was clear. Well, somewhat clear.

Sitting down at the table, she hoisted her bag off the adjacent chair to pull out her purse and then her cell phone. The red x over the icon bar wasn't what she wanted to see but couldn't do anything about it, so she clicked on the text symbol to re-read Vivi Anne's messages. Whether Rance was mad at her or not, she wasn't going to let this place become a nuclear dump site. Nor would she quit caring about him. That would be impossible. Meeting him had changed that about her. He'd brought out the ability to care inside her.

She had no idea how Vivi Anne had discovered the nuclear dump site information but was one-hundred percent sure about the accuracy of it. She read through the text again and learned nothing new, other than Vivi Anne didn't mentioned either of Lou or Nate's names.

They were behind it, at least one of them. Probably both.

She swiped the screen, scrolling through Vivi Anne's other messages. Stopping the rolling screen, she re-read another message.

—Beth Livingston died on May 25, 1901 in a train wreck shortly after it left Billings, where she'd been visiting her family. Her body was never recovered.—

While reading the message again, Liz pulled the cigar box out of the bag. She set her phone aside and laid the pictures on the table, examining each one. Her remarkable resemblance to Beth was no longer startling. In fact, she sensed a kinship with the woman. Could almost imagine how much Beth had loved Rance. How much she'd missed him while visiting her family in Billings.

Vivi Anne's message made no mention of a bridge, or water, but those were the images that entered Liz's mind. They came about so quickly, her breath stalled and panic gripped her chest as water seemed to engulf her.

She pushed away from the table, gasping as her legs began to tremble, and put her head between her knees, hoping to escape the overwhelming dizziness. It was far worse than it ever had been. And there was no reason. The trunk was nowhere near here.

Even with her eyes open images flashed. Swirling water seemed to be everywhere, towing her down into a dark abyss. Fear engulfed her as she pushed further away from the table. The panic was so great, so real, she couldn't think of anything except escaping. She had to get out of here. She tried to stand, but her legs were so heavy, paralyzed, that she dropped onto the floor and used her arms to drag herself toward the door. The powerful force pulling her backward was familiar, she'd experienced it before and her panic grew. Frantically, she clawed harder and faster.

Her heart pounded, and air wouldn't catch in her lungs by the time she reached the door. A great sickening of nausea welled inside her, and Rance filled her mind. She wanted to shout for him but couldn't. It took tremendous effort, her last bits of strength, of willpower, to push the screen door open.

As soon as her head crossed the threshold, the heaviness lifted and the darkness surrounding her disappeared as if she'd just crawled out of a rabbit hole. Relief welled as air entered her burning lungs. She gasped and panted, but with each breath her terror dissolved, and she crawled onto the porch, letting the screen door slam behind her.

With her back braced against the side of the house, she leaned her head back and breathed, just breathed.

It was several moments before she had the wherewithal to wonder what had happened. She'd never experienced anything like that before and hoped to hell she never did again. That was too real. Too vivid. Too familiar.

Eeriness washed over her, and she closed her eyes as memories she hadn't known existed came forward. What had happened in the house had happened before. She had been engulfed by water and had fought to find a way out of it.

Memories of the accident that had taken her parents had never surfaced before. At five years old, her little mind had known the terror had been too much for a child to bear and had wiped it away. Other than a few faint images of people she assumed had been her parents, and the odd ball horse ones, she had no memories of her life before going to live with Gladys and Norman.

May 25th.
May 25th.

Vivi Anne's message said Beth died on May 25th. Didn't it? Could it be the same date? Not year, but month and day? Much like the accident, dates hadn't been imbedded in her mind. She'd been to her parent's grave site several times. There was no headstone, no granite marker, but the little metal stakes held her mother and father's names, birthdates, and death dates. May 25, 1994. Their accident, her accident, had happened on the same date as Beth's. Many, many years apart, but the same date.

No longer gasping for air, she kept her eyes closed and contemplated what else she could pull forward from her early life. There was something there. Something she wanted to remember but couldn't. Telling herself to relax, she tried harder.

Frustration is what came. She sensed the interruption before actually hearing the vehicle coming up the driveway. "What is this? Visitation day?" she mumbled upon opening her eyes.

Huffing out a breath at not being found sitting on the back stoop, she rose to her feet before the truck rolled under the faded *Rocking L* sign. For a flash of a moment, she saw what that sign had looked like when Rance had first hung it. The wood had been golden brown and the letters black from how he'd burned them into the wood. The image of what it had looked like fresh and new brought a smile to her face and a warmth around her heart.

"Happy to see me?"

She turned toward the truck that had parked beside the house and the man climbing out. "Not so you'd notice," she told Nate. "Did Lou call you?"

"No, why? What did you find?"

Dollar signs flashed in his eyes as boldly as a cartoon. He jumped up the couple of steps and crossed the porch to pull open the screen door. Disgusted, she followed, but paused before crossing the threshold.

"Where is it?" Nate asked. "What did you find?"

What had happened was still too fresh in her mind. Holding the screen door open, she remained on the porch. "Nowhere. I didn't find anything."

Frowning, he glanced around. "Then why'd you ask if Lou called me?"

She shrugged. "Because I told him the same thing I told you. I need more time."

He ran a hand over the back of the chair as he walked around it to the table, the heels of his boots clicked loudly against the floor. "Well, darling, I hate to burst your bubble, but you don't have it. I got the confirmation from the fire chief today. This place will be burned down on Saturday. The good news is they'll use it as training for the volunteer firemen, so it won't cost me a dime and most everything can stay." He turned around to look at her. "Other than the stuff you say is worth something. I've hired some men to come out and haul that stuff to town on Saturday morning."

Dread filled her. It wasn't as frightening as the panic earlier, but it was just as real. "That's not enough time." A heavy sigh escaped. Forever might not be enough time to convince Rance of what he needed to do. Must do. He was too focused on Beth to even consider what the future could hold. Consider how to stop all this from happening.

"It's gonna have to be," Nate said.

His distracted tone had her stepping forward. The room didn't spin, no images flashed behind her eyes, and she took another step toward the table.

"Who are these pictures of?" Nate asked.

"That's Rance and his wife, Beth, on their wedding day," she answered. "Haven't you seen a picture of him?"

"Old Rance died long before I was born," Nate answered, picking up the picture of Beth. He glanced between it and her several times. "Wow. You could almost be her twin."

"No," she denied. "I couldn't."

"Her relative for sure." He flipped the picture over as if looking for a name or date, and then back again. "Maybe you are. Some claim Beth wasn't supposed to be on that train that crashed. Her original plan had been to leave the next day, but she'd changed her mind."

"In order to come home early."

He shook his head. "To not come back at all. When she and Rance got married, they lived in the log cabin out back. Beth wasn't used to that and grew homesick. That's why she went to Billings, and story goes she hooked up with a previous boyfriend and headed east."

Not even beginning to believe such a thing, she said, "Whose story? Yours?"

"I don't know who started it, but it was around long before me." He set the picture down, stuck both hands in his back pockets and rocked on his heels. "That would be some crazy coincidence, wouldn't it?"

His T-shirt and jeans, once again, were black and tight. His stance did nothing for her. "What would be a coincidence?"

"You. You're from Billings, right? That's what

Buzz said." Without waiting for her to confirm or deny, he continued, "That you came down here looking for antiques and discovered a long-lost family member. Maybe she'd returned to that area at some point, or her children did and you're Beth's great-great-granddaughter or something." He pulled one hand out of his pockets and tapped the picture with a finger. "You sure do look like her."

Liz refused to rub at the chill rippling her arms, but couldn't stop the fingers of one hand twisting the ring on her other. Why were there so many coincidences? She did resemble Beth, and the band on her finger was an exact duplicate to the one Rance wore. It all seemed impossible. Yet, everything that was happening was impossible on so many levels. But they were happening, she couldn't deny that. Not needing another avenue to travel down, she moved to the table and put the pictures back in the box. "Everyone has a twin, or so it's said."

"Or maybe they have the same genes and just don't know it."

She closed the lid on the box and changed the subject. "If Lou didn't call you, why are you here?"

"I saw your car down by the gate."

The day had been so busy, she'd forgotten about leaving her car at the gate. As well as how she'd been in such a hurry to see Rance this morning she couldn't wait for someone to open it. A lot of good that had done her. He'd been gone for several hours. Ever since she'd insisted she wasn't Beth. "And, I suppose, you were just driving by?"

Nate shrugged. "Why is it parked down there?"

"No one was here to open the gate when I arrived."

Twisting about to lean a hip against the table, he tipped the brim up on his hat. She'd noticed he was handsome, it was hard not to, but she hadn't noticed how dark his eyes were. As dark as Rance's. Maybe because he'd said she could be Beth's ancestor, she wondered if he was Rance's. There were similarities. Just like Lou, Nate's build was similar to Rance's. Her stomach did a little dip. Was that where Rance was right now? With Cindy?

"I never got a call."

While half of her mind was twirling sadistic ideas of Cindy, the other half was able to focus on Nate. "I called Lou. Not you."

Nate shook a finger at her. "That was a mistake. Lou's not an early riser."

Of the two, she'd pegged Nate as more of the play boy, and that held true, even after seeing Lou in action last night. Nate's grin said so. "And you are?"

He chuckled and his eyes twinkled as he winked one eye. "When I need to be."

She didn't want to like Nate, and therefore brought up what Lou had told her. "In order to not get caught with someone's wife?"

Nate shook his head. "Touché. Lou was spilling his guts, was he? Looking for a shoulder to cry on? Let me tell you something, darling. The apple doesn't fall far from the tree. Aunt Janice was Uncle Leonard's third wife for a reason. He just couldn't keep it in his pants." Leaning closer he lowered his voice. "Between you and me, I think the only reason that stopped was because he was afraid Janice would cut it off if it came out when it shouldn't."

She bit her lips together and tightened her throat

against the absurdity of that, but throw in the way Nate had one brow lifted and despite her efforts, she couldn't keep in a laugh. Disguising her laughter, she asked, "So, the men in your family are afraid of women, are they?"

"Some, but you are about as frightful as a Pomeranian."

Not overly sure where she'd heard it, or if it was true, she chose to use the belief anyway. "Ask any burglar and they'll say little dogs are more frightening than big ones. They hide and bite at the Achilles' heel."

"If you say so." Nate's attention had gone to a phone that had jangled. He pulled if from his back pocket, and the look on his face said he wanted to answer but didn't because she was standing there. He silenced the ring and slipped the phone back in his pocket. "I gotta run. Do you want a ride to your car?"

"I'm not ready to leave." She wasn't and wouldn't be until after speaking to Rance again. If it meant she spent the night out here, she would. Saturday was the day after tomorrow. He hadn't returned. She'd have felt him, which meant he was still outside in his time.

"I'm not saying you have to leave."

She pulled her eyes off the door. "You're not?"

"No. The fire department is going to burn this house down on Saturday. The barns and outbuildings, too. Have you looked through them yet?"

She shook her head. Her little exploration of the cabin really didn't count.

"Then you still have a lot of work to do before my guys arrive on Saturday morning." He'd walked to the door. Rather than push open the screen door, he pulled a key ring with a single key out of his pocket. "I'll give you a key to the gate so you can come and go as you please. Stay as late as you want." Grinning he added, "It's a mile walk to your car."

Skeptical, she asked, "What about protecting your assets?"

Nate opened the door with one hand while waving the other for her to exit. "That was Lou. I'm more afraid of you scaling that gate. I don't think our insurance will cover a broken leg."

The fact she currently didn't have any insurance didn't elude her. The cost of COBRA coverage had been far too extreme. Stepping over the threshold, she grabbed the key he dangled. "I had no intention of breaking a leg, and I still don't."

He followed her to the passenger side of his truck and opened the door. "Most people don't intend on breaking anything, but it still happens. All sorts of things just happen. And we regret them."

She clamped her lips shut and waited for him to walk around and climb in behind the wheel. "Are you referring to sleeping with Sandra?"

"Lou really was looking for a shoulder to cry on." He adjusted the air conditioning vents to blow in her direction after starting the truck. "I wasn't the first or the last, but yes, I regret sleeping with Sandra. She and Lou have been on and off for years. One is no better than the other, and I knew better than to get tangled up in it. What can I say? It just happened. Just happened."

Sleeping with someone she shouldn't have had almost happened in college. And she'd been full of guilt and regret afterward. There had been no love, just hormones and curiosity, and though she'd stopped before it had happened, she'd been emptier than ever afterward. Yet, still knew that hadn't been what she'd been after. Loveless sex. It still wasn't. No matter how wonderful people claimed sex was, and she did believe it could be wonderful—with the right person—she knew there was more to it than that. There had to be an undeniable connection, one that formed long before sex ever came into the picture, and stayed long after sex made it stronger. She'd been called a prude, and frigid, but she didn't care. She knew deep down she was right. It was odd how so many things about her had grown with clarity the past couple of days. Things she'd accepted, but never fully understood before.

As they rolled beneath the *Rocking L* sign, her thoughts shifted to Rance. She should be hoping it had been Cindy who had arrived in his time earlier and that the two of them were forming a relationship—a lasting one that would provide him with future generations. However, the idea of things happening between the two of them—things that led to sex—bothered her greatly. In ways it never had before, and far more than the idea of Nate sleeping with Sandra.

"It's a family curse."

"What is?" Her mind had been elsewhere but had heard his last words.

"The ability to have a happy marriage."

While telling her about Robert, Edith hadn't said much about his or Lou's parents. "Your parents weren't—"

"Divorced?" He shook his head. "No, but they should have been. They fought constantly. I'm sure the only reason they stayed together was to prove to Leonard it could be done." His laugh was bitter. "That and the money. My father was a financial broker during a time when there was money to be made. He made plenty and invested it well. Neither one of my parents were willing to disrupt that by having to divide it and pay lawyers."

He slowed the truck as they approached the open gate. "Mother liked to dangle that under Leonard and Janice's noses as much as everything else. She was the one who claimed Beth Livingston never died but ran off with another man. Most likely because Aunt Janice was spouting off about how Rance was Robert Dixon's real father. They tried to outdo each other on everything. Storytelling was no different."

"Do you believe he was?" She swallowed the lump in her throat that had come out of nowhere. "R-Rance. Do you think he was Robert's father?"

"I don't think it matters one way or the other." He stopped the truck next to her car. "That was a long time ago, and it has no impact on my life whatsoever." He shrugged. "If Rance wanted people to know if he was or wasn't Robert's father, he'd have said so."

The sinking feeling of her stomach said her entire plan had been flawed from the get-go. She couldn't make someone do what they didn't want to do. Namely Rance. "You're right." Holding up the key with one hand, she opened the truck door with the other. "Thanks for the key. I'll make sure I lock the gate when I leave."

"No problem. If I don't see you before then, I'll see you Saturday morning."

She nodded and climbed out. Saturday. She couldn't change the world. At least not Rance's world. He didn't want it to change, so why was she trying?

As she climbed into her car, Nate rolled down his window.

"If you see old Rance, tell him I said hi." He winked and drove away.

Chapter Twelve

Rance had regretted walking out of the house, away from Beth, the minute the door had slammed shut behind him, but being his foolish, stubborn self, he hadn't turned around. Instead, he'd spent hours in the barn, not doing much besides wearing out the bottom of his boots. Now, standing in the empty kitchen, he was more than frustrated.

She was gone. He didn't blame her. She'd been mad at the way he'd yelled at her, but damn it, he didn't know what the hell he was doing. The first time around, Beth hadn't needed to be courted. He hadn't needed to make her fall in love with him. She'd insisted that had happened as soon as she'd seen him. He'd expected it to be that way again. But it hadn't. She didn't remember him, so she couldn't love him. She didn't even remember herself. It made sense. He supposed. A person who had been reborn would have to relearn all about themselves.

He hoped he was right. He sure as hell didn't want her to be right. The idea of partnering up with Cindy made his skin crawl. Listening to how her beau had died had made him feel a bit sorry for her, considering he could relate, but not enough to marry her. Heartbroken or not, that woman was trouble, and he didn't need any more troubles.

He scratched his head and glanced at the handful of

yellow flowers he'd plucked from the ground beside the corral. It was hard telling when Beth would be back, so he walked to the cupboard to find a glass.

Picking them had seemed like a good idea, at the time. Now, it seemed foolish. She wouldn't be able to see them. Going to town to find her wouldn't work either. He wouldn't know where to start looking, and roaming the streets with a hand mirror would have people thinking he truly had gone crazy.

Maybe he had.

After filling the glass with water, he stuck the flowers in it and turned around to carry them to the table. The mirror sat there. So did the box of pictures he'd sent with her last night. The ones he'd wanted her to see. To remember their wedding day.

It hadn't worked. Instead she'd insisted she wasn't his Beth.

As he set the flowers on the table, other things appeared. Strange things. They appeared sheer at first, like a curtain with the sun shining through it, but the harder he stared at them, the more clear they became. A cloth bag with an odd metal strip on top that held the sides together, beside it sat a pad of paper and the pen she said didn't need to be refilled. There was also a narrow, black rectangular-shaped box looking thing. Another larger cloth bag sat on a chair. That was the one she'd pulled the book out of that had pictures and prices of items like those in his house.

He reached down to flip the edge open of the bag, but like when he touched Beth, his hand went right through the material. He tried the pen and paper and small box but wasn't able to touch any of it. The picture box he could touch, and open, and pick up the photos.

Having those photos memorized, he closed the lid. The pad of paper, held together with a spiraling piece of wire along one side, was the pad she'd used yesterday to write down things. She'd held it up for him to examine, along with that newfangled pen she just threw away when it became empty and bought a new one. He'd told her that seemed like a waste. Still felt that way, but his heart started to race as he continued to stare at the items.

If they were here, it meant Beth was too.

The house was empty. His instincts said as much. However, just to be sure, he darted in and out of each room, upstairs and down. Each vacant area increased the alarm building inside him. She had to be outside. What if she'd gotten hurt? Tripped, or fell, or got herself locked inside of one of the outbuildings? She'd said things were different in her time. Hinges could have rusted off, boards rotted away.

He hurried back to the kitchen, pausing only long enough to grab the mirror off the table. He'd be able to see her, but she wouldn't know he was there, not without the mirror. How to help her was something he'd have to figure out once he found her.

He was almost to the door when Beth appeared. Faint at first, as she walked through the screen, then she became as clear and real as the rest of the room. His relief was so great his arms came up to engulf her in a hug. He didn't move though. The look on her face had frozen his feet to the floor.

As her eyes settled on the mirror, her voice sounded as sad as she looked. "You're back."

His heart took a hit as solid and painful as any punch he'd ever received, and he gave himself a moment to reflect upon that. Arguing hadn't worked. Anger hadn't worked. He was going to have to court her. Coax her gently into seeing things his way. The way they were supposed to be. That wasn't all that new to him. He trained horses into doing what he wanted. A woman couldn't be that much different.

Confidence put a smile on his face and he held the mirror out for her to grasp. His entire being felt the moment her hand touched the handle. "I was worried about you," he said softly.

She frowned. "Worried about me? Why?"

"The house was empty."

A tiny smile tugged at the corners of her mouth. "I'd left my car at the end of the driveway this morning and went to get it." She closed her eyes and shook her head. "I don't know what to do, Rance. I want to help you, but I don't know if I can, I don't know—"

"I want to help you, too," he interrupted. The desire to pull her close, to comfort her, to chase the sadness from her eyes and heart frustrated him because he couldn't hold her. Couldn't hug her.

Her sigh echoed inside his head. His heart.

"Does that mean you've reconsidered marrying Cindy?"

Mentally committing himself not to argue, he said, "I've thought about all you've said."

"And?"

"And Cindy's gone through a tough time lately," he said, purposefully not answering her question.

"So that was her who arrived earlier? You've spoken with her?"

"Yes, that was her." He took note of how sad she still sounded. "Come, sit down at the table."

A half-smile appeared again. "So you can make yourself some coffee?"

"No, so you can tell me what this stuff is."

She glanced at the table. "What stuff?" Her eyes grew wide. "My purse? My notebook? You can see them?"

"Yes, I can see them but can't touch them."

"But you can see them. Could see them even when I wasn't in the house?"

He grinned at the excitement in her voice. "Yes, I can, I could. What are they?"

They moved to the table and sat with the mirror lying between them.

"This is a purse." She pointed to the cloth bag. "Women keep all their essentials in it. Money. Credit cards, which I have none, but do have a debit card. Relatively the same thing, I just have to have money in the bank rather than a set amount some company will loan me for an exuberant interest rate. I don't believe in that. Credit has caused a lot of problems for a lot of people in my time."

Credit had caused problems for people in his time, too, but he didn't say that. Nor did he say she felt the same way about credit as him. Always had.

She'd let go of the mirror to pull on a tab that separated the metal strip.

"What's that?"

"I just told you. It's a purse."

"How you'd open it? How'd you separate the metal strip?"

"Oh, that's a zipper. They were invented early in your century but didn't become popular until after World War I, mainly on rubber boots and jackets."

Interested in the mechanics of how it worked, he said, "Do it again."

When she grasped the bag with both hands to hold it closer to him while opening and closing the metal strip, his attention was drawn away. His heart started pounding as his eyes settled on the ring on her finger. Why hadn't he noticed it before?

He lifted his gaze, and as their eyes met, for the breadth of a heartbeat, he knew she was remembering the exact thing as him. The day he'd put that ring on her finger, and she'd put the identical one on him.

She twisted away. "Now days they use zippers for everything." Her voice was shaky. "Clothes, furniture, bags, tents. Some are metal, some plastic or nylon."

Setting the purse aside, she picked up the small black rectangle and touched the screen, making miniature, colorful pictures appear. "And this is my cell phone I told you about. A phone that doesn't need a cord. I don't have coverage here, so I can't show you how it works."

She set the phone down but didn't look his way. "That's not unusual. Cell One doesn't have the best service. I know. I managed their customer service division until a few weeks ago when another larger company bought them out. None of us knew about it until that morning. Those men who'd entered the Cell One building that day, and stood along the corridors, watching to make sure everyone only carried personal possessions out the front doors, had no idea how many lives they were affecting. Nor did they care."

He knew she was avoiding him and let her.

"Everything's connected," she said. "Like dominoes. When one falls, it knocks over the one beside it, and the one after that, and the one after that. There were people there who needed those jobs. They had kids to feed and mortgages to pay. That hadn't mattered to the powers that be. For them it came down to the all mighty dollar—the ones in their pockets."

If he hadn't already been convinced this was Beth, he would be now. She was always concerned about others. He'd told her once that she cared too much. She'd disagreed, said that she was honest, and liked other people to be treated honestly, too. And that the only person she'd ever really, truly care about would be him. He'd be the only one she ever loved, too. He'd agreed with that, even while knowing she cared about and loved others—family and friends, just like he did. He also knew the love they shared would surpass all others.

She glanced around the room, still avoiding looking his way. "I didn't have a mortgage and had—have a savings account. They also gave me a severance package. Most of that is still in the bank, too. I went to work at the antique shop the day I got laid off."

"You like antiques?" he asked, knowing she wasn't ready to tell him about the ring.

"Yes. I've always been interested in history. Majored in it in college. But I also like Vivi Anne. She's eccentric, and I think a little bit psychic. She doesn't tout around a crystal ball or set up a booth at fairs, she just has an uncanny wisdom that had intrigued me from the moment I met her. She opened the store last spring, when she moved to Billings from out east somewhere, she's never said exactly where."

"What does she look like?" Rance wasn't sure why he wanted to know that, but he did.

Beth looked at him then, and there was a twinkle in her blue eyes. "You would be surprised by her. She's tall with long gray hair, but she always has it piled on top of her head with a large claw clip." She smiled. "What would surprise you is how she dresses."

How she dressed surprised him, but he liked it. "Oh? Why?"

"She always wears dresses that go clear to the floor, we call them maxi dresses, and they are colorful. So bright they can hurt your eyes. Psychedelic. That means they are covered with all sorts of colors. Greens, yellows, reds, blues, purples. She wears lots of jewelry, crystals and such, and her nails, both fingernails and toenails are always painted either purple or pink."

If he had one wish, it would be that her eyes were always lit as brightly as they were right now. They used to be. Especially when she'd talk about him and their life together. "She sounds colorful," he said, knowing she was waiting for a response.

"Oh, she is, but she's also very down to earth. Literally. She rarely wears shoes. Says going barefoot keeps her grounded."

"And she's your friend."

She frowned slightly before nodding. "The best friend I've ever had." With a shrug, she added, "I've never gotten very close with too many people. None, really. I always preferred to be alone."

That didn't sound like Beth at all. She had several friends, good friends, both up in Billings and here in Cody. People were attracted to her like bees to pollen, and she cared greatly about others.

"Why?" he asked. "Why would you prefer to be alone?"

She shrugged but then frowned. "Because I never belonged."

Recognizing her thoughts were going deeper, and not sure that would help, he asked, "What else do you see on the table?"

"My notebook and pen."

"What else?"

She gestured toward the chair on the other side of the table. "My other bag."

"What's in the center of the table?"

She shook her head. "Nothing."

He picked up the mirror and tilted it until a reflection of the flowers appeared. "What do you see in the mirror?"

With a puzzled look and caution, she touched the mirror. Slowly a gentle smile appeared on her face as her gaze went from the mirror, to the table, and back to the mirror.

"A glass of yellow daisies," she said softly.

"Do you like them?"

Still holding the mirror with one hand, she used one fingertip on her other hand to touch the reflection. "Yes."

"I picked them for you."

She licked her lips, an action that stirred him deeply.

"Thank you," she whispered. "No one's ever picked flowers for me before."

He withheld the fact he had on several occasions, choosing instead to say, "I'll pick them every day for you."

Half expecting her to protest, to say that wasn't possible, he searched his mind for an appropriate response. He hadn't come up with one when her eyes met his. The longing there, the authenticity, tugged at his heart.

"Tell me about Beth," she whispered. "Tell me everything about her."

The request took him by surprise, and for a second, seemed impossible. How could he tell someone all about themselves?

"Please?"

He set the mirror on the table and nodded, both for himself and her. He'd just have to pretend he was talking to someone else. "She's the most beautiful person on earth. Inside and out. Her laugh could make birds sing, and her smile…" He paused, trying to describe something that was purely indescribable. "Her smile was brighter than the sun. Everyone loved her. She was kind and friendly, and thoughtful and generous. She didn't have an enemy. If she did, it wasn't for long, and she won them over."

"So, she had lots of friends."

He nodded. "Too many to count." That was the truth. There had been so many people at their wedding; the pews wouldn't hold them all. People had to stand in the back of the church.

"She had to have some faults."

He grinned. "Oh, she did. She was full of herself. Her confidence scared me. I wanted to jump in her path and say slow down before you get hurt." This was easier than he'd thought it would be. "I did more than once. It was never because she was doing anything bad, she would just act before thinking. Once, I had tied a horse to the corral, but left too much lead and it got tangled around its leg. Beth saw that and went running to untangle it. I was on the other side of the corral and thought she was going to get trampled before I could get there. She said she didn't want the horse to break a leg. I was so scared, and relieved, all I could do was hug her. Just hug her."

"How'd you meet?"

The idea of her not remembering hurt, but he refused to dwell on that. "I'd taken a pair of mustangs up to her father. Conrad, her father, and Millie, her mother, along with Beth and her sister, Abigail, had seen one of Buffalo Bill's shows up in Billings, and Conrad wanted a pair of white horses just like the ones used during the opening of the show for Millie. Beth had perched herself on the top rung of Conrad's corral to watch while I demonstrated how the horses could bow and back up, and prance. I was there for two days and before I left, she told me I was in love with her."

Her genuine smile filled her eyes. "You were."

He nodded. "I was." Warmth and pressure on the back of his hand had him looking down. Her hand was lying atop his, and he felt it. Genuinely felt it on top of his. Not through it. On top. Excitement zipped through him. "I was in love with her. Always will be." Afraid she'd pull her hand away, he continued, "I asked her how that could be. How I could be in love with her, when I hadn't even gotten up the nerve to touch her. And she said I had touched her. That I'd—"

"Touched her heart," she said, quietly, but thoughtfully.

His excitement doubled. "Yes. Touched her heart. And then she said, when—"

"You touch someone's heart, touching their hand is easy," she said, once again finishing his statement.

Their eyes both went to their hands and as he gently laid his other one atop hers, a lump the size of a boulder lodged in his throat. The hand between his two was solid and real, and soft and gentle. He curled his fingers around the side of her hand, as excited to feel the warmth of her skin beneath his as he was afraid to let go. To ever let go.

Hoping and praying, he leaned toward her, so ready to feel her lips against his. To taste her sweetness, to lose himself while kissing her, holding her, loving her. She was leaning toward him, too, and her eyes fluttered slightly as the lids closed.

"Rance, you in there?"

The shout came from outside the house but shattered the connection between him and her completely. Though the image of her hand was between his, her flesh and blood hand wasn't.

She was looking at their hands and frowning. "What's wrong?" she asked. "What happened?"

Unable to even whisper without being seen or heard, he shook his head.

Cliff had already pulled open the screen door. "You are in here. Didn't you hear me yelling? I've already searched the barn and the cabin for you."

"Sorry, Cliff. I didn't hear you," he answered, still looking at her.

She smiled. He wanted to ask if she could see Cliff, but already knew the answer. She couldn't see into his world anymore than he could see into hers.

"What are you doing?" Cliff's gaze roamed the table.

The flowers, the mirror, the box of pictures, how his own hands sat upon each other. He pulled them off the table. "Nothing."

"Just thinking?" Cliff pulled out a chair.

He shrugged. Beth's bag had been on that chair, but it was no longer visible. Her other items were gone, too.

Cliff sat. "Got any coffee on the stove?"

"It's cold. From this morning." He tossed around a few ways to shoo Cliff out the door, but none of them would work. Cliff was too intuitive.

"That'll do." Cliff set his hat on the table. "I don't mind cold coffee, especially on a hot day."

"I was just getting ready to go back out to the barn."

A faint hint of a giggle tickled the inside of his ear. Though her image had faded to the point it was translucent, she stood and grabbed her notebook. "I'll be back." Her words were barely a whisper.

He didn't want her to leave. He wanted Cliff to leave. Cliff had stood, but he wasn't headed toward the door.

"You want some, too?" Cliff asked on his way to the cupboard.

"Sure." She'd disappeared, and he couldn't follow her, not with Cliff here, and telling the other man to leave because he wanted to be alone with his wife would have Cliff setting down roots.

Cliff carried two cups to the table, and as he sat on the chair again, he nodded toward the glass beside his hat. Wrinkles formed between his dark eyes. "Flowers?"

Rance shrugged.

The cup Cliff was lifting toward his lips stopped midway. "You didn't pick them for someone, did you?"

"Why?" It was none of his business, yet Cliff seemed really worried about that little clump of flowers. Could he have seen Beth? Her ghostly image?

"I-uh-I met Cindy coming into town." He set down his cup without taking a sip and swiped one hand over his thick mustache. "Guessed she'd been out this way. Came to apologize about that."

"She thought Horse was limping."

"There is nothing wrong with that horse," Cliff said. "I checked that animal over this morning myself."

Because his mind was so full of Beth, and the excitement of touching her still flowed through his blood stream, Rance was able to muster up a bit of the sorrow he'd felt for Cindy earlier. "She's having a tough time of it. Losing her beau and all."

Cliff sputtered into his coffee. "Losing her b— what beau?"

"Eugene." He never minded drinking cold coffee and took a swallow. "The guy that died last year. They were engaged to get married."

"Last year? Engaged Cindy?"

Rance nodded.

"I never heard about that."

"Maybe Nan never told you." Even before he said it aloud doubt had formed.

Cliff shook his head. "She lied. Whatever Cindy said, it was a lie. There was no pending marriage. That girl's got problems. She'd rather lie than tell the truth. For the life of me, I can't figure out why."

The idea of Cindy's story being a tale wasn't hard to swallow, except that she'd appeared sincerely heartbroken, and knowing the depth and breadth of the aching rawness he'd experienced upon hearing about

Beth's accident, he couldn't imagine someone pretending that. There was no reason to even imagine pain like that. Sorrow like that. "Maybe she doesn't want sympathy." He certainly hadn't. He'd wanted Beth.

"Don't let her fool you, Rance. Please. Don't let her fool you." Cliff rubbed a hand over his forehead. "She's…well, she's—just don't let her fool you."

"No one's gonna fool me, but thanks for driving out." He'd wasted enough time. Beth was in the other room, and that's where he wanted to be. With her.

"Rance, I—"

He held up a hand. The last thing he needed was advice from one more person. He pushed away from the table and stood. "Thanks for riding out, Cliff. I appreciate it, but I do have work to do."

Cliff's expression said he wasn't ready to leave, but he downed his coffee and then stood. "I'll make sure Cindy doesn't bother you again."

"Good enough," Rance answered while walking across the room. He still couldn't completely believe Cindy had lied about her beau. She'd seemed too sincere. "But don't be too hard on Cindy. She'll come around." He held the door open for Cliff's exit. "I'll stop by your place soon."

Cliff walked out the door, but held it open with one hand. "Are you doing all right, you look better, sound better, but…" He said no more, just shook his head.

"I'm fine. Thanks for stopping out. I'll see you next time I'm in town."

"You're sure?"

"I'm sure." He may not be fine, but he was far better than he'd been a few days ago.

****

The hum of Rance's voice still vibrated the air around Liz, and that was a comfort like no other. He soothed her very being. Even while trying to figure out why she'd been able to feel his hand, real flesh, against her real flesh. That had been amazing. Truly amazing. The warmth of his hand had filled her from head to toe. Still did.

She'd left the kitchen when his company had arrived in order to contemplate that but hadn't made it any farther than the front room. A horse had caught her attention out the window. It stood in the pasture, staring at the house as if it expected to be seen, to be acknowledged. A liver and white mustang mare.

She couldn't say how she knew it was a mustang mare anymore than she understood how she'd known what Rance had been about to say when he spoke of Beth. How she'd said he'd touched her heart. The words had simply left her mouth without her even thinking them.

The image of Beth and him exchanging rings had been the same. It had appeared without thought, almost as if she'd been there. Claiming that was impossible didn't lessen an internal authenticity that was far too real to question.

Her heart rate increased, and a smile pulled at her lips before the mirror appeared in front of her face. A comforting weight surrounded her, like a warm blanket had been draped around her. She knew it was his arms even before touching the mirror.

He was standing behind her, with his arms around her shoulders, and without any fear or question, she leaned back, knowing he'd support her.

"Your company left," she said unnecessarily.

"Yes."

"What did Cliff need?"

The skin covering the top of her ear tingled, and her stomach fluttered at the wonderful sensations slowly growing inside her. She didn't need the reflection in the mirror to know he'd kissed her ear, and that the hand not holding the mirror was pressed against her stomach.

"Just checking up on me," he said.

"He's a good friend."

"Yes, he is, always has been."

Her mind was not on Cliff being a good friend, or any other man. She wanted to spin around and kiss him. Hold him and kiss him and make love with him. The desire was as crazy and powerful as the notion that it had happened before. That they'd made love in this room, with the flowered wallpaper surrounding them.

His reflection in the mirror was looking at her and the smoldering gleam in his eyes said he was recalling the same thing. That should be mortifying, but instead it thrilled her to the core.

The pressure around her increased, his arms tightening. His lips never moved, but she heard him whisper, *"I love you."*

Her response was silent as well. *"I love you, too."*

Chapter Thirteen

Not being able to express how much he loved her, how much he wanted her, was about the hardest thing Rance had ever experienced. His lips lingered as he kissed the side of her face, and though he could taste her, feel her, he still couldn't. It was crazy, but she wasn't really there, inside his arms. Not yet. A part of her hadn't fully come home yet.

Not knowing how or when that would happen added to his frustration and pain.

"Do you see that horse out there?" she asked quietly.

Her reflection said she was gazing over the top of the mirror, and he lifted his head to look out the window. "Which one?" A herd was in the front pasture.

"I only see one," she said. "A liver and white mustang."

"Esmeralda," they both said at the same time. They laughed together too.

"You don't like that name."

"I never said that," he answered.

"You think it's a silly name for a horse."

"That I did say."

"But Beth named the horse," she said. "Therefore, you never considered changing it. That was Beth's horse, wasn't it? A liver and white mustang mare named Esmeralda."

They were looking at each other in the mirror again. "Yes," he answered.

She closed her eyes, and when she opened them her brows were knit together. "Why do I know these things? How do I know these things? How can I see that horse?" She broke out of his hold without him feeling it and turned around to face him, while still holding the mirror. "I came here to inventory antiques, and then I met you, and I wanted to find a way to save you from a lonely, solitary existence." A tear slid down her cheek and she shook her head. "But now, now I…I…"

His heart tightened in his chest. "You what?"

Confusion filled her eyes. "I don't know. I don't know what I'm supposed to do. What I should do or how to do it. I-I don't even know who I am. I'm different when I'm here."

He reached for her hand, but his went through hers as easily as it did thin air. He balled his hand into a fist before trying again, but it was to no avail. It made no sense, how one minute he could feel her and the next he couldn't. It was almost as if she was floating in and out of his world. Of his time.

Like a beacon of light on a dark night, Hiah's voice came to him. *"She must find her spirit home."*

She frowned. "What?"

He hadn't meant to say Hiah's words aloud and shook his head. "I know it's hard to grasp, even for me, but, Hiah, a Shoshone Medicine Man," he added assuming she didn't remember, "says you've been reborn, but that your spirit needs to find its spirit home."

She'd taken a step back. "Reborn?"

The fear in her eyes told him to use caution. "Yes. The Shoshone believe we have many lives, and—"

"I'm not Shoshone," she interrupted. "And Hiah isn't a real medicine man. He portrays one in Buffalo Bill's Wild West Shows. I've seen posters of the show with him in them."

"Yes, he is in Buffalo Bill's shows, and he's a medicine man. He's also my great-uncle."

"But this isn't about me." It's about him. And saving his ranch. And… She attempted to take a deep breath to calm her bouncing nerves. It was like she was a kernel of corn in a popcorn popper, being shot from one extreme to the other. She could feel his touch, then she couldn't. She knew things, and then didn't. And she wanted things, impossible things that made no sense what so ever. But reborn…

Her head started to swirl and her chest clench. Dread bubbled in her stomach, and her skin turned cold and clammy. "No," she muttered. "Not again."

Knowing what would come next, she let go of the mirror and ran for the kitchen. "This is too much. It's just too much. I can't do it. Don't need to do it." Grabbing her bag off the chair, her purse and cell phone off the table, she spun for the door.

The mirror floated before her. "I'm not Beth," she said overly loud. "I haven't been reborn. She hasn't been reborn."

A hum filled the room and the mirror shook. She refused to touch it even though it made her heart ache.

"I'm sorry, but I can't be her," she said, hurrying to the door. "I've never cared about anyone, about anything. And she did." Her breastbone stung from how hard her heart pounded. She shoved open the door. "I'm sorry, Rance. I'm truly sorry."

She ran to her car, climbed in, hit the ignition, and stomped on the gas pedal. She had to get away. Couldn't have another panic attack. Wouldn't have another panic attack.

If she didn't hurry, she'd change her mind. The hum still echoed in her ears, and she could imagine Rance yelling at her from the yard, chasing her car.

She bounced about as the car sped over the ruts in the road but didn't slow until she was through the gate. The idea of not stopping crossed her mind, but her better judgment, if she had any left, forced her to hit the brake pedal.

Hurrying, as if the devil was chasing her, she jumped out and ran back to the gate. It was heavy and awkward, but she swung it closed, threaded the attached chain around the pole, and latched the paddle lock. The thud of hooves had her glancing up. It wasn't the little mustang she'd seen earlier. This horse was big, and as gray as storm clouds, and racing toward her.

She ran back to her car and stomped on the gas as the door slammed shut. The car shot onto the pavement so fast her tires squealed. Her heart was racing just as fast, and she drew in several breaths, trying to slow it down.

Gradually, everything slowed. Her heart. Her breathing. She eased her foot of the gas, letting the car slow to a safer speed. Glancing in the review mirror, at the empty road behind her, she sighed. These panic attacks were getting out of hand. She'd never had two in one day.

By the time she arrived in town, she was more in control. More reasonable. Her phone dinged several times, signaling both text messages and voice mails awaited her attention now that she had coverage.

Needing some time to gather her thoughts and nerves, she pulled into a café parking lot. She hadn't eaten all day, and it was after six. No wonder her head hurt. Her stomach hurt. Her heart hurt.

Eating may not have anything to do with her heart, but she was probably dehydrated and that would. Wouldn't it?

Either way, she parked and climbed out of her car.

She sat in a booth of cracked red Naugahyde and placed an order with a young girl wearing shorts and cowboy boots. The décor was the usual for the area, western and rustic, and she wondered if the lack of other customers was a warning. After downing the glass of water the waitress had carried over, she headed for the powder room and splashed cold water on her face. Looking at her reflection as she finger-combed her hair, she wondered about heatstroke. That did odd things to a person. Maybe that's what was happening. It was hot outside and inside Rance's house. As if her image was a different person, a sneer formed, telling her she wasn't having a heatstroke.

"Fine," she whispered at the mirror. "Then I'm crazy. Flipping crazy. Happy now?"

She grabbed her purse off the counter and headed for the door while muttering, "So flipping crazy I'm talking to myself and expecting answers."

Back at her booth, she watched people filing in, families and couples, and by the time her burger and fries arrived, she figured she'd simply beat the rush—which was a very sane and rational thought. Reality. This was reality. She wasn't having a heatstroke and she wasn't crazy. She was just hungry.

A family sat at the table next to her booth. A young couple with a girl and boy. The boy was little more than a baby and kept twisting around in his tray-less high chair, pointing at her. The father kept trying to gain his attention, but the boy found her more interesting.

"Sorry," the father said. "He's hungry and loves French fries."

"Well, here, then." She pulled a napkin from the metal holder and used her knife to sweep a few fries onto the napkin. "I have far more than I can eat and don't mind sharing if you don't mind."

"That is so sweet of you," the mother said, reaching for the napkin. "And we're sorry to have interrupted your meal."

"Don't be sorry. I truly have more than I can eat." She'd eaten most of the burger that had been just shy of huge. "There's more if he wants them."

"These should tide him over," the mother said. "Thank you."

"Tell the nice lady thank you, Rance," the father said to the boy.

Her ears were ringing, but she waited as the child, sucking on a French fry, chatted something that resembled thank you before she asked, "What's his name?"

"Rance," the mother answered.

Her stomach somersaulted and she had to swallow to keep the hamburger where it belonged. "That's unusual, isn't it?" She wasn't sure if that was an appropriate way to fish for more information, but truly didn't care.

"Yes, but it's well known around here," the mother

answered, smiling at her husband.

"Oh? Why's that?" Calm and in-control—somewhat, she pushed her plate toward the edge of her table in case the child needed more fries, hoping to entice more answers.

"Rance Livingston was horse breeder in this area during the early nineteen hundreds," the father answered.

Nodding toward her husband, the wife continued, "Dale's family's cattle ranch butts up against the Livingston property. Since the first time I heard the name Rance, I've loved it."

"It's a nice name." The once tasty burger swelled to three times its quarter-pound weight inside her stomach.

"My great-grandfather knew Rance and bought several hundred acres from him before he died. Clair and I have tried to buy more, Rance's home place, but the people who own it now are asking too much for it."

"There's an old house and other buildings on the property that the fire department is going to burn down this weekend," the wife, obviously named Clair, said. "It's sad, but I guess they've had someone out there inventorying the antiques so hopefully a few things will be salvaged."

"Are you new to the area?" the husband, Dale, asked.

She shook her head. "Just passing through." Although little Rance had been sucking on French fries the entire time, he'd never taken his eyes off her. They were as big and brown as his namesake's and as memorizing.

"The blue Mustang from Montana?" Dale asked.

"We parked next to you," Clair explained a moment later.

"Yes," she answered before flipping the conversation back to Rance's property. "Why are they burning the buildings?"

Dale shrugged while Clair said, "There are plenty of rumors circulating."

She wanted to ask what those rumors were, but the waitress appeared at their table. As soon as plates were set before the children, both parents had their hands full. In spite of wanting to know more, interrupting their meal would be too rude. She gathered her purse and stood. "Thank you for the visit." Unable not to, she ruffled the boy's dark hair. He was still looking at her even while his mother tried to make him turn around. "Bye, Rance."

The boy waved while the parents thanked her for the fries and wished her safe travels. At the counter, she paid for her meal. The same waitress who'd waited on her took her money, and she noticed the girl's T-shirt said, *Save a horse, ride a cowboy*. She added a couple dollars to her tip, for the girl to buy a new shirt, but as the waitress dropped the tip into a jar full of money, Liz figured maybe the girl didn't need a new shirt. That one seemed to be serving her well.

She climbed in her car and took note of the pickup truck parked next to her. *Rolling Hills Cattle Company* was painted on the door. She couldn't help but think of little Rance, and how living next door to a nuclear dump site might affect him. His family. The community as a whole.

Those thoughts lingered as she drove to her hotel and continued after she entered her room. She considered calling Vivi Anne, but her mind was in too much turmoil for that. Thoughts of Rance, and what he'd eaten for supper, if he had, and if he was still mad at her, mingled amongst all the others.

Flopping onto the bed, she stared at the ceiling. She wasn't cut out to save the world. To save anything. She couldn't even save herself.

****

"What the hell am I doing?" Rance asked himself as he brought the big gray horse to a stop where his driveway met the road that led into Cody. He could ride all the way to town, search every street, but he'd never find her. Beth had disappeared as soon as she'd walked out the kitchen door. He shouldn't have mentioned Hiah, of being reborn, but Beth had understood and accepted such things, even encouraged him to explore his heritage more.

The Beth he'd known and married had.

Maybe this one was right. She's not Beth.

He turned the horse and started back up the driveway, but midway, angled their route across the pasture. It was a fair distance, but he needed more than the vague answers his great uncle had provided last night. There had to be a way for him to convince Beth she'd been reborn.

His thoughts took a tumble. Even if that happened, if she believed, she'd still be in her century, and he'd be in his. What good would that do either of them?

Despite all his doubts, all the ifs and buts, he still needed more answers, and continued forward.

The sun had long ago set, leaving the moon to guide his way the last few miles. In that golden glow, as his uncle's squat cabin came into sight, Hiah could be seen standing in front of the cabin, waiting for him.

Rance rode into the yard and dismounted. "You knew I'd come."

"You have many questions."

"Yes, I do."

"I cannot answer them," Hiah said.

He pulled the bridle off his horse before moving to relieve the horse of his saddle. "But you can help me understand them."

"Only you can help you understand them," Hiah said.

That was not what he wanted to hear. "I don't know how." The frustration inside him was so strong it angered him and broke loose the pain beneath it all. "I can't live the rest of my life without her." His throat burned. "Don't want to live the rest of my life without her."

"Come." Hiah waved an arm. "We sit."

He piled his riding gear on the ground and let the horse roam where it may. His uncle didn't lead him into the cabin. They walked around it, to the back side where a small fire glowed in the darkness. The ground around it was worn smooth and hard. Hiah collected a few small logs from a pile nearby and tossed them into the smoldering coals before gesturing to sit.

Hiah sat across the fire, with his legs folded, his hands resting on his knees, and his chin forward. "You loved your woman very much."

"Yes, you know that."

"You must be thankful. Not many know this kind of love."

He shook his head. "How can I be thankful when she was taken from me?"

"She has come back to you."

Holding back the anger, the pain, pushing inside him, Rance shook his head again. "No, she hasn't. She's a ghost. She lives in a different time. I can't hold her. Can't love her."

"You do not love her?"

"Yes, I still love her." Frustration bawled his hands into fists. "What good is that when I can't touch her?"

"Do you not love the sun? The light it gives you. The warmth and nourishment it gives the earth."

"I appreciate the sun," Rance answered, instead of pointing out the glow in Beth's eyes had filled him with more light and warmth than sunlight ever had. "The earth couldn't survive without it."

Hiah nodded.

Rance waited for his uncle to say more. After a weighted length of silence, he asked, "What does the sun have to do with Beth?"

"You cannot touch the sun."

He ran both hands through his hair and squeezed at his temples. This was doing him less good than searching through Cody would have. "I know I can't touch the sun. I don't want to touch the sun. I want to touch Beth. Love her like a man loves a woman again." He slapped both knees. "Can you tell me how I can do that?"

"No, I cannot."

He withheld the desire to jump to his feet. "What can you tell me?"

Silence once again weighted each minute that ticked by. He wanted to leave but had nowhere to go, no one else to help him figure out what he needed to do. Accepting that, he bowed his head. "Is there anything I can do? Is there anything you can tell me?"

"I can tell you your woman has found her spirit home. It is you. You must welcome her home."

"I did welcome her home." He shook his head. "But I want more than her spirit."

"Why?"

"Because I love her."

Hiah took a deep breath before saying, "A love so great it lasts many generations is a gift many never receive. You do not know of this because you do not think Shoshone."

"Then tell me how to think Shoshone," he pleaded. "Tell me how to understand this great love."

"I cannot tell you how to think Shoshone." Hiah stood. "Come, I have prepared a place for you."

Confused, he asked, "Prepared a place? For what? Where?"

His uncle did not answer but led him a distance away from the cabin to a dome-shaped hut. There Hiah removed his clothing and instructed Rance to do the same before entering. Willing to try whatever he could to understand more, he obeyed. The heat of the interior of the hut was intense, and beads of sweat popped out of his skin before he sat down.

"We will call to the four winds, the earth, and the sky," Hiah said.

Rance didn't know how to call to anyone. His grandparents had forbidden him to embrace any of the Shoshone ways. Hiah knew that and had never suggested otherwise. Even after moving away from his grandparents, when Rance had a choice to explore his heritage, he'd chosen not to. His father had been half Shoshone, he was only a fourth, and considering the way people looked down upon anyone with Indian blood, he'd shied away from acknowledging any flowed through his veins.

Instead, he'd focused on his horses, until he'd found Beth. Besides Hiah, and possibly Buffalo Bill, who never commented on it either way, she was the only one who knew Hiah was his great uncle.

"Do not think, nephew," Hiah said. "Do not question. Close your eyes and repeat after me."

He copied the chanting noises Hiah made. He felt unconscious humming sounds that meant nothing but continued. He tried in earnest to follow each direction Hiah gave him, even while doubting any of this would help him. Help Beth.

Chapter Fourteen

Liz awoke with a start and glanced around to see why. Other than a thin strip of light above the curtain, the room was dark, and quiet. Her heart was pounding, but not overly hard, and she closed her eyes. Knowing she'd been dreaming, she tried to focus on what the dream had been about.

A knock on the door had her opening her eyes again. She glanced at the clock beside the bed. Twelve-thirty. The knock sounded again, and she flipped her legs off the edge of the bed. She was still completely dressed. Including her sandals. The very ones she'd cursed while scaling the gate this morning. Or yesterday morning.

She was running her hands through her hair when the voice that said her name on the other side of the door had her jumping to her feet.

"Vivi Anne?" Sure enough, the gray-haired woman, dressed as colorfully as ever, was on the other side of the door. "What are you doing here?"

"I've been calling you all day, finally just had to drive down here to make sure you were still among us," Vivi Anne answered, walking into the room.

The overhead light came on and over a hundred watts temporarily blinded her. Liz rubbed her eyes, and then while closing the door, noted the porch light wasn't on. Vivi Anne's truck was parked beside her car, and although they were off now, it had to have been the headlights of the truck shining above the curtain a minute ago. "How long have you been here?"

"Just pulled in. Knocked twice before saying your name. I didn't want to wake anyone else."

Figuring it had been the dream that had awakened her, Liz closed her eyes again. Something about that dream still lingered, just below the surface where her mind couldn't reach. It was no use. She couldn't remember anything. "Why are you here?"

"I just told you." Vivi Anne patted the bed. "Sit down. I must have awakened you out of deep sleep."

Liz sat on the bed. "I fell asleep after I ate. I must have been really tired because that was five hours ago."

"Why didn't you answer your phone?"

"I didn't hear it."

"All day?"

She shrugged. "I don't have service out at Rance's place."

"How are things coming along there?"

The dream tried to come forward again, but it was still too faint. "Fine, I guess."

"You guess?"

She reached for the bag she'd dropped on the bed earlier and then remembered her notebook was still in Rance's front room. Her hands started to tremble, and she released the bag. "I don't think I can go back out there."

"Why?"

"It's so complicated I don't even know where to start." She stood and paced the small area between the foot of the bed and the dresser holding the dark-ages television set. "Rance doesn't care about any of the things in the future. He loves his wife too much to care about what happens to his property decades after he dies."

"But you do."

"No. Yes." She growled at her own confusion. "I don't want little Rance to grow up next to a nuclear—"

"Little Rance?"

She shook her head. "A family I met at the café. But who am I to stop it? How do we even know that's true? Neither Lou or Nate have mentioned it."

"Have you asked either of them?"

"No, it didn't come up in conversation. They both have enough of their own issues. One's sleeping with the other one's wife, and—"

"You know who they are sleeping with?"

She let out a gust of air. "Yes. They told me. This entire thing is a convoluted cluster—"

"Mess."

That wasn't the word she'd been about to use, but the f-enhimer wasn't in Vivi Anne's vocabulary. "Yes. A mess." And I'm to the point I don't care what Lou and Nate want to do with the property." Meeting Vivi Anne's gaze, she asked, "How'd you learn about the dump site?"

"Certain board meeting minutes have to be made public, you just have to know where to find them." Vivi Anne had already kicked off her flip flops, and lifted her feet onto the bed, tucking them beneath her purple skirt. "If you don't care about that, what do you care about?"

She had to pinch her lips together in order to fight the burning at the back of her eyes. Nothing, she wanted to say, but that wasn't true. Might never have been true. She'd wanted to believe she didn't care about others because of this very reason. It hurts. Hurts like hell.

"Rance. I don't want him to live the rest of his life in that little cabin. Sad and lonely." She swallowed a sob. "But he loves Beth so much, he refuses to do anything about it." Sniffling, she pressed a finger to the corner of her eye. "He won't even talk about anything else, and because-because I look like her, he thinks I am her."

The tears forcing their way out stuffed-up her nose. She took the Kleenex Vivi Anne handed her.

"It's heart breaking," she said. "Literally heartbreaking."

"For who? You or Rance?"

"Rance." She'd spoken without thought and had to retract it. "Me, maybe. I don't know. I've never given a shit about anyone, anything; yet, my heart is breaking for this man. I find myself wishing I was his wife. That somehow, someway, I'm here because of him. That he's my…" She didn't know how to explain it, and the tears gushed out again. "I think I've fallen in love with him, Vivi Anne. How flipping crazy is that? I don't even believe in love. Don't even know what it is."

"It's not crazy at all." Vivi Anne held up a hand for her to stop pacing. "None of us know what love is until we find it. Rance could be your soul mate. That's what you were going to call him."

She had been about to call him that. "That's impossible. We don't even live in the same century."

"Stranger things have happened," Vivi Anne said.

"Tell me one."

Vivi Anne shook her head but then patted the bed.

"Sit down."

She kicked off her sandals before climbing on the bed to sit cross-legged, ready to listen. She needed answers of some kind and believed Vivi Anne was the only one to give them.

"What I told you about Otto's accident is true. I saw it before it happened," Vivi Anne said.

Liz nodded but held her silence, waiting to learn more about Vivi Anne's husband and her powers.

"But the part I left out is that things like that had been happening to me for years, and it sucked. I'd walk into a room, and my head wanted to explode. I'd know what people were thinking. I couldn't look them in the eye because I'd instantly see things about them. That their spouse was cheating on them, or their credit cards were maxed. I'd see flashes of their pasts, of their futures. Worse than that, I'd see people. Dead people. Like that kid in that movie years ago. Old spirits, new spirits, happy spirits, grumpy spirits. It was constant. There was no switch I could turn on or off. No way to stop those spirit cocktail parties from appearing." She let out along breath. "Until Otto's accident."

"What happened?" Liz asked, truly concerned.

"I told myself I had enough, and I called a psychic."

"*You* called a psychic?"

"Yes. I didn't know what else to do, but I was never, ever going to have what happened with Otto happen again. That was before cell phones, and I had no way to call him, to warn him. I just sat there, waiting for the deputy to show up at my door. I knew one would. I'd seen it."

"Oh, Vivi Anne, I'm so sorry. I can only imagine

how terrible that must have been."

"It was hell. Living hell. After Otto's accident, I couldn't take any more and called a friend I'd met through my *psychic community*, one who was very comfortable with her abilities, and she walked me through learning how not to see dead people, and not hear people's thoughts, and not see futures. It wasn't easy, but slowly, it worked. I made a conscious promise, gave myself permission to believe that it would work, and it did."

"What worked?"

"Belief in myself."

"But…" Liz wasn't sure how to say it other than, "You still have psychic abilities."

"Yes, I do, but so do you and everyone else on this earth."

Liz shook her head. "Not like you do. I Googled you. There are people on line who insist you helped them find their soul mate, brought them together after years of being apart."

"I know, and I let them use my name because it is what they believe. What they need to believe, but in truth, they were just people I crossed paths with, or encountered for different reasons. All I did was help them lift the weight holding them down. People know what's holding them back from going after what they want; they just need to recognize it. Then they usually need validation to lift it, to exhume guilt or excavate themselves out of sorrow, or whatever it is keeping them from getting what they truly want."

To say Liz was disappointed put it mildly. She wanted some sort of distinct validation on what was happening to her, why she was here in Cody falling in

Lauri Robinson

love with a ghost—if she truly was falling in love with a ghost. What Vivi Anne was saying reminded her of all the time she'd spent trying to find out information about her past, her family. There had been nothing but dead-ends. No answers. No long-lost family connections. Nothing, which had left her as empty and dissatisfied as she was right now.

She sighed. "So you're not a psychic, you're a life coach."

Vivi Anne's smile was empathetic. "I'm me. That's what I am. Who I am. Right now, that means I'm an antiques dealer and will be until I'm ready to try something else. I've also been a bartender, a belly dancer, a truck driver, a massage therapist, a journalist, a travel agent, and several other things. I even taught third grade my first year out of college. Which meant after being a student I was a teacher." With a shrug, she said, "People are what they believe they are, and society relates that to the job they have. The way they earn money. I've never earned money by helping people, so no, I'm not a psychic or a life coach."

Liz didn't want to sound selfish, but she was so flustered. "So you can't help me. Can't help me figure out what to do about Rance. You're only here to sell his antiques."

"That's the reason we are both here," Vivi Anne said. "But as your friend, which I am, I can tell you a bit about soul mates."

"Soul mates."

"Yes. That's what you were going to call Rance a few minutes ago, before we got off track."

"I don't want a ghost to be my soul mate." Although it did seem par for her life.

"Why not? Soul mates come in many forms. It isn't always the love of our lives. Otto was the love of my life, but he wasn't my soul mate." Vivi Anne smiled softly. "A soul mate is a member of our soul family. A group of souls who have a karmic relationship. Some aren't easy, but soul mate relationships always include important life lessons. A brother, sister, mother, father, any family member can be our soul mate. So can a best friend. Someone you instantly connect with, have recognition, a bond that is deep and solid. One that never goes away. You can sense your soul mate even when separated by space or time. Take that man I met from Helena."

"The one you met about antiques?"

"It wasn't about antiques. He heard about me from someone, and he's looking for his son whose plane went down in Alaska last year. He swears his son is his soul mate and believes he didn't die in the accident."

Curious, Liz asked, "Did he?"

Vivi Anne shrugged. "I'm not a psychic. I don't find lost people. But this man believes his son isn't dead, and he's searching for someone to validate his belief."

"Can you?"

"No one can validate what another believes. Beliefs are internal. Two people can be presented with the same facts, one may believe them, another may dispute them, either way, the choice is theirs." Vivi Anne lifted a painted-on brow. "If you believe Rance is your soul mate, sincerely believe it, then he is."

Liz slapped her knees. "I don't want him to be my soul mate. Why would I want the love of my life to live in another century? That makes no sense."

"I already said, soul mates aren't always the love of our lives. That man from Helena, his son may be his soul mate, but not the love of his life."

Squeezing her temples, Liz let out a growl. "You are making my head hurt."

Vivi Anne laughed. "I don't mean to be, I'm just pointing out the facts."

"Fine," Liz said. "If Rance isn't the love of my life or my soul mate, then what is he? Why do I care so much about him? Why do I care what happens to his property? It doesn't make sense. I feel like I'm going crazy."

"If you believe you are going crazy, then you are. Just like if you believe you don't care about others, then you don't, despite your actions."

Liz jumped off the bed. "Stop. Just stop."

"I'm only saying that whatever you believe, that is what you'll manifest."

After pacing the small space at the foot of the bed several times, Liz stopped. "So, if I stop believing that I'm seeing Rance, I will no longer see him?"

Vivi Anne shrugged.

Liz's stomach tightened as a deep and very real fear settled there. "I don't want to stop seeing him. I-I don't know. Maybe I do love him. I know that sounds crazy, even to me, but it's the only way I can explain how I feel about him. I've never felt this way about someone before. I've never cared this much about someone."

"Then don't stop." Vivi Anne stood. "Just know, that once you believe, truly believe, you have to be prepared, and you have to be careful. If you decide Rance is your soul mate or the love of your life, are you willing to give up the possibility of ever finding a man who loves you with all his heart in this century?"

Liz wasn't overly affected by that idea. "Maybe that person, that man, doesn't exist."

Vivi Anne shrugged. "Maybe he does."

Frustration boiled inside her. "So you're saying that Rance isn't—

"I'm not saying anything," Vivi Anne said. "He very well could be your soul mate. Soul mates are forever. We are reunited with them no matter how many times we are reborn."

A shiver rippled Liz's spine. "Why did you say that?"

"Because it's true. Loves of our lives are only for our lifetime, soul mates are forever."

Shivers raced up and down her arms. "Rance claims I'm Beth reborn."

Even her painted-on eyebrows seemed to smile as Vivi Anne drew in a deep breath.

"I'm not," Liz argued. "It's not possible. I can't believe that."

"Yet, you can believe I'm a psychic, and I saw Otto's car accident hours before it happened?"

Chapter Fifteen

Rance had tried blocking the woman's path, had shouted and jumped up and down, and done anything he could think of to get her attention, but she ignored him.

Yes, ignored him.

She knew he was there. Every once in awhile, she grinned and shook her head. Especially when he'd shaken the mirror before her face.

Dressed in a tent-like outfit that was as colorful as a gypsy's, she'd entered the house earlier today and roamed through every room, checked every closet, cupboard, and drawer. Afterward, she'd walked outside, and then re-entered.

"That's my wife's trunk," he shouted, once again trying to block her path.

"I know."

He stumbled backward. "I knew you could see me. Where did you get it? The trunk, where did you get it?"

"I can't see you," she said, "because I don't want to. Therefore, I won't."

"What the hell does that mean?" Not really caring, he asked, "Where did you get that trunk?"

"Billings, Montana. I'm putting it back where it belongs."

He followed her up the stairs. "Where's Beth? Have you seen her? What century do you live in?"

"Are you always this friendly to intruders?" she asked before heading down the hallway.

He paused to scratch his tingling scalp. Suddenly, he knew who this person was. The friend Beth had told him about. She was exactly as Beth had described. He ran down the hall and right through the woman, which caused his insides to jolt and quiver momentarily. Stopping in the doorway to the bedroom, he braced both hands against the door jams to block her path. "Where is she? Where's Beth? I know you know her."

Smiling, the woman walked right through him.

The force that caused, though it wasn't painful, made him buckle over for a moment. Cursing, he had to wait for his insides to collect themselves before he stood straight again and then spun around.

"Beth, as you know her," the woman said, "Liz as I know her in the twenty-first century, is at the motel in Cody, sleeping after a night of trying to figure out what she believes and doesn't believe." She set the trunk on the floor near the foot of the bed. Where it had always sat. "I'm hoping this trunk being here will help her. Lord knows I didn't want her to see it in the back of my truck."

"Is she coming back?" Excitement raced through him. "I have to know, is she coming back?" He reached down to open the lid on the trunk. "I can help her believe. I know how."

The woman sat down on the trunk. "Don't open it. Let her."

That hadn't been necessary. His hand couldn't grasp the lid. It went right through the wood, as if it wasn't there anymore than this woman. Confused, he tried again. Nope. It wasn't there in his time, much like the items Beth had brought with her. Her bags and such. "When is Beth coming?"

"Soon," the woman said. "I have to leave now. Get back to the motel before Liz, Beth, wakes up."

She'd stood and walked toward the door. Her gray hair was piled on top of her head by a big, odd looking hair clip, and her shirt held more colors than a rainbow. It reached almost to her knees, over the top of the skirt that swished around her feet. Exactly as Beth had described. Why could he see her, when he hadn't been able to see Nate or Lou?

"Who are you?" he asked.

"Vivi Anne, Beth's friend from the future."

"I know that. She told me about you. But who are you? Why can I see you?"

She made no comment, which had his blood boiling. He followed her down the hall and the stair steps. "She's mine. No matter what century you know her in, she's my Beth. Mine."

The woman turned around and smiled. "I'm not the one you need to convince of that, Rance. She is."

He didn't follow her out the door. There was no need. She was right. Beth is who he needed to convince. The one who needed to believe in him, in their love, and in herself. That was going to be the hardest part. The Beth he'd married had believed in herself, had the confidence of an acorn dropped onto the ground by the wind. She'd known she could grow into an oak tree and had. This Beth of the future didn't hold that belief, and he didn't know how to give it to her.

He did know it was possible though. If it was possible for Hiah to guide him in order to look inside himself, to see with his heart rather than his eyes, it was possible for Beth to do the same. To regain her confidence. To believe in herself again. To believe in love.

The sweat lodge he'd entered last night had been foreign to him, and he'd been skeptical. Although he couldn't completely explain what had happened, how it had happened, Hiah had guided him on a rite of passage that left him with a deep and significant insight. When he'd left the lodge early this morning, he was not only wide awake, he was filled with understanding.

For some things.

Others were still unclear.

Like when Beth might appear.

Therefore, he didn't want to leave the house. Couldn't take the chance of not being right here when she arrived. The horses would be fine, they had access to water and feed. The chickens would have to find themselves some bugs today.

He made himself some coffee, and fried a couple of eggs later on, when his stomach growled, and then another pot of coffee.

In the midst of wondering if he'd wear out the floor boards, he practically tripped over his feet when Beth appeared just inside the door.

Catching his footing, he rushed to the table and grabbed the mirror. The sight of her filled him, and though he'd always felt that sensation, the love she'd planted inside him and nurtured its growth, this time it was stronger, more valid.

Because he believed.

A wave of sadness washed over the shine inside him. Her eyes were puffy, as if she'd spent hours crying.

As soon as she touched the mirror, he said, "I missed you." He knew what he had to do, and swallowed an ounce of pride. "Liz."

Her eyes widened. "What did you call me?"

"Liz. That's your name, isn't it?"

"Yes, but—"

"It's a nice name." Grinning, he said, "And is easy to rhyme."

"What?" She frowned while shaking her head. "Rhyme?"

He was tripping over his own tongue, mainly because he was trying to make her smile. Grabbing words out of nowhere, he said, "Yes, like Liz is his, or when you get yourself all flustered, I can say, oh, oh, Liz is having a tiz."

Her expression, a mixture of a scowl and a frown made him shrug at his behavior.

"Have you been drinking?"

"No, but I probably should have been," he answered honestly. He'd had so much coffee, his piss was probably brown. He hadn't noticed if it was or not when he'd relieved himself off the front porch a short time ago. He'll go to his grave with that bit of information. Beth would be in a tizzy if she ever learned about it, but he hadn't wanted to leave the house. This wasn't about him, it was about her. All about her.

She had to believe that. Had to focus on herself, so he changed the subject and tried to sound as if he still had a bit of sanity. "Tell me about yourself. When you aren't cataloguing antiques in haunted houses, what do you do? Where do you live?"

Eyeing him closely, she asked, "You sure you haven't been drinking? How about smoking? Have you been to Colorado lately?"

"Haven't been to Colorado in years," he answered. "Have you?"

"I've never been to Colorado. No reason to go there."

"Why did you want to know if I've been there?"

She grinned then and shook her head. "No reason. It was a bad joke."

"A joke on who?"

"Forget it," she said. "No, I've never been to Colorado for any reason."

"Good to know." Every little bit of information was good to know, and he needed a lot more. "Where do you live?"

She frowned, and looked him up and down, until eventually answering, "Billings, Montana. I've told you that."

"Yes, yes, you have." He drew a deep breath to collect his thoughts, which were a jumbled mess. "You live with your folks, then?"

"No, my parents died when I was a small child. I've told you all this already."

She had, but he hadn't been listening. Not really. Not like he should have been. Not like he would now. "I know. I just want to hear it again."

"Why?"

"I just do." Yesterday, it would have been hard for him not to tell her that Conrad and Millie, her parents, were alive and well, and missed her almost as much as he did. Today, he could accept she didn't know that. Didn't remember that. "How did they die? Your parents, how did they die?"

"A car accident," she said. "It was, storming. My father must not have seen the train coming. It hit our car and killed my parents."

"But not you?"

"No. Not me."

Her lack of emotion was unlike her. No, it was unlike the Beth he knew. Choosing not to contemplate that, he asked, "Who raised you? Who did you live with then?"

"A foster family. Gladys and Norman Walker. They took in dozens of foster children over the years. Some only stayed a few days, others like me, lived with them for years."

"Do you still live with them?"

She shook her head. "They both passed away earlier this year, but I moved into my own apartment years ago, right after high school. That's where I still live. It's small. Not much bigger than your little cabin out back, but its home."

"Is it?" He wanted to bite the end of his tongue, and quickly added, "In Billings?" He wanted his house, their house, to her home, but she had to want that.

"Yes."

Searching for another question, he shifted his feet. "Do you have any sisters? Brothers?"

"No." She frowned and glanced from him to the mirror and back again. "Why are you asking me all this?"

The truth was the best answer he could think of. "I want to know all about you." The century she lived in made no difference. Neither did the name she called herself. This was the woman he loved. Would always love. Her spirit was the same. The very essence that made her remarkable, unforgettable, loveable, was connected to his with a bond stronger than time and too powerful to be broken by even death. He'd known that before, but this morning, he believed it profoundly.

"Like Beth did you when you first met," she said. "She almost wore out your brain with questions about you and your family."

That's what he'd told Beth shortly after they met— that she was wearing out his brain. "Yes."

He reached for her as she let go of the mirror. His hand encountered nothing, but relief washed away his concern as she sat down in one of the chairs. Her face was full of sorrow, and he knelt beside her, placing the mirror on the table within her reach.

It was a moment before she touched the mirror and turned to meet his gaze. "It doesn't matter, Rance. Whether I believe in reincarnation or not. Whether somehow, someway, Beth and I share the same soul doesn't matter. You are still in the twentieth century, and I'm in the twenty-first."

That was a dilemma. One he didn't know how to solve. Yet, didn't doubt there had to be a way. Grasping the notion the woman from this morning had delivered the trunk for a reason, he said, "Come upstairs with me."

"Why?"

"There's something I want to show you."

"I've seen everything upstairs. I know where everything belongs. I even know where things came from originally." Frowning slightly as she glanced around the room. "Other than that stove."

He grinned. Beth had never seen the stove. "Come.

Please."

She sighed, and shook her head, but the smidgen of a grin on her lips kicked his heart beat into a faster pace. Beth never could hold back when someone said please. Especially him.

"All right," she said. "But it's not going to matter. Whatever it is."

That was Beth, too. She'd argue her point until the last dog was hung when it was something she truly believed.

He shifted his hand on the mirror, placing it over the top of hers holding the handle, and the warmth that filled his palm gave him more hope. The sensation wasn't as strong as it had been yesterday, but in his heart, he was touching her. Holding her hand.

Her gaze met his as she stood, and then glanced down to the mirror. "I can feel that," she whispered. "Your hand. I can feel it."

"Once you touch someone's heart, it's easy to touch their hand," he whispered.

She closed her eyes for a moment. Her breath came out shaking, as was her voice. "Yes, it is."

He was getting close, or rather, she was. He could feel it, and that filled him with urgency. "What else do you feel?"

She licked her lips and closed her eyes. "I don't know. It's hard to explain."

"It's strange, isn't it," he said. "How you always thought you knew most everything there was to know about something, and then, one day, everything changes and you realize you didn't know everything, in fact, you didn't know much at all."

Her frown was back. "What are you talking

about?"

"Life. Before I met Beth, I thought I knew things. What I wanted. Within hours, things changed, and then, when that train accident happened, things changed again. And then you appeared, and things changed again, and they have every day since." His blubbering was confusing her, and him. "I know you aren't in my century, but at times I feel as if you are. I can almost believe you are as flesh and blood as me. Not with my hands, but inside, with my heart." He searched her face, confirming his belief. "You feel that way at times, too, don't you?"

She nodded. "Yes, at times I do almost believe you are…" She shrugged. "Real."

"I am real. And so are you."

Silence surrounded them as they stood there, holding the mirror, yet looking at each other and feeling. He knew she was feeling him as deeply as he was feeling her, inside himself, inside his heart, where she'd lived before and would again. Completely. He believed that with all he had and would make her believe it too. When she blinked and offered a tiny grin, he whispered, "Come."

Liz's entire being shook. Not trembling with fear or pulsating with excitement. This was different. Almost as if she was on an uneven surface that was about to give way. She'd never been in an earthquake, but imagined this could be what it felt like, yet it wasn't the ground beneath her shaking. It was her. Inside her it was as if something was being separated, shaken apart. Not destructively, but gently, lovingly.

She'd spent the better part of the night contemplating souls, reincarnation, past lives. It was a concept she could grasp. Vivi Anne once pointed out over two-thirds of the population experienced déjà vu. That had been back at the antique store when she'd first seen the half-done saddle. The tooling, the initials, had looked familiar, and as she'd rubbed the leather, she commented it was as if she's seen it before. That's how she felt now. As if he had led her up these stairs many times before, and she'd been happy about that. Excited.

She'd experienced déjà vu many times the past few days, especially while seeing certain things in the house, but, this time it was different. Rather than just knowing where an item came from or experiencing a hint of familiarity, this time excitement danced deep in her belly. He had led Beth up these stairs many times. Every night they'd lived in this house, and once upstairs, once in their bedroom, he'd made love to her with deep and profound passion.

She swallowed and pressed a hand to her chest as her heart began to thud. Her body was remembering things, not just her mind. It was crazy. Mainly because she was seeing herself, not Beth. With Rance. Making love.

"Are you all right?" he asked as they paused at the top of the stairs.

She had to nod, whereas in truth, she was far from all right. She was a million miles away from sanity with her foot still on the gas pedal. Holding her breath in an attempt to quell the fiery desires of the pole dancer that had come to life inside her, she told herself it truly didn't make a difference what she saw in her mind, what she felt, she and Rance were centuries apart and always would be. Sex was as impossible as everything else.

As they walked down the hall, she once again told herself she hadn't been his wife in a past life. That was impossible. As impossible as flying monkeys and little green men. She'd contemplated all those things last night, as well as others. Believing Vivi Anne was a psychic and had foreseen her husband's death was easy. People all around the world believed in such things. There were TV shows dedicated to such beliefs and phenomena. Not that everything on TV was true. There were shows about past lives and time travel, too, but they were considered fiction. Imaginary tales some creative writer produced while deep in the throes of writing tales of what-ifs that are meant for nothing more than entertainment.

It was easy to see the difference. Or at least it had been last night while lying in the bed at the motel. While walking next to him, it wasn't easy. Nothing was easy. Other than believing he was as real as any other person walking this earth—even though he wasn't living in her century. Last night she'd concluded believing she'd never been his wife would be the easiest thing to believe and hoped that would make the erroneous pain of living without him not so overwhelming. Not so soul-crushing.

All the thoughts racing through her mind collided when she stepped into the bedroom. The simple wooden trunk with metal hinges and single latch sitting at the foot of the bed was as recognizable as her own hand, and seeing it made her heart tumble, yet, ironically, panic didn't well inside her. That was where the trunk belonged. Where it had always belonged. At the foot of the bed.

She'd been in the room numerous times over the

past few days, and the trunk had never been there. "How did this get here?"

He knelt beside her but she didn't wait for his response.

"Vivi Anne was here, wasn't she?" Liz asked. "This morning, while I was sleeping."

Knowing he wouldn't have been able to see her friend, she explained, "Vivi Anne is the friend that I told you about. The one who owns the antique store. The day before I came to Cody, the church that Norman and Gladys left their property to had called Vivi Anne about selling some antiques, this must have been part of that lot and she brought it down here. I wonder why she didn't mention it to me." The trunk didn't scare her, not like it always had in the past. It probably wasn't the *same* trunk, just similar. Although that would make sense, she knew it wasn't true. This was the same trunk she remembered.

Cautious, yet not able to restrain herself, she reached out a hand and touched the curved top. Fuzzy, a fleeting image of emptying the trunk flickered in the recesses of her mind, as did refilling it with material— clothes or blankets. The thoughts, or memories, were too far away, too obscure to grasp, but there was excitement, happiness behind filling that trunk. Therefore, those memories could not be hers.

She'd only ever seen the trunk twice, once in the attic and then when Norman had carried it downstairs. Both times had frightened her, and neither time had she put anything in it. As far as she knew, it had never been opened.

Looking up, she asked, "What's in it?"

"I don't know," he said. "I've carried it up and

down the stairs, in and out of the buggy, but never looked inside it."

The very center of her chest seemed to expand, to open a door that had long ago slammed shut. "Of course you didn't," she said, running a hand over the wood. He not only loved Beth with all his heart and soul, he respected her and trusted her. He would never have needed to look in her trunk because he would never have wondered what was in there. If he'd wanted to know, he'd have asked, and she'd have told him. He'd never asked, though, because in the scheme of things, during his life with Beth, they'd had far more important things to focus on. Their love. Their lives.

She swallowed at the lump forming in her throat. The apprehension in his eyes all but stole her breath, as did his silent communication. He still didn't need to know what was in the trunk, but he wanted her to know.

She didn't want to know. Never had wanted to see what was in that trunk. It was her Pandora's box. Had been from the moment the rescuers had found her floating atop it.

What was she thinking? A trunk from his century would never have lasted until hers. Not one that had been submersed in water. That's what had happened to Beth's. It had been on the train with her when the bridge collapsed almost a hundred years before the car accident that tossed her into the same water. A wooden trunk would have long ago rotted. Dissolved into nothing.

"Open it," he said quietly.

The trunk no longer filled her with panic, but that could change the moment she lifted the lid. "I don't want to."

"You need to. For both our sakes, you need to."

He would have to point that out. If it was just for her, she'd never lift the lid, but for his sake, if it would make a difference in his life, she'd crawl inside the damn thing. She clenched her teeth together to keep from growling at the frustration filling her. This caring about others, loving someone, sure had its consequences. No wonder she'd never wanted to do it before.

"Open it."

"I'm getting ready to," she snapped. "Don't rush me." Normally not so quick to temper, she flinched slightly.

His snort, the way he held in a laugh, struck her in an unusual way. He wasn't offended. There was a twinkle in his eyes.

She had to pinch her lips together to hold in a giggle. There was nothing funny about the situation, but the desire to laugh, along with a rare sense of happiness filled her so fast, so completely, she pressed a hand to her lips in order to contain a giggle.

He laughed, too, and as she watched that, him laughing, his eyes twinkling, his smile growing, she laughed harder. It was crazy, ridiculous, to be sitting on the floor laughing with a man who was over a hundred years older than her, but it was wonderful at the same time.

She'd fought this the entire way. The idea, the fact, that she'd somehow crossed a dimension, an unexplainable barrier that most people didn't even know existed. But what if she truly had? If that really was the case, and she was starting to fully believe it could be possible, she should be embracing it.

Shouldn't she? Experiencing it to the fullest. It had happened for a reason.

He was that reason. She had no doubt of that. He had loved Beth so fully, so completely.

Was that the reason she was here? To learn love did exist. Not in the casual, flippant way people of her time believed it to be, but in the purist way possible. Untainted love that lasts through the ages, beyond time and all the barriers people put in place.

Her mind stopped momentarily. Beth had loved him as strongly as he had loved her, and she hadn't been ready to leave him. Hadn't been willing to leave him. In fact, she'd gone beyond human capacity to not leave him. Her soul had anyway.

This wasn't all about him. It was just as much about Beth. And how hard, how long, her spirit had fought to be reunited with him.

The breath she took was once again shaky, uneven. She wasn't certain how she knew it, but the realization was as solid and real as everything she knew about herself. She'd been chosen, chosen by Beth to be the catalyst to reunite these two—if only for a moment. If only to say their final good-byes.

She had to close her eyes against the sensation of being pulled apart inside again. It was stronger than before. Almost painful. More so than even her panic attacks and that told her it was time to get this over with. Her hands were balled into fists, and it took conscious efforts to move them toward the trunk. It was just a trunk. An old trunk that couldn't hurt her. But it could help him. There had to be a message inside of it. Something Beth wanted him to know.

The quaking inside her eased as she opened her

hands, spread her fingers over the trunk lid. She drew in a deep breath, and then used a thumb to unclasp the hitch.

There was no creaking of hinges as she opened the lid, no spring-loaded Jack-in-the-box surprise leaping out to scare her. She let the air out of her lungs and reached down to push aside the sheet of old tissue paper to reveal a stack of neatly folded items. She picked a tiny garment off the top.

It was old, the silk and lace yellowed by age and deteriorating, but it was clearly a child's christening gown.

Her hands shook as she laid the gown down, and she held her breath, afraid to look at Rance. Her stomach clenched as an overwhelming sadness brought tears to her eyes. Beth had been pregnant when she'd died. This couldn't be Beth's final message to him. It just couldn't be. He'd suffered enough pain. He didn't need to know he'd lost his child along with his wife.

Did not need to know.

"What is it?" he asked. "What's in there?"

Her first instinct was to cover the gown with the paper again, but she couldn't. Just couldn't. She loved him too much.

She bit down on her trembling bottom lip and sucked in a deep breath before turning his way. Reaching for the mirror lying on the floor, her hand froze before it touched the handle.

The mirror was on the floor. He wasn't holding it. Neither was she. Yet, she could see him. He was a bit translucent, but she could see him. At this moment, she didn't know if that made things better or worse.

Chapter Sixteen

"Beth?"

He hadn't called her that since she'd entered the house, and the sound of his voice echoed inside her head. The fingers on one hand curled over the edge of the trunk as the air in her lungs turned fiery and her vision blurred.

The sensation of falling into a dark abyss over took her. It was suffocating, but unlike before, it was peaceful, serene. The further she fell, the more tranquil she became, as if on the edge of entering a deep, welcoming sleep.

On the verge of giving in completely, of letting the sleep overtake her, she was broadsided by a powerful force.

Panic hit her just as hard. Making her thrash. Her lungs burned as she was propelled upward so fast water rushed up her nose, stinging. She opened her mouth to scream, but it instantly filled with water, choking her.

Another unexplainable force overpowered her then. Stole all her abilities. It commanded her arms and legs to move, making her body swim through the water faster and faster. There was no fighting it. No denying it.

When her head broke through the surface, her lungs were scorched and couldn't hold the air she gasped before the waves pushed her head back under.

She wanted to give up, to float back into the darkness still clutching to unknown parts and dragging her back downward, but that obscure force inside her shoved her upward again. This time it was as if someone was holding her, dragging her upward, through the water with great urgency. When she broke through the water's surface this time, she was thrust into the air and hoisted over the top of something hard.

Air filled her lungs, causing her to cough and spit water, and to shiver.

She was cold, so cold, and tired. So tired.

Rance tried again and again, and again, but his hands went right through her, couldn't grasp onto anything. She'd collapsed on the floor in front of him. Worse than that, he feared she'd stopped breathing. The gasping had stopped. The thrashing of her arms and legs had stopped.

He tried again, but his hands only dragged across the floorboards, splinters catching beneath his fingernails. His heart pounded and his mind swirled. Frantic at how blue her parted lips had turned, and unable to do anything else, he leaned over her and blew into her mouth.

He blew and blew and blew.

The idea of losing her again enraged him. So furious, so raw, he pounded a fist on the floor. "No, damn it," he bellowed. "I won't let you take her from me again! I won't!"

He had no idea who he was shouting at, no idea who he challenged, but he'd win. This time he would win. This was his wife, and he'd fight hell and high water to save her. "She's mine! You can't have her."

Tears blurred his vision as he blew into her mouth

again. "You're my wife. My wife, and I won't lose you again," he said between breaths. "I don't give a damn if your name is Beth, or Liz, or Esmeralda, damn it. You're my wife, and I won't let you go. I won't."

Wanting her to hear him, he grabbed her shoulders and was instantly shocked when his hands folded around her flesh. He pulled her off the floor, onto his lap, and shook her, pounded on her back, and shook her again. "Come back to me, Beth. Come back to me."

The hint of a whimper made him freeze. Cautiously, for he very well could be imagining things, he carefully tilted her head upward, and then cried in earnest when her breath mingled with his.

After a moment of thankful bliss, of hugging her, he scrambled to his feet and carried her to the bed. Not wanting to let her go, to ever let her go, he crawled onto the mattress and laid his head on her chest, listening. The steady beat of her heart, the rise and fall of her chest elated him. After scooting her up until her head rested on a pillow, he laid on his side. Holding her face with both hands, he kissed her forehead, her eyebrows, the tip of her nose.

"Wake up, honey," he pleaded. "Please, please, wake up."

Her lips were no longer blue, and as he kissed them, he whispered again, "Please, Beth, wake up."

The fluttering of her eyelids sent his heart racing fast enough to make it explode. He barely had the wind to say, "Beth?"

Her eyes opened and closed as a smile spread across her face. "Hello, my love."

For the blink of an eye his heart stopped. Completely stopped. Her whisper had been faint, but he'd heard it. The exact same words she said to him almost every morning of their married life.

With a jolt that would have knocked him on his ass had he been standing, his heart started beating again, and he attacked her. Attacked his wife with an array of kisses she couldn't keep up with.

Almost.

Her lips were as crazy as his. She kissed every inch of his face, as he did hers, and when their lips finally collided, it was a homecoming like no other. Their mouths were open, their tongues curling and twisting around one another. He hadn't forgotten how wonderful she tasted, or her delicious nectar that made him want more and more.

He pulled her close, so the length of her body was flush against his. Her arms folded around him and she pressed her breasts firmly against his chest while gently rubbing his crotch with one knee.

She loved teasing and taunting him with her body. Loved working him into an aching responsiveness that could only be satisfied by one thing. He was no better, he loved fondling and caressing and kissing her until rousting desire overtook her so completely she'd beg him to take her.

From the first time they'd mated, on their wedding night, their unions had been as explosive as lightning.

Plunging his tongue deeper into the slick, sweet corners of her mouth, he kissed her until there was no air left his lungs. After drawing in a breath, he whispered, "Lord, I've missed you."

She smiled and cupped his cheek with one hand. "Missed me? I haven't left yet."

"No—" An eerie sensation had him glancing

around, noting the pale light of dawn filling the room, his heart started to pound. Her dress was draped over the back of the chair. That's what she always did when they got ready for bed. Took off her dress and draped it over that chair. It was blue with little pink flowers, and his favorite. He'd told her that while unbuttoning the row of buttons running down the front of it that day in the front room, when the flowers on the wall paper had come to life.

A wave filled with everything from relief to excitement washed over him. It hadn't happened. She hadn't gone to Billings, hadn't been in a train accident. It had all been a nightmare.

"Thank you!" he shouted to whoever, whatever, deserved his gratitude.

He rolled onto his back while tightening his arms to pull her on top of him, to kiss her, to love her fully, completely, all day long.

But at the very moment his lips should have found hers, her body should have rolled atop his, the room lit up as if a bolt of lightning had struck the floor, and he swore he heard Beth shout his name. Faint and faraway.

His arms became empty. No weight lay upon his chest. Nothing but air touched his lips.

He bolted upright, ready to shout, ready to curse, but he wasn't alone.

She laid there. Beside him. He could hear her gasping for air. Or was that him?

The rise and fall of her chest said she was breathing quietly, restfully. Her hands were on her stomach, and that's where his eyes stalled, staring at her hands, at her stomach. Her clothes. A pair of those odd short pants with the cuffs turned up at her ankles and a white shirt that didn't have sleeves.

That was impossible; yet, as he glanced toward the chair sitting beside the wall, the empty chair, he knew it wasn't impossible. That it was indeed true.

Depressed, disappointed, he dropped his head back onto the pillow and shifted his gaze to the ceiling. He'd felt her. He'd kissed her. It had been Beth. Completely Beth.

He let out a long exhale before taking a chance. Slowly, he reached over, and without looking, lowered his hand in the vicinity of where hers laid upon her stomach.

His palm met nothing but the quilt.

The air in his lungs caught and twisted as it made its way up his chest and out of his mouth. His desire, the blistering hunger inside him that only she installed or could satisfy was still there. Now it ate at his insides like a wolf devoured a carcass. There would be no release, no satisfaction. It was more than that. More than a need for release or satisfaction that was tearing him apart. It was the love. The amazing love they shared that he wanted back in his life.

"How did I get on the bed?"

Turning his attention away from the carnage happening inside him took considerable effort, but he found enough to say, "I carried you."

"You carried me?"

"Yes. For a short time, I could feel you. Touch you."

Silence bathed the room. He was grateful it gave his body time to collect itself, but also hated it because it gave him time to remember holding her, tasting her. For a moment, his life had been whole again.

"Beth saved my life."

He twisted enough to look at her.

She rolled onto her side and placed both hands beneath her cheek. "I don't know how it was possible, but Beth saved my life."

Whether she was wearing different clothes or not, nor his inability to hold her hadn't changed his love for her. He shifted onto his side to lie face to face. "Why do you say that?"

"Because she did. The accident I told you about, the one when my parents died. The train pushed our car into the river just south of Billings. I've never remembered anything about it. Never really remembered much about my life before living with Gladys and Norman, but…" She held her breath for a moment and when she released it, a little frustrated-type grunt came out. "I don't know how, but I saw it all, felt it all, when I opened the trunk."

He tried laying a hand on her side, just for reassurance, but his palm once again passed right through her image and landed on the quilt. "Saw what? Felt what?"

"The accident. Me. I was little. Barely five years old, and I felt myself falling to the bottom of the river. I wasn't frightened, or trying to swim, I was just sinking…" She shrugged one shoulder. "And falling asleep. I was tired. Exhausted. I must have given up and I was drowning. I guess. I-I don't what else to think."

"But you didn't drown?"

"No, before I sank all the way to the bottom, Beth caught me, or-or." Her eyes turned misty as she shook her head. "It's hard to explain."

"It's all right. I'm here. I'm listening."

She looked away and back again. "It was as if she entered me and forced me to swim to the top—which makes no sense because I never learned to swim. I still don't know how." She shook her head. "But I swam to the top and after I did, when the waves kept pushing me under, she pulled me through the water and up into the air again." She shivered slightly. "I hate water. Hate rivers."

"Rightfully so." He flinched at his own words. He wasn't trying to make light of her story but could understand someone who had almost drowned would never want to get back in the water.

"She, or we, swam until we found the trunk, and then she hoisted me over it. I was so tired, so cold, I wanted to go to sleep, but she wouldn't let me." Sliding her hands out from under her cheek, she held up the left one. "She put this ring in my hand, and told me not to let go of it. That I couldn't go to sleep because I might drop it, and that I couldn't drop it, because then it would be lost forever."

He held his hand before hers, palms facing each other. It was strange, because he couldn't feel her hand, but he could feel his ring touching hers. Her eyes said she felt it too, and they both saw how the sunlight shining through the window glistened against the gold.

"I told her I was tired and cold. She said she'd keep me warm, stay with me until someone came. Until someone found me."

"And she did."

She shrugged, and tears shimmered in her eyes. "Beth's soul, her spirit, must have been under the water for almost a century waiting to save someone. Waiting to give them the ring." She lowered her hand and pulled the ring off. "She must have wanted you to have it."

He shook his head. "She must have wanted *you* to have it."

"I was just a little girl, and—"

"I can't touch it," he pointed out. "I can't take it because I can't touch it."

She bit her bottom lip as she slid the ring back on her finger. "I forgot that part."

"I didn't," he said with a sigh. There had to be a way for him to touch her again. He hadn't imagined that. Hadn't imagined kisses her, and wouldn't give up until he could kiss and touch again. He hadn't imagined something else, either. This was and wasn't his Beth. She was just who she said she was. Liz Baxter from the future, while also being his Beth from the past. From his time. The two had become one in the river the night of her car accident. "What's in trunk? What made you remember all this?"

Her face scrunched as she squeezed her eyes tight. He couldn't read her thoughts but knew whatever they were; she didn't want to tell him.

"You can tell me," he coaxed. "There's no reason to be afraid. Even if I could touch you, I'd never hurt you."

"I know," she said sadly. "It's just that sometimes, words hurt the worst."

"Yes, they do. "But you can still tell me. I can handle it."

She licked her lips and drew a deep breath. "Beth—" She swallowed as if her throat burned. "The trunk is full of baby clothes. Beth was pregnant when she drowned."

She'd said it all in one breath, as if knowing she

275

wouldn't be able to tell him if she didn't hurry. Despite the pain of knowing their child had been taken along with Beth, he smiled. She was his Beth.

"I know."

"You do?"

The grimace on her face was nothing shy of adorable.

"Yes, I do." He cleared his throat, needing to push aside the handful of gravel that had settled there. "I knew Beth's body as well as my own. I loved it more than my own. Over the past few weeks, it had changed. Nothing had interrupted our nights together, and I'd guessed why."

"But you never told her."

He shook his head.

"Why?"

"Because she wanted to surprise me. That's why she wanted to go to Billings. I thought about telling her to just see the doctor in town, but knew she wanted her mother with her when the doctor examined her, so…" He shrugged. "She went to Billings."

"She didn't know you knew."

"No, I made sure she didn't. I didn't want to spoil her surprise."

"She was hoping for a boy, and to name him Rance."

He smiled. "How do you know that?"

"I know a lot of things." After a brief shake of her head, she added, "More than I should. I guess because we share the same soul. I have memories of you and her. Memories of her parents. Conrad and Millie. And her sister, Abigail."

His mind clutched onto one thing she'd said. "You

believe you share the same soul?"

"We must. How else would I know all this?"

Excitement gathered ground inside him. This was progress. "You believe you are Beth?"

She closed her eyes. "It doesn't matter what I believe." A tear slid out from beneath her lashes as she whispered, "It doesn't change anything."

"It might."

"No, it won't. No matter what I believe, the fire department is going to burn this house down tomorrow, and I'll never see you again."

He shot up and flipped his legs over the edge of the bed.

"Where are you going?"

Looking over his shoulder as he stood, he said, "To stop them."

"Rance—"

He spun around. "No one will take you away from me again."

She climbed off the bed. "It's not a matter of taking me away. We live in two different centuries."

His hands balled into fists at the need to take her shoulders, to make her understand just how deeply his love for her lives inside him. "I don't care if we live a thousand years apart, we belong together."

"But that's not possible."

"Like hell it's not." He'd felt it a moment ago. Felt her in his arms, tasted her lips, and he would do that again. Arguing wouldn't get them anywhere, so he walked toward the door. "Come on, I may need your help."

She followed. "I already tried helping, you wouldn't listen."

He continued into the hallway. "There is another way, one that doesn't include me marrying anyone else."

Liz grabbed the doorway to keep her balance. The idea of him marrying Cindy, or anyone else, had never pleased her. Now it tore at her heart as if someone had shoved it inside a paper shredder. Probably because her libido was still in drive. She'd awoken more hot and bothered than a pole dancer, or the person watching the pole dancer—whichever way that went. She'd never seen a pole dancer in person, but certainly had been thinking about their provocative moves lately, which was as out of character for her as everything else when it came to Rance.

Such as the sex high she'd just experienced. No, sex hadn't happened, but it had been about to. Somewhere in time, and the memories still dancing in her head said Rance was an exquisite lover. He and Beth had held nothing back when it came to the bedroom. That was part of what she meant when saying she knew more than she should. Parts of her where still overheated because she knew what it was like to make love with him, and that left her so hot and bothered, she might remain that way for the next twenty years.

Which was enough to tell her she couldn't live the rest of her life loving a ghost. One way or another, she'd need these cravings satisfied at some point. Sighing, she asked, "What other way?"

He was already on the other end of the hallway and spun around. With a grin that made her heart flipped, he held out a hand. "We have to figure that out together."

She took a step but stopped in order to press a hand to her temple, where a sharp pain briefly shot. It disappeared as quickly as it had formed, but her heart sank as she opened her eyes.

The hall was empty, but the familiar hum said it was only empty in her time.

Anger arose. This seeing him, then not seeing him could very well put her on the criminally insane list. If it kept up, she could go postal.

She grabbed the mirror that floated in the air. "How'd you know I couldn't see you?"

His grin was enough to make her toes curl. "You quit arguing with me."

"No, I haven't," she said, walking down the hall beside him. "The only way to make sure this house isn't burned down, is to make sure Lou and Nate don't inherit it, and the only way to make that happen, is to—"

"I'm not marrying Cindy," he interrupted.

"I don't want you to," she snapped.

The mirror became stationary, and that caused her to stop mid-step.

"Good. I'm glad we finally agree on that."

She shook her head. His eyes told her this was as frustrating for him as it was for her. "I never wanted you to marry her. I just thought that was the only way. If Robert isn't born, there—"

"Will be no Lou and Nate," he finished. "That's our ticket. We have to make sure Cindy doesn't get pregnant."

He was moving again, down the steps quickly and she had to hurry to keep up. "How are you going to do that?" she asked.

"I'll go to town and talk to Cliff. Tell him to keep an eye on her."

"I'm sure Cliff is already keeping an eye on her, she is his niece."

"Then I'll keep an eye on her."

The idea of completely eliminating Lou and Nate's existence seemed harsh, and wrong. So wrong. When they arrived in the kitchen, she said, "I don't think that's the answer."

"I don't either. But it's a start. We have to start somewhere."

They both stood near the table. Rooted together in this room, yet separated by years and years.

She searched for a way for thing to be different, for any possible solution, and knew he was too. "What if," she said aloud as an idea formed, "you discover who is, or was, Robert's real father? If he marries Cindy, then Cliff and Nan won't raise Robert, and Nate and Lou won't inherit this place."

He lifted a brow and gave her a rather saucy look. "You don't think it was me?"

Heat flushed her cheeks as her heart fluttered. "I never did."

"Good." His grin disappeared as he glanced around the room. "If Cliff and Nan don't raise Robert, who will inherit this place?"

Deflated of the ounce of excitement that had formed, she sighed. "I don't know." Another thought flashed. "What's in your will?"

He shrugged. "I don't have a will. I haven't written one yet."

"Maybe you need to put that your property can be sold."

"Then I won't be here when you arrive."

"You're right." She rubbed her forehead. Beth had

saved her from downing—that's what had happened, she'd seen it—for a reason. He already knew about the baby, so that wasn't it. "We need more time. That's what we need. Time to see what works and what doesn't."

He nodded. "Tomorrow's fast approaching."

"Then it's up to me," she said. "I have to find a way to stop the firetrucks tomorrow. Postpone them."

"How will you do that?"

"I don't know, but Vivi Anne will help me. We'll figure out a way."

He waved toward her bag still sitting on the chair. "You still have some of that water in a bottle you like?"

"Yes, why?"

"We could sit down, have a cup of coffee and a bottle of water and try to come up with something."

Urgency said she had to leave, but she didn't want to go. Didn't want to go anywhere that he wasn't. Not ever. "All right."

He nodded toward the table. "I'd pull out a chair for you, but—"

"I got it," she said, resting her free hand on the back of the chair. She wasn't sure where to look. He was setting the mirror down, but whether she could see him or not, knew he stood beside her. The flowers reflected in the mirror as it settled on the table and she smiled. "I really like the flowers. Thank you."

"You're welcome," he said. "I really like you."

"I really like you, too, but I'm not—"

"I'm going to get a cup of coffee."

She didn't blame him for not wanting to hear her protest again. It was getting old and nauseating, but it was the truth. Beth's soul may have saved her from drowning, but she wasn't Beth. She could become more open minded about many things, but that was still unfeasible. There was no way she and Beth could be the same person. Absolutely no conceivable way. They were as different as night and day. Born in different centuries.

Sensing his arrival even before the mirror shifted beneath her fingers, she sat down. Sunlight shining through the windows made the flowers reflecting in the mirror more cheerful than any she'd seen, and that made her smile. He was trying so hard and all she'd done was dispute the one thing he wanted.

She pulled out the chair and sank onto the seat and while running her free hand through her hair. Giving him what he wanted was impossible, but there had to be a way to stop the fire department. There had to be.

"Do you like music?"

His question caught her off guard. "Everyone likes music. In my time we listen to it in our cars, in our homes and work places, even while on hold."

"On hold?"

"When you call someone on the telephone, there's often music to listen to while you wait for the other person to answer. Cell One's had been awful. I'd made them change it to be more pleasant for the customers to listen to while waiting to be connected."

"The phone doesn't just ring? That's what the one in Cliff's office does."

"Yes, it rings, too. Why did you ask about music?"

"No reason," he said. "Just wanted to know."

The victrola in the other room said either he or Beth liked music. As soon as the thought crossed her mind, an image of Beth sitting on the sofa listening to scratchy music flashed behind her eyes. Glancing into the mirror, she said, "Beth brought the victrola with her when she moved here, didn't she?"

"Yes, her mother gave it to her."

"But she never liked it. Beth didn't like it."

"She said it sounded too scratchy, but she liked other music."

She nodded, once again knowing more than she should. "She loved to dance. The two of you danced a lot, at events...like barn dances."

"We did. Do you like to dance?"

"No."

"Why not?"

"I never learned any specific steps, mainly because I didn't like being that close to someone. Didn't like them touching me." There it was again, insight as to why she'd been the way she was. Is. The way she is.

"You'd like dancing with me."

She laughed at his confidence. "Really?"

"Yes, really."

He was right, and that made all the things that couldn't be once again weigh heavy. Even her hand felt heavy and as she glanced down at it, excitement once again appeared. She could see his hand lying atop hers.

Slowly, cautiously, her gaze traveled up his arm, over his shoulder and neck, to his face. He was faintly translucent, but he was there. All of him. The sight of him sent a ripple of happiness throughout her system. "I can see you again," she whispered. "I can feel your hand on mine."

He cocked his head and glanced toward their hands. "Let go of the mirror."

Praying she wouldn't be disappointed, she closed

her eyes and concentrated on the sensations of feeling his hand lift hers off the mirror as she released the handle.

"Open your eyes," he said quietly. "Can you still see me?"

Hearing him increased her excitement and gave her hope as she lifted her lids. "Yes. Yes, I can see you. Hear you. Feel you."

From the moment she first saw his reflection in the mirror, she'd admitted he was a handsome man, but seeing him in the flesh, albeit a bit see-through-ish, was amazing. His body was trim and fit and tall and buff, and as close to perfect as a man could be.

"I can feel you, too," he whispered while his fingers wrapped around her hand.

"How? I don't understand how this can happen and then not happen just as quickly."

"Perhaps it's not something we need to understand." He pushed his chair away from the table.

She saw that too, the chair in his time. The table, the cup sitting next to the mirror, and she could still see her things, too. "This is crazy."

"No. It's wonderful." He tugged on her hand. "Come."

A flashback of what had happened upstairs had her shaking her head.

"Just into the parlor, this time," he said, as if reading her mind.

"Why?"

"You'll see."

Half afraid he'd disappear again, while also hoping he didn't, she stood and followed through the arched doorway into the parlor. They crossed the room and he stopped next to the victrola. "What are you going to do?"

"We are going to dance."

"I can't dance."

"You can with me. I'll show you." He knelt and opened the door. Lifting out a record, he held it up for her to see. "Find this one in your time."

"I—"

"Please?"

"All right, but don't blame me if I step on your feet."

He laughed. "I won't. I'll be happy to feel it."

Smiling, she agreed. "Me, too." It was as crazy as everything, but she wanted this to work. She wanted to dance with him. Knew it would be memorable.

She found the same record, but as she lifted the lid to put it on the machine, she said, "This is old. It might not work. The baffles and rubber seals, or the spring, might be too dried out."

He grinned. "We'll find out, won't we?"

"But if I break it, it could lose value."

"It's mine to break, isn't it?"

"Yes, but, I'd be the one breaking it."

"With my permission. Now put the record on and wind it up."

It would take both hands and she was hesitant to let go of his. He was too, that reflected in his eyes, and they both grinned when he let go of her hand and could still see each other. "Am I thin to you?" she asked while putting the record on the turntable. "Not skinny, but see through thin."

"Yes."

It was odd, how their arms and hands merged

without colliding while they each made the exact same movements putting the needle on the record and then cranking the handle on the side of the box. Within moments scratchy music started to play softly.

"Can you hear that?" he asked.

"Yes. Can you?"

"Yes."

She grinned. "The sound is coming from your time and my time, at the same time."

His smile made her stomach flutter.

"It's coming from our time," he said softly.

The most marvelous thing happened then, he literally swept her into his arms and across the open space in the parlor. It was heavenly, as if she was a well-trained ballroom dancer. Her feet instinctively knew what to do, how to follow him, as did the rest of her body. His shoulder was firm and solid under one hand, the other hand felt the warmth of his palm pressed against hers.

"See, you know how to dance."

"But I don't know how—" Suddenly it was as if she had two left feet.

"Yes, you do know how to dance," he said while not slowing their movements despite her instant loss of rhythm. "Say it. Say you know how to dance."

"I know how to dance," she said mainly to please him while struggling to keep up.

"Say it again."

"I know how to dance."

"Again and again. Keep saying it."

"I know how to dance. I know how to dance." Her feet were following his again and she could feel the rhythm of the two of them and the music. "I know how to dance. I know how to dance." Each time she said it, the movements no longer took thought, they just happened. "I do know how to dance." Excitement flared inside her. "I do!"

"I knew that all along," he said.

"I think you are just an excellent teacher."

"Nope. You knew all along. You just didn't realize it."

His smile was enough to make her believe that may be true and she no longer cared how or when she learned to dance. Sashaying around the room in his arms was too wonderful not to enjoy it.

That's exactly what she did, enjoyed it like nothing ever before. Her entire being grew content and happy, like sunshine filled her very soul as he led her around the room. When she took a moment to contemplate that, faded and far off images flashed behind her closed eyelids. She tried to bring them closer, to concentrate on them, but they were too fleeting, too elusive. Yet, she sensed they were of him and Beth. Images of the two of them dancing just like she and he were, but he'd been the one unsure.

She opened her eyes as understanding flooded her foggy brain. "Beth taught you how to dance, didn't she?"

He nodded. "She did."

A strong desire to laugh tugged at her. "And you thought it couldn't be done."

Once again, he nodded. "Yes, I did."

"She proved you wrong."

"That she did."

He said that with pride, and with love. Something she'd always claimed to know nothing about, but now concluded that was because she'd never had anything to compare it with until this very moment. Her heart actually felt full. Vivi Anne was right. A person didn't know how to love until they experienced it.

The music had stopped and so had they. He didn't look as translucent. She could see the fine lines near his eyes created by his smile. See how dark brown his eyes were and how the sunlight caught in his dark hair, making it glisten. She drew in a deep breath, simply enjoying the sight of him, and the vaguely familiar scent that teased her nose caused a shift inside her.

It smelled like leather and horseflesh and sunshine, all mixed together to form an aroma that as unique as it was wonderful. And one she knew. Knew very, very well. The idea, and the scent, snagged inside her brain. She hadn't noticed anything familiar to it in the house before so where was it coming from? Why did it thrill her in ways she'd never really been thrilled before?

She bit her lips together, clearly recognizing the thrill as a deep and specific one. It was Rance. And he smelled wonderful. Especially at night while they…Sex again. She was true-blue crazy.

The smile on his face grew, as if he knew her thoughts as clearly as she did. He leaned forward, too.

At this moment, being crazy was exactly what she wanted. Closing her eyes as his lips met hers, she looped her arms around his neck and kissed him. Truly kissed him. She could feel his lips, and parted hers to slide her tongue along the thin seam of his lips.

His lips parted and excitement exploded inside her as his tongue met hers.

Now, this, actually feeling him, tasting him, was indeed crazy, but too wonderful to make her stop. She could feel his body as he pulled her closer, pressing her against him from hip to chest. His hands roamed over her back and then up to cup her cheeks as he took control of the kiss.

Her fingers spread deep into his hair to hold on, keep herself grounded as his kiss practically lifted her off the ground.

It felt that way, as if his kiss was drawing her upward, beyond herself into a familiar yet unknown dimension. Not so unlike what had happened in the water, when Beth had saved her. As her feet nearly left the ground, a slice of fear ripped through her so fast she jolted backward, ripping her lips away from his.

The room was spinning, and she pressed the heels of both hands to her temples. He called to her, but the pounding in her head made him sound faint and faraway. Growing wobbly, she reached for him, for something to hold onto. Her hand caught the edge of the victrola, but it wasn't enough. Her knees buckled and she went down. Not hard, but fast enough hitting the floor stung her tailbone.

She sat there as the spinning slowed. Panic wasn't clawing inside her. There was no fear or terror. Realizing that, she lifted her head. The room was empty.

"Rance?" She rose onto her knees first, testing her equilibrium. "Rance?"

As a mirror appeared before her face she sank back onto her bottom. Disgust filled her. For as lovely as it was, there were moments she hated that mirror. With plenty of loathing, she grasped the handle.

"What happened?" he asked.

"I don't know. My fantasy must have gotten away

with me."

"What?"

She had never felt so pouty. Never wanted to scream and demand injustice stop picking on her. "Nothing."

"Are you all right?"

"Yes, I'm fine."

"You're sure?"

No, I'm not sure, she wanted to shout. *I'm not fine. I was fantasizing about kissing a ghost to the point I could actually feel it!* Knowing that wouldn't get her anywhere, she said, "I'm sure." She shook her head. "I just don't understand how I can see you one minute, and then you're gone."

"I can see you all the time."

"You don't have to rub it in."

"What?"

She pushed herself off the floor. Needing a moment, she let go of the mirror in order to take the record off the turntable. The mirror waving before her face couldn't be ignored, and she grasped the handle again.

"Want to dance again?"

"No. I don't want to dance again." Whether she wanted to or not, she wasn't going to. Dancing with him, seeing him, kissing him, wasn't getting them any closer to solving this entire escapade. If there was some rhyme or reason to all the strange occurrences, she might be able to figure things out, but there wasn't. "What are we going to do?"

"I don't know."

His honesty, along with how it was laced with disappointment, tested the small amount of willpower she had left. She'd never been so despondent. Being around him didn't help. It made her want things that could never be. Things for her that is. For him things could be different. She still believed that.

"I think I need to leave," she said. "I need time to think. To talk to Vivi Anne. To…I don't know. Figure something out." That seemed impossible, but she couldn't deny there was a spark of hope inside her. That there was an answer, if only she had more time to figure it out. She didn't. They didn't. "The fire department will be here in the morning."

Still holding the mirror, she used one hand to put the record away and close the victrola. "I'm going to go to town. Talk to someone about putting a stop to the burning. The fire chief, or the mayor, or the sheriff. I don't know. I'll think of something."

"All right," he said. "I'll see what I can do on my end. In my time."

"I'll be back." Her fingers refused to release the mirror as much as her eyes refused to meet his reflection. "As soon as I know anything, I'll be back."

"You'll be careful?" It was half a command, half a question.

"Yes, I'll be careful. I'm always careful."

The wiggling of the mirror forced her to glance at the glass. His brows were lifted and his expression said he didn't believe her, and as crazy as that was too, it made her smile.

"Don't worry. I will be careful. I won't slash any tires or…" She grinned. "That's not a bad idea."

"What are tires?"

"Rubber wheels."

He nodded but clearly wanted to say more. She

best leave before he did.

"I'll be back."

He bit his lips together momentarily before saying, "Liz, I—"

"I don't mind when you call me Beth." Who was she to deny him that small amount of pleasure?

His eyes glistened as he grinned. "All right, then."

He took a step closer, and her heart—that damned organ that hadn't given her any trouble up until she'd stepped foot in this house—sensed his closeness. It started beating faster, fluttering. Her lips tingled, too, remembering his pressed against them. If only that could truly have happened. If her fantasies could be real.

"Beth," he said softly.

The blood pounded through her veins with such force she gripped the side of the victrola again. "Yes?"

"I love you."

Her heart melted, along with the rest of her insides, leaving her legs so weak they wobbled. Those were words she'd never imagined hearing. Never thought she needed to hear. Whether it was possible or not, she couldn't deny it any longer. Blinking at the tears forming, she couldn't deny something else either. This was why she forced herself not to care about anyone, ever, because it hurt. Loving him didn't hurt, but losing him had, and would again. With her last bit of courage, she whispered, "I love you, Rance. I truly do."

Chapter Seventeen

Liz flicked on her blinker to pull into her motel, but a honk had her shutting off the turn signal in order to switch lanes and pull into the big chain hotel across the road. She'd sat in her car at the gate for a good half hour or more, wondering about what had happened, or hadn't, and what she could do about any of it. And crying. Crying because she wanted to be Beth, but wasn't and wouldn't ever be. Her only hope was Vivi Anne, and she hadn't wasted anytime on her drive to town. The fact no flashing lights had appeared in her review mirror had to be a sign of good things to come.

After maneuvering around the parking lot full of cars, she slammed her car into park before it had rolled to a stop. Jumping out she flung the door shut with one hand while pulling open the passenger door of Vivi Anne's truck with the other.

A ballad about coming home to a place they'd never been before, and being born again, filled the cab. She reached in and turned off the music. Vivi Anne played John Denver music nonstop. It had never bothered Liz before, but it did right now. "You really need a new CD."

"That is new. I just bought it at the gas station," Vivi Anne said. "A person can learn a lot from Johnny's songs, if they'd actually listen. Let him do the singing."

Dropping that subject, Liz nodded toward the iPad propped against the steering wheel. "What are you doing?"

"Stealing Wi-Fi," Vivi Anne answered. "That fifteen minute dinosaur computer at our hotel made me want to pull my hair out. I'd look awful being bald." She set the iPad on the seat beside her. "I rented my own room so you don't have to share. Les said he's thinking about ordering the internet for guests, but he'd have to raise his rates, and customers won't like that."

"Yeah, I know. He told me all about it."

"What are you doing back here? I didn't expect you until dark." Vivi Anne raised a drawn-on brow. "Or later."

Catching the insinuation, she sighed and climbed in. "He's a ghost."

"A handsome one."

Excitement made her stomach bubble. "You did see him. When you brought the trunk out there."

"Of course." Vivi Anne used a hand to fan herself. "No wonder Beth fell in love with him."

"There's more to Rance than a handsome face." Her stomach clenched. He wasn't only a ghost, he was married. She was in love with a married man. This wasn't any better than being in love with a ghost. Or was it?

"I know," Vivi Anne said. "His broad shoulders, muscle bound arms. I bet those pecks can dance, and the way that stomach narrows onto those hips—"

"Stop," Liz said.

"A man's body, just like a woman's, was meant to be admired."

"You don't have to tell me that. I'm already

twisted as tight as a Sunday paper rubber band." Turning an air conditioner vent to blow directly on her, she shook her head. "And there's more to Rance than his body. He's kind and gentle, and smart and driven, and talented, so talented when it comes to his horses." A sadness formed inside her. "He has so much to live for and he's so devoted."

"He has a lot to be admired."

"Yes, he does. And I have to help him."

"What are you going to do?"

"I'm not exactly sure, but I need your help." Trying to explain, she continued, "There's something I'm missing. Something a bit elusive. It's there, but I don't know what it is. I know that sounds crazy, but this is all crazy. I can't explain it, but I've never felt this way before. Felt this driven."

"Well, I just sent an email to the local newspaper reporter and posted a link to the board meeting minutes about the nuclear dump site on several social media sites."

"We need more than that," Liz said. "We have to stop the firetrucks from going out to the ranch tomorrow. I need more time to figure out what I have to do."

"Figure out what you have to do?"

"Yes. What we have to do. I need your help. I know that's a part of it. You're the reason I'm here in the first place."

Vivi Anne nodded while drumming her fingers against the steering wheel, and Liz gnawed on her bottom lip, waiting to hear what her friend was conjuring. It would be good, had to be, and would work.

After glancing in the review mirror, Vivi Anne said, "Jump in your car and meet me across the road."

At that moment, she was more thankful that she'd met Vivi Anne than she was for air to breathe or the sun, or moon, or anything that she took for granted, without a conscious thought, every single day. Her instincts had been right. Vivi Anne was the answer, and time was of the essence. Excitement flared as she jumped out of the truck and into her car.

Minutes later, as she opened the driver's door of her car parked in front of her motel room, Vivi Anne stopped her truck behind the car. "Climb in."

Liz complied, and while clicking on her seat belt, asked, "Where are we going?"

"To eat."

That didn't correspond with any of the ideas bouncing about in her head. Confronting Lou and Nate, or perhaps the fire department was more in line with what she'd been considering. Slashing a few tires still wasn't far from her mind, except for the fact that was sure to give her an arrest record. Which she could live with if it meant Rance didn't live in that old cabin for the rest of his life.

"To eat," Liz repeated, mentally attempting to dig deeper into the suggestion.

"Yes."

"Why?"

"Because I'm hungry, and you are too. You haven't eaten today, have you?"

"No." She stopped herself from adding it seemed like a waste of time. Several fast food restaurants lined the highway, and driving through one wouldn't take much time. They could brainstorm while eating in the truck. Gesturing toward a drive thru near the intersection ahead, she said, "Mexican sounds good."

"Then Mexican it is," Vivi Anne said while driving through the intersection.

Liz stared at the fast food restaurant as they drove past.

"I don't want heartburn afterward. There's a much better place downtown," Vivi Anne said.

Downtown meant a sit down and be waited on place, which meant at least an hour of valuable time. Every ounce of her being was noting each minute she wasn't at Rance's house, wasn't with him, and that left her longing for things she'd only recently come to want. To need.

"It won't take that long."

Liz tried to pull up a smile but wasn't in the mood to put too much effort into it. Rance needed help. She needed help, and that made her stomach scream for more than food. Patience, or lack of, had never been an issue for her in the past. Then again, plenty of other things had never been an issue either.

All she could do was hold belief in Vivi Anne, and that was easy. She'd believed in the other woman since meeting her. Believed she'd seen her husband accident...Her thoughts waned and shifted to other ones. Internal ones. If she could believe that so easily, why couldn't she believe in other things? Why couldn't she allow herself to believe she and Beth shared the same spirit?

Beth had saved her from downing. That she did believe that. So what about reincarnation? Could she be Beth reincarnated? The Beth of the twenty-first century? How else could she know all the things she did? All the antiques in the house she *knew* about. Where they had come from. Which ones Beth had brought with her from Billings and which ones had been Rance's. Which ones he'd bought for Beth.

And the trunk. How did she know Beth had been pregnant? Only Beth had known that. She had to have lived it in a past life. Had to have been Beth.

"I opened the trunk," she said as they followed the highway to downtown. Testing her theory.

"What's in it?"

A solid pit formed in her already twisted stomach. "Baby clothes. Beth was pregnant when she died." She glanced out the side window. "You already knew that, didn't you?"

"I looked in the trunk," Vivi Anne answered.

"Did you know Beth saved my life?"

Vivi Anne glanced her way and then back out the windshield. "How?"

She wasn't certain if her friend knew or not. "In the river. After the car crashed."

"That was the same place Beth died."

"Yes. Her spirit had been there since then. Since the train bridge collapsed. Waiting for someone to come along." Glancing out the window again, but reliving the images she'd only seen internally, Liz twisted the ring on her finger. "She stopped me from drowning and draped me over the trunk. That's when she gave me this ring. Her wedding ring. I thought it had been my mother's. That it was the only thing they'd been able to salvage from our car, from my parents."

"Why did you assume that?"

"I don't know. Probably because that's what Gladys told me when she gave it to me." She twisted the ring again. "I thought I'd lost it until it showed up in my suitcase the other night. It was in the outer pocket."

"You rarely use the suitcase."

"I've never enjoyed traveling."

"Because of what happened to Beth in the past."

Liz let that settle for a moment before nodding. "Probably." She stared out the window, but wasn't really looking at anything. "Wilma Harris was right. She was a friend of Gladys', and I remember her telling other people at church that her son had saved my life. That he'd given me CPR when they found me. Beth stayed with me until the rescuers arrived, and as soon as she left, I-I died. Today, when I opened the trunk and remembered all of this, I felt someone blowing air into my mouth. Into my lungs. I don't remember the hospital or moving in with Norman and Gladys. Actually, I have very few memories until getting older. I guess it all had been too traumatic for a child."

"Probably."

"Why didn't Beth ever come to me before? Why didn't these memories appear, and why was I so afraid of the trunk?"

Vivi Anne pulled into a parking lot and found a parking spot. "What do you think?"

Liz sighed, but ultimately went with her gut. "Because it wasn't time. I wasn't ready to believe the possibilities."

Vivi Anne's smile was rewarding enough for Liz to smile in return. Being Beth, or sharing a spirit with her, wasn't so bad. In fact, it was sort of special.

They both climbed out of the truck and made their way into the restaurant. Feeling less confused, more aware, the assault of delicious aromas made her stomach growl.

"See how hungry you are?" Vivi Anne asked.

"It does smell good,"

Once seated at the table, she scanned the selections, made her decision, and set the menu aside. It was time to get down to work. "Rance and I need more time."

"For what?"

"To figure out a way to save his ranch. We considered several options, like making sure Robert is never born, therefore neither are Lou and Nate, or for Rance to change his will, but those options could also eliminate the possibility of me finding him at his house."

Confusion or possibly disbelief crossed Vivi Anne's face before she smiled at the waitress who appeared at the table. They both placed their orders, but before the waitress left the table, Vivi Anne grasped the woman's hand.

"That's a lovely ring," Vivi Anne said.

The waitress, a young woman with her brown hair twisted into a messy bun, smiled. "Yes, it is," she answered with a hint of sadness.

"Have you been married long?" Vivi Anne asked.

"Five years," the waitress answered.

An undercurrent that Vivi Anne was about to become more involved with the waitress than necessary rippled Liz's nerves. The woman was already married; she didn't need a match maker. More so, Liz wasn't interested in sharing Vivi Anne's attention, not while she needed her. A hint of shame had her bowing her head. She may not have been over caring in the past, or at least thought she hadn't been, but she'd never been that callous. That self-centered. Nor did she want to be.

"He's overseas," the waitress said. "In the military. Other than a few months here and there, we've been apart the entire five years."

"That's hard," Vivi Anne said.

"Yes, it is," the waitress said. "But as my mother says, I made my bed, now I have to lie in it."

"She didn't want you to marry him?"

The woman shook her head. "She loves Drew almost as much as I do, but my father was in the armed forces, too. Mom knew that makes for a lonely marriage and didn't want me to have that."

"That's understandable," Vivi Anne replied.

Empathy filled Liz. The woman's mother should be more caring, more understanding and supportive.

"Letters, phone calls, even video chats, don't warm a person's bed at night," the waitress was saying. "Some days, seeing him and not being able to touch him, makes it worse."

Liz almost groaned aloud and bit her tongue to keep from saying she fully understood.

"What can you do about that?" Vivi Anne asked.

"Not much," the waitress answered.

Vivi Anne nodded. "I suspect he feels the same way you do."

"He does."

"Just like all other roads, love's a two-way street," Vivi Anne said.

Liz had to let out the air she'd been holding as Vivi Anne's words echoed in her head.

"I'll go put this order in," the waitress said. "It won't be long."

"Thank you," Liz replied.

"This salsa is excellent," Vivi Anne said, dipping a chip. "Try some."

"What—" Liz started, wanting to know what Vivi Anne knew about the waitress.

"Eat," Vivi Anne insisted. "It'll clear your mind."

She opened her mouth, but Vivi Anne shook her head and pointed toward the small dish.

Liz tried the salsa and ate several chips, while Rance once again filled her thoughts. She hashed out ideas that only resulted in an occasional nod from Vivi Anne, especially once their meal was delivered.

After eating a fair amount of chicken enchiladas, Liz set down her fork, and waited impatiently as Vivi Anne all but licked her plate clean. The waitress arrived and asked if they needed the check separated.

"No." Vivi Anne held up at hand as the waitress walked away. "My treat. After all, this is a business trip."

Liz had long ago forgotten the business aspect of the situation, but consented by saying, "Thank you. It was delicious."

As if she had wings rather than feet, the waitress appeared again. Laying the receipt on the table, she said, "I feel I owe you an apology. I usually don't unload on guests. I'm sorry, and I hope I didn't interrupt your enjoyment."

"Oh, not at all," Vivi Anne said. "Not at all. It added to our enjoyment."

Liz smiled, and then noted the number of bills Vivi Anne handed the waitress.

Holding her silence until they exited the building, she then stated, "That was an unusually large tip."

Vivi Anne's smile never faltered. "She'll need it

for her trip overseas."

"Overseas?"

"Yes, to see her husband. She hasn't gone to see him because she thought they couldn't afford it. My tip is seed money."

"How do you know—" Liz stopped herself and change her question to a statement. "Maybe she can't afford it, even with your tip."

"People can afford what they believe they can afford."

They arrived at the truck, and Liz waited until they'd both climbed in and buckled up before saying, "Are you always matchmaking?"

"No, and I wasn't matchmaking. They are already married." Vivi Anne started the truck. "They just needed a push in the right direction to stay that way."

"What do you mean?"

"The bartender has been pursuing that waitress, and she'd been contemplating an affair. Only because she's so lonely. And she'll regret it the rest of her life."

"How can you possibly know all…" Liz let her question trail away.

"There's never room for three in a marriage." Vivi Anne steered the truck onto the highway.

****

Rance glanced around the table. This had been a bad idea. Cliff looked like he'd just set a bead on a bank robber. Nan's lips were pinched tight and from the fury in her eyes, steam could start spitting out of the top of her head at any moment. Cindy, the one who should appear uncomfortable at the very least, was batting her eyelashes like they were fly swatters. The only two eating were Ralph and Randy. They consumed food with the gusto of boys their age, asking for second and third helpings to be passed their way.

He, on the other hand, had barely lifted his fork. Entering the house a short time ago had been like stepping foot into an icebox. He'd tried for a fast exit, but Nan would have none of that.

So here he sat, waiting for the next shoe to fall, and hoping it didn't hit him.

"You boys go on outside and play now," Nan said.

"You mean it?" Ralph asked.

"Without doing dishes?" Randy asked.

"Yes," Nan said. "And don't come in until I call for you."

"Yes, 'em," the boys chorused to the sounds of chair legs scraping and boots running for the door.

The weight inside the room increased as the door slammed shut. Nan was the one to break it. "So, Rance, who told you of Cindy's condition?"

He shot a glance at Cliff. "Condition?"

Cliff nodded.

"Who told you?" Nan asked.

The truth wasn't an option. "No one told me about her condition," Rance said. "Cindy, however, told me about Eugene."

"I'm afraid there was no Eugene. At least not one Cindy was engaged to." Nan cleared her throat. "My sister asked if Cindy could come stay with us because her condition will soon become visible." She shot a serious glare toward Cindy. "My brother-in-law, her father, is seriously ailing, and my sister does not want his last days to be festered with scandal."

A shivered slowly crawled its way up Rance's spine as Cindy smiled. She was more of a fool than he'd first imagined, or more manipulative. He'd go with fool. Only a fool, a large one, would think they'd win going up against Nan.

"Now, of course we are not going to lie about this," Nan was saying. "And Cindy has been informed we won't stand for foolishness. Her only option, besides staying with us, is a home for unwed mothers."

"What about the baby's father?" Rance asked, looking toward Cliff. "Why not just find him and make him marry her?"

"Unfortunately," Nan said, "the baby's father is already married and has other children."

Rance drew in air through his nose. He was getting the answer he and Beth had discussed, but it sure made for uncomfortable conversation. "What about once the baby's born?"

Cliff answered this time, after Nan had nodded toward him. "Nan and I have agreed to raise the child. It's not his or her fault the way they came to be and no child should have to pay for the mistakes of their parents."

"Although we know you are not the gossiping type, we must nip any rumors before they get started," Nan said. "When people ask, and they well, we will simply state Cindy made a mistake and is now facing the consequences."

And he thought he had troubles. From the looks of her, Cindy had never faced consequences and wasn't about to start now. If she had an ounce of brains, she'd have already figured that out.

"I was quite surprised when Cliff mentioned you knew of Cindy's troubles, and even more surprised when you knocked on the door this evening," Nan said.

"However, I am glad you are among the living again."

"I'm among the living all right," Rance said half beneath his breath. People living in another century, but living nonetheless. And he hadn't mentioned Cindy's condition to Cliff. The lawman had simply assumed he'd known. From what he'd said at the house evidently. He couldn't quite remember what he'd said. "I just stopped by because I told Cliff I would." As an afterthought he added, "And to thank you for the meals and such."

"What happened to Beth, and you, was tragic, nothing more than tragic, and you've been in my prayers every single day," Nan said. "You'll remain there."

Rance nodded, and without glancing toward Cindy again, hoped others were praying for Nan and Cliff. They'd need it.

After spending some time on the front porch, visiting with Cliff about nothing particular, especially Cindy, Rance left for the ranch. Cindy's baby would be raised by Cliff and Nan. There was no changing that. Nan's mind was set as firmly as a mountain. He briefly considered visiting Hiah again, but he wouldn't find any answers there either.

His great uncle had helped him last night, but in truth, it hadn't come from any medicine or even the Shoshone blood in his veins. Hiah had simply guided him to look inside himself. To surrender to the battle that had been going on between his heart and his mind. The sweat pouring off him had forced him to a survival place, a place where the mind had no control. In that purification, in that wisdom, while stripped of all other thoughts, he'd found his answer.

Beneath his heart that had pounded against the heat, against the extreme conditions he'd forced upon his body, he'd seen the one thing he desired above all else.

Love.

It was simple as that.

When he'd found Beth, when they'd found each other, all the rest of his life had become meaningless. They'd loved each other unconditionally and would continue to. Beyond the limits of this life.

He believed that, believed she'd been reborn to return to him, and he believed he'd be able to keep her with him this time. How is what he must discover, and just like the answers he'd already received, that would have to come from within.

Making things happen through hard work and sweat was a hell of a lot easier.

How was he going to come up with an answer, figure out what had to be done by tomorrow? Before they burned his house down a hundred years from now.

His horse snorted, and Rance patted its neck. "I know boy. Maybe Cliff's troubles aren't so bad. At least Cindy lives in this century. Nan would have one hell of a time explaining the consequences of my troubles."

Huffing out a breath, he shook his head. "So would I."

Chapter Eighteen

Liz woke several times throughout the night. For different reasons. Feverish and throbbing after an erotic dream about Rance. So bitter and angry after one concerning him and Cindy that she'd punched the pillow. Scared and frantic when another included flames eating away at his house. The worst though, was the last, where she was empty, too full of sorrow to even wipe at the tears that fell down her cheeks and onto the pillow.

After a time of wallowing in self-pity, she tossed aside the covers. She climbed out of bed and without bothering to so much as splash water on her face, opened the door and stepped outside.

A tint of red in the pre-dawn gray on the horizon hinted a promise of what was to come. Sunshine. Warmth. Happiness perhaps, for the extremely lucky.

The T-shirt and shorts she slept in didn't provide warmth against the chill of the air, but it covered her adequately enough, so she walked to the end of the building where a couple of plastic lawn chairs sat.

Sitting in one, she pulled her feet up, wrapped her arms around her shins, and rested her chin on her knees as she stared at the horizon. Disappointed weighed as heavy inside her as sorrow, and anger. Vivi Anne hadn't been any help last night. After helping the waitress with her love life, Vivi Anne had done little more than suggest the answer to her problems was inside her. Just as it had been inside the waitress.

That made no sense at all.

Finding a way to stop the firemen this morning wasn't inside her. She'd given up on the slashing tires idea, and considered a standoff, which included her finding a place that sold assault rifles. That could certainly put her in jail, or prison.

"Ask yourself why it's a problem," Liz whispered, repeating the words Vivi Anne had said last night. The same thing she'd said before. When all this had started.

"It's a problem," she said aloud, "because the firemen will burn the house down. And that's a problem because then I'll never see Rance again. And that's a problem because I love him. End of whys."

She sighed and stared at the sky turning pink. Why couldn't she have been born normal? Maybe she had been, but that had changed when the train hit her father's car. And Beth had entered her life. Beth's spirit anyway. That's when she became this shell of a person. Never caring, never wanting, just existing.

Until meeting Rance.

Vivi Anne arrived beside the chairs. "You're up early."

Liz nodded. "Couldn't sleep."

"Here."

The cup wafted steam.

"It's full of sugar and creamer just like you like it." Vivi Anne sat in the other chair. "I brought a coffee pot with me."

Liz couldn't help but grin as she took the cup. "Thank you."

"You're welcome."

After several sips of coffee, she said, "I've tried, Vivi Anne. I've asked myself why until I can't ask any more, and I haven't discovered a solution."

"Maybe it's not a solution you should be looking for."

She took another drink, letting the warm coffee chase aside the chill inside her. "I'm not like you. I don't have the instincts you do, the insight. I really wish you'd just tell me what I have to do."

"I can't tell you what you have to do, honey. There's this thing we all have. It's called free will. It's what gives us the ability to choose between possible paths. If I gave you the answer, that's the route you'd take, so therefore your actions wouldn't have been freely chosen. Not by you."

"It would be if I think it's right."

Vivi Anne took a long drink off her cup of coffee while staring out at the horizon. The hotel across the road blocked much of the sunrise, and the increase of traffic the last half hour disrupted the solitude, which goaded at Liz's already flustered mood.

"When you moved out of Gladys and Norman's house, did they tell you it was time for you to go?" Vivi Anne asked.

"No, they said I could stay the entire time I went to college."

Vivi Anne nodded. "You went because it was your free will. Inside you, you felt it was time to move on so you did. And it was your free will to research your parentage, to find something out about your parents, their history."

"And hit only dead ends."

"Because you only dabbled in it," Vivi Anne said.

"Because deep down, it wasn't as important to you as you thought it should be. If it had been a burning desire, you would have pursued it and continued until you found the answers you sought."

That was true. She hadn't had a burning desire, not like the one she felt when it came to helping Rance. "What if I'd never found the answers?"

"You would have, or died trying. That's how it is when something is truly important to us. If someone told me they'd give me a million dollars for the antique store, I'd sell out in a heartbeat, but if offered a million dollars to never help someone find happiness again, I'd have turned them down." She let out a short laugh. "I might have to think about it, but ultimately, I'd turn them down. It's who I am. I love helping people. *Three things will last forever—faith, hope, and love. But the greatest of these is love.* I'll never forget the first time I heard that passage and how it resonated with me. Of course, at the time, I didn't know it would lead me on the path it has. I was only six, and in Sunday school."

Vivi Anne turned, looking at her with an extremely serious expression. "If I offered you a million dollars right now to leave this morning go back to Billings and forget about Rance, would you do it? Would you leave?"

"No," Liz answered instantly.

"Why?"

"Because Rance is depending upon me."

Vivi Anne shrugged. "He lived a hundred years ago. In our time, right now, Rance is dead."

Instantly irritated, Liz said, "He's not to me. He's alive, and it's up to me to make sure his future is one he deserves."

"Why?"

Liz bit the end of her tongue in order to give her mind a moment to consider her answer. Time didn't matter. The answer wouldn't change. It was because she loved him. Trying to give Vivi Anne a more thoughtful, complex answer, she said, "I've been given this amazing opportunity to help him. It'll all be for not if I don't."

"And that matters to whom?"

"To Rance."

Vivi Anne's expression said she wanted more.

"And to me. It matters to me."

"Aw, finally, we get to you. Why is that?"

"Why is what?"

"That you're thinking about Rance and not yourself."

"Because I love him," Liz answered without thought or doubt. "I've already said that. I know it's crazy, perhaps delusional, but I've fallen in love with a ghost."

"And if you so manage to save his house from being burned down, what then? You'll live there the rest of your life? With a ghost. Someone you can't touch. You can't have a physical loving relationship with? What kind of life is that going to be for you?"

Liz opened her mouth, but then shut it. Eventually, as her chest burned, she admitted, "I don't know. That's why I need more time."

"I'm sorry, honey, but time isn't what you need. Think about it, how will you afford to live there? Lou and Nate aren't going to let you stay there for free, and as far as I know, you don't have the funds to buy the property and keep it up until you die of old age."

Jealousy burned. "Why were you so fast to help that waitress last night, but just throw road blocks at me?" As soon as the words were out, she regretted them. "I'm sorry. That wasn't fair of me to say. You've been a lot of help."

"Don't be sorry," Vivi Anne said. "We are only angry about things we are passionate about. Your problem is more complex than the waitresses. She already knew the answer, just needed someone to validate it for her."

Not sure how to respond, but not wanting to be a lost cause, Liz said, "Well, I could live with a ghost. I could find a way to come up with the money I'll need."

Vivi Anne's eyes grew sorrowful as she leaned forward. "What about Rance? Is that what he wants? To live with a ghost the rest of his life?"

Her throat welled. "No, he wants his wife back. He wants Beth."

"And where does Beth fit into all of this?"

Liz had a brain freeze. Not the eating ice-cream too fast, but a real, black out where nothing existed, not time or space, and it was as disorienting as it was peaceful. Then, as if they appeared from nowhere, the words Vivi Anne had said last night hit. There's never room for three in a marriage.

The reality of that saturated every cell in her body. She wasn't what Rance wanted. Beth was. He wanted Beth. Not her.

"I'm going to go jump in the shower," Vivi Anne said. "It'll be time to head out to Rance's soon. To meet the moving guys."

Liz acknowledged she'd heard with a nod. As badly as she wanted to see Rance, she didn't. She had no answers for him. No solution. She wasn't Beth.

****

Fury drove every footstep Rance took. Thieves. He'd been gone a matter of hours last night and thieves had hit. The saddle he'd been working on for Beth was gone, as were a couple of half-made halters and bridles. They'd been in the barn, and he hadn't moved them. Granted, he hadn't spent much time in the barn lately, not with Beth's arrival, but he'd checked the cabin and woodshed, just to make sure he hadn't stashed them someplace out of sight, out of mind.

He hadn't.

Stomping up the steps and into the house, he roamed from room to room; making sure nothing else was missing inside. Everything was in order, making him believe the thieves hadn't entered the house, which only confused him more. What sort of fool would steal a half-tooled saddle and parts of halters and bridles?

Fools, saddles, and bridles left his mind as a familiar sensation took root inside him. He retained the urge to run, knowing Beth was in the kitchen. The idea of sneaking up behind her thrilled him, just as it always had. Soon surprising her would include kisses like the one they'd shared yesterday. He'd dreamed about that kiss last night, and was counting the minutes until it happened.

The unfulfilled needs that had encompassed his body yesterday hadn't totally left yet. He'd missed her so much. Missed the taste of her. The feel of her. And having that all again yesterday convinced him she'd be back in his arms, in his life, every day very soon.

Anxious to see her and learn what sort of plan she'd come up with, he hurried down the stairs. The fact he hadn't had much luck in town with Cliff and Nan didn't deter him. They'd figure it out. What's meant to be is meant to be. He and Beth had been meant to be from the get go.

As he'd known, she was in the kitchen, running a fingertip along the handle of the mirror. Slowly, he crossed the room, taking time to examine her from head to toe. She wore another set of short pants, a shade of blue that was so light, they looked almost white, and her shirt was purple. This one had sleeves, but they didn't come down as far as her elbows. The way those odd-fangled clothes she wore molded her body like a tailored leather glove had grown on him.

"I know you're there."

He grinned and reached around her to touch the mirror. "And I know you are here."

They lifted the mirror together and the sorrow on her face tugged at his heart.

"You weren't able to stop them," he said.

"No, I wasn't," she replied quietly.

"We will think of something."

She pinched her lips together.

"Yes, we will," he insisted. "I love you. You love me. You were reborn to be with me, your husband. I won't believe otherwise."

"It's not possible. I wish it was true, but it's not. It's—it's just not possible."

He wanted to grip her shoulders and spin her around and had never been so flustered that he couldn't. "You never used to say that. You always insisted everything was possible. As long as a person believed, everything was possible."

"That was before, before Beth died."

A deep breath did little to calm his nerves. He thought they were over this. Over her thinking she wasn't Beth. She was. Liz and Beth are the same person. Why can't she see that?

"They can start in the barn."

Instinct had him letting go of the mirror and walking toward the door. Glancing around the empty space, he asked, "Who are you talking to?"

Pressing the mirror against her breast, she walked toward the parlor. "I'll be upstairs."

He followed and waited until they were in the bedroom before asking, "Who is here?"

She'd walked straight to the window, and that's where they stood. "Men. They are taking out the antiques."

"We don't need it. Whatever they take, we don't need it. We can buy more. Replace anything. Everything."

She shook her head. What bothered him was the lack of light in her eyes. There was no belief in them. No belief in her.

"What happened last night? What happened to steal your belief?"

"Nothing happened. I just faced the truth. And that's what you have to do, too. You have to face the fact Beth died in that accident. That she'll never come back to you. You have to get on with your life. Find someone else, get married again. Love again."

A flaming tremor made him quake in his boots. He was growing tired of pointing out the obvious. "Love again? What do you think I've been doing these past few days?"

"I don't mean love Beth again, I mean love

someone else. Find someone else and have a family so today doesn't happen a hundred years from now in your time..." She shook her head. "In whatever time, whosever time, men don't come clean out your house. So the fire department doesn't come to burn it down." Letting go of the mirror, she whispered, "So I don't lose my sanity. If I have any left. I don't even know anymore."

She walked away, to other side of the room and covered her face with both hands.

He pulled his hat off and threw it on the bed. She was back to being Liz completely. This bouncing back and forth was wearing, and frustrating, and...exasperating for both of them. The tears she swiped aside said more than that. It was hard.

More for her than him. Being two people at the same time had to be hell. If this happened every time someone was reborn, it was amazing a sane person walked on this earth. It didn't happen. Most people didn't know they were reborn. She only did because Beth was so determined to come back to him. She'd been fighting to come back to him for over a hundred years, but in doing so, she was destroying another person. Another human being.

That wasn't right. Beth wouldn't want that.

Beth wouldn't want that.

His heart sank to his knees, then further, onto the floor where he might as well stomp on it.

Acting before he couldn't, he crossed the room and held up the mirror.

She pinched her lips together and clutched her hand into a fist.

He waited and swallowed at the bile working its

way into his throat. He'd come to love her, as Liz and as Beth, and letting her go, this time on purpose, may prove to be harder than the first time. But it was the right thing to do. The only thing he could do for her.

Hesitantly, she grasped the mirror.

"You're right. This, what's happening, isn't right. I shouldn't have dragged you into it." He shook his head. "It was just so easy for me to believe that—" He stopped himself. It no longer mattered what he believed or why or how. Not much mattered a whole lot. "I'll make you a promise, if you'll make me one."

She nodded, and the tears streaming down her face said it wasn't any easier on her than it was on him. He was proud of her for that. Proud of her strength and righteousness.

"I promise to get on with my life, as you said. I won't wait for Beth any longer. I can't promise I'll get married again, that will depend on how things go. I'm not Robert's father, but I'll do my damnedest to make sure Lou and Nate don't inherit this house. I'm not sure how that will change things, but I hope it'll mean you'll never have to come here to catalogue antiques."

The pain on her face tore at him, and he planted his feet firmer on the floor to combat the aguish eating him inside out. "You have to promise me you'll walk out that door and forget you ever met me. Look deep inside yourself, and find what's beneath your heart, what makes you smile, and laugh, and live. When you find what that is, don't let it go. Don't ever let it go."

Not waiting for her answer, he let go of the mirror and left the room while he still could. His vision was blurry, his heart broken, but he kept walking.

Down the stairs, across the room, and out the door.

Chapter Nineteen

There was nothing to find beneath her heart because she didn't have a heart. Just an empty hole where one used to be. Liz didn't even know why she was still alive. Still breathing. She didn't want to be. Not at this moment. Rance was gone. The emptiness of the house echoed around her, inside her. "Damn you, Beth. Why'd you save my life to just have it filled with such pain?"

She laid the mirror on the bed. "If I'd been you, I'd never have died on that train. I'd never have gone to Billings. I'd never have left Rance for any reason."

With tears scalding her face, she walked to the door, and like a zombie in a B movie, continued down the hall. Down the stairs. Across the kitchen. Out the door.

"Liz?"

She walked past Vivi Anne and down the outside steps.

"What's wrong? What's happened?"

She held up a hand, stopping the questions as she continued forward, to her car. The tears came in full force then. Feeling her way, she found the door handle and climbed in. If she'd thought the eye of the hurricane consuming her had already hit, she was wrong. It hit with such force, such magnitude, her entire being shook hard enough to shatter bones.

Crumpled against the steering wheel, she shook and sobbed and cried until there were no tears left, no part that wasn't encrusted with pain. She stayed there a while longer, numb and uncaring.

When the car door opened, she didn't even lift her head.

"The firemen are here."

Hands pulled her upright and cupped her cheeks. She didn't have the strength to pull away.

"What the hell happened?" Vivi Anne asked.

"He's gone." She wasn't numb. Saying that hurt like hell.

"Rance?"

Anger flared inside her. "No, Santa Claus." Vindictive, unrelenting pain twisted her insides harder. "Yes, Rance, who's not any more real than Santa Claus. A cruel trick played on kids to make them behave."

"Hold up," Vivi Anne shouted to someone behind her.

Liz pushed the woman's hands away and fumbled at the keys hanging off the side of the steering wheel. "Let them come. Let them burn the place down."

Vivi Anne grabbed the keys and pulled them out of the ignition. "Not until you tell me what happened."

"I told him he had to get on with his life. That Beth was dead and wasn't coming back."

Vivi Anne grabbed her face again, and twisted her, forcing eye contact. "Love sometimes gets you into trouble. Up-to-your-waist-deep trouble. It can hurt like hell, and twist you inside out and upside down, but in the end, it's worth it."

"No, it's not."

"So you want to live the rest of your life without it?

Work for me, selling bits and pieces of other people's lives, living in a one-bedroom apartment until you're too old to climb the steps?"

"You don't know—"

"Like hell I don't! I know you're in love with the man you just sent away. You've loved him for centuries."

"And I can't have him!"

"He's the only thing you've ever been passionate about."

"I know that!" Rance would forever be the only person she'd ever love with this intensity. "And as I just said, I can't have him. We live in two different worlds. Two different centuries."

"Love is timeless. It has no barriers."

Frustrated, Liz grasped handfuls of her own hair, pulling at the roots. "What part of this don't you understand? Whether I love him or not, he lives a hundred years ago, and he's in love with someone else. His wife!"

"Beth."

She snapped her head up. "Yes. Beth." She slapped the steering wheel. "Someone I'd give everything I own to be right now."

"But you are her."

"No, I'm not. I'm Elizabeth Baxter."

Vivi Anne squeezed her face more firmly. "Elizabeth Baxter died at five years old in an accident with her parents."

A chilling sensation rippled Liz's spine. "No, I didn't."

"Yes, she did. That little girl, along with her parents, was supposed to die in that accident. You. Beth wasn't supposed to die in that train accident. Wasn't supposed to be on that train. That's why your soul was still there, waiting for a chance to get back. To make things right."

"That's not—" For some reason, Liz couldn't say that wasn't possible. It didn't feel right. Or she just wanted to be Beth so badly, the words wouldn't form. She had said it so many times, but couldn't. Just couldn't. "It took over a century?" she whispered.

"Time has no boundaries," Vivi Anne said once again. "No hours or years, only moments that are either acted upon or forever lost."

Just then something peculiar resonated inside Liz. It stole her breath and made things swirl. Not outside of her. Inside. Almost as if the little twisted pillars of her DNA started bouncing off one another. It was reminiscent of when Rance had danced her across the room. She hadn't paid it much attention then, because she'd been in his arms and that had been too wonderful to think of any else. It had felt as if her true self had come alive while dancing with him. As if Liz had been a figment of her imagination. An illusion her spirit had created until the time was right for her to know the truth.

That she wasn't Liz Baxter but Beth Livingston.

Something inside her shattered with such force she doubled over. Her forehead hit the steering wheel as she pressed both hands to the burning in her chest. Her lungs rattled and then tightened as she tried to breathe. Visions formed, all sorts of images that flashed across her mind like a movie on fast-forward.

She recognized the people, the places, the events. Especially the train wreck, the water, the pain, and how she'd shouted for Rance. When a child appeared in the water, her heart started racing as she swam toward the sinking tiny body.

Hands grasped her shoulders, shaking her.

Her heart was racing and hot tears fell from her eyes as she looked up at Vivi Anne. "You're right," she whispered. "Liz Baxter died in that car accident with her parents. That's why there's no information about her, about her family. She never survived the accident. And that's why, why I was so aloof, my heart only knew him. I had to find him to find myself."

Tears fell from Vivi Anne's eyes as she nodded.

"I'm Beth. I always have been. I—" Alarm had her scrambling, grabbing the steering wheel to maneuver out of the car. "Rance! I have to find him. Now, before they set the house afire."

"Go," Vivi Anne ordered. "I'll hold them off as long as I can."

Beth started for the house, but stopped. Spinning around, she wrapped her arms around Vivi Anne. "I may never see you again."

"You won't ever see me again," Vivi Anne whispered. "But I'll never forget you."

A part of her had connected with Vivi Anne, a friend in a time of need, a counterpart, an ally she owed much. As appreciative as she was for all that, there was no drawing need to remain behind. She didn't belong here. Never had. "I'll miss you."

"You'll be too busy to miss me." Vivi Anne kissed her cheek. "Now go!"

Beth started to run, but stopped again to spin around and say, "Rance isn't Robert's father. If needed let that be known."

"I will!" Vivi Anne shouted before she grabbed a fireman's arm.

Beth grinned and ran to the house. She grabbed the door handle, shouting, "Rance! Rance! It's me, Beth! Where are you?" A miniature explosion rattled inside her chest, like a top of a canister under pressure letting loose, flying skyward, releasing freedom, and more. It summoned hope and truth, and most of all, love. Pure, unfiltered love like she had known before. Had experienced. And it was right there, where it was supposed to be, at the base of her heart. Its very foundation.

Drawing upon that, she raced up the steps to see if the mirror had been left behind. More alive than ever, and driven, she ran down the hall. "Rance! Rance!"

Sunlight shone onto the bed, and a beam, precise and bold, reflected off the glass, shooting a prism of colors onto the ceiling. She leaped over the trunk that must have been inadvertently pushed aside when the armoire had been carried out and grasped the handle of the mirror. "Rance! Rance!"

There was no hum. Instead shouts rattled off the walls. Vivi Anne's protests. Arguments from men.

Beth closed her eyes, searching deep within. Rance's love had shown her who she was, but getting back to him was all up to her. Had been all along. She had to believe. Believe she was Beth. Believe she had been given a second chance. Been reborn so she and Rance could live right here in this house until they were too old to climb the stairs.

They would. They'd live here for decades, raising children and horses, and loving one another until the end of time, because love knows no boundaries. Has no barriers.

It conquers all as long as one believes that with all their heart.

She did. She believed.

She. Believed.

Her eyes flew open at the pounding of footsteps on the stairs. Vivi Anne's protests were getting closer, as were the men telling her to get out of the way.

"Rance, please!" Beth shouted, begging him to appear.

His reflection didn't appear in the mirror, and she spun about, to run for another room in search of him, but tripped.

The air whooshed out of her lungs as she landed on the trunk. Draped over the top, she reached for the handle that slipped from her hold. "No!" she screamed as the mirror hit the floor and bounced out of reach.

On the second tumble, the mirror shattered, splaying glass into the air. Tiny shards rained onto the floor like hail. Tinkling and clanging as they settled upon a final resting place.

"No," Scrambling off the trunk, she crawled to the bits of glass. "No. No. No."

The pounding footsteps drew closer as she clawed at the broken glass, searching for larger pieces, ones that could hold a reflection.

There were none.

"No. No," she sobbed.

All the love she held for Rance, the love she'd harbored for more than a century, let loose like a dam no longer able to hold back a river. Water rushed forth, and terror filled her as she was pulled downward, into a dark abyss she'd known before. Fighting, gasping for air, she cried, "Rance Livingston, you're my husband. I'm your wife. We pledged our love forever. Forever. You promised." With her last bits of air, she whispered, "I promised."

****

Rance grabbed the door frame, freezing in the bedroom doorway as his heart stopped, flipped, and started beating fast enough to steal his breath. He'd heard Beth shouting for him all the way out in the barn. The sight of her crumpled on the floor, surrounded by shards of glass had him lunging forward.

Kneeling beside her, his hands shook as he reached out. "Yes!" he shouted to the heavens as his hands grasped a hold of her. "Beth, Beth!" He pulled her onto his lap, kissing her hair, her forehead, her cheeks.

She was limp, her arms dangling, her head hanging sideways. "No!" he growled as pain sliced through his chest. "No! Not again!"

Grabbing her chin, he blew air between her parted blue lips. He blew again, and again, and again. He didn't stop until she coughed.

Then he froze momentarily before he pulled her against his chest and started pounding on her back.

She coughed another time, and another, and then moaned, "Stop. Stop."

Grasping her shoulders, he yanked her off his chest. Her face was twisted in a frown, her breasts heaving with each breath she took.

"That hurt," she muttered.

"I'm sorry," he said, although sorrow was the one thing he wasn't feeling. "But you have to stop doing that to me."

"Doing wh—"

326

The shine that appeared in her eyes, the smile that overtook her entire, beautiful, face kicked his heart into a gallop.

"Rance!" She wrapped her arms around his neck and continued repeating his name while kissing him. His chin, his cheeks, his neck, anywhere her lips touched.

His were just as busy, kissing anything they came in contact with until they finally found her mouth. Their union was feverish, intense, and completely consuming. He could think of nothing but her. How wonderful she tasted, how fragrant she smelled, how remarkable and right it was to hold her in his arms.

When they separated, they were both gasping, and laughing.

"Goodness." She sighed and rested her head against his chest. "Oh, goodness."

"What happened?" He gathered her legs away from the broken glass covering the floor. His heart skipped another beat as he made sure no glass was on caught on her skirt. Her skirt!

"I was looking for you and tripped over the trunk and the mirror broke." She stiffened and lifted her head off his shoulder. "I wanted you to carry the trunk downstairs, didn't I ask you to?"

This was Beth, in the flesh and wearing the blue dress with the pink flowers he liked so much, yet, a part of him was afraid to accept that. As if she might disappear if he did. At the same time, he knew she'd never leave him. Not on purpose. Swallowing, a bit confused by the answer on the tip of his tongue, he said, "Yes, you did. I was hitching up the buggy. You're taking the trunk to Billings. Leaving on the noon train."

She looked down at her dress, and then gathered a handful of her skirt to splay it out and examine it. A moment later, she dropped the material and scampered off his lap. "Get up! Get up, Rance. Get up!"

He did so, while holding his breath. She was remembering. So was he. In unison, their gazes roamed around the room until their eyes met and locked onto each other's.

"It hasn't happened yet," she whispered.

"No." His heart pounded. "It hasn't."

As if they were surrounded by ears, ones they didn't want to know their secret, she whispered, "I haven't gone to Billings yet." She shut her eyes. "The train, the bridge hasn't collapsed yet."

Pulling her close, he placed his mouth next to her ear. "And I haven't been haunted by your spirit yet."

She giggled.

He chuckled.

When their gazes met again, light literally danced in her eyes. "I'm home, Rance. I'm home."

He ran his fingers into her hair, pushing out the pins holding the long tresses atop her head. As her hair tumbled over her shoulders, he kissed the top of her head. "Yes, Beth, you're home."

She squealed and leaped, wrapping her arms around his neck. "I'm home!"

He'd caught her waist, and while shouting, "You're home!" he pivoted, twirling her around.

"I'm not going to Billings," she said as they spun, her feet and skirts flaying in the air between the dresser and bed.

The bed. That thought shot a bolt of lightning from his head clear to his toes. One so hot it probably burnt a hole in the floor. "You better believe you're not, darling," he said. "Not today."

She laughed as he gathered her legs in one arm and threw himself backward, onto the bed. The springs creaked and clanged as his bottom hit the mattress, and she bounced in his arms, but his hold was tight. He'd never let her go. Never. Ever.

Beth flipped around and pushed Rance until he was lying flat on the bed, his head on a pillow. The need, the desire inside her had long ago grown uncontrollable. She grasped the front of his shirt and ripped it open. "I'll sew the buttons back on," she said, as the threads broke and buttons flew across the room.

"All right." He grabbed the front of her dress, sending her buttons flying as far as his. "God, I've missed you," he growled as her camisole ripped in-two.

"You've missed me?" she mocked while tugging his shirt out of his pants with one hand and fumbling with his belt with the other. "I've waited over a hundred years for this."

The way he fondled her breasts, teased her nipples into hard nubs, was exquisite, but she didn't need any tender caresses to arouse her. She was already on the brink of explosion. What she needed was him filling her, completing her, satisfying her.

She crawled off him, giving no mind to the damage she was doing to her dress—his favorite—as she ripped it off her shoulders and shoved it over her hips. "Get your clothes off, Rance Livingston," she demanded. "Your wife needs you, now."

One boot, then the other hit the floor. "My wife will always need me."

"You better believe that!" She kicked off her

drawers.

Their clothes flew, landing where they may, and once they were both bare, both aroused and impatient, they jumped back onto the bed. Laughing and kissing and laughing some more.

They didn't bother climbing beneath the covers, there wasn't time. Rance came home to her in a swift, all-encompassing thrust that had her shouting his name at the joyous pleasure.

Beth wept at one point, at the beauty, the splendor, the cataclysmic atonement of loving him so fully, so completely, that nothing could ever keep them apart. She clung to him, abandoning herself unto him for pleasure and a fulfillment so great and freeing it was impossible to comprehend. For some perhaps. Not for her. She'd come home. She was home.

The inferno that built was so hot, so bright, it challenged the sun, and when it exploded, it sent them reeling, tumbling, and gasping for air between the open-mouthed kisses that had been as demanding as their mutual thrusts.

Beth kept her eyes closed as the calm after the storm of their lovemaking settled around them, and when she lifted her lids, and her vision cleared, she let loose the joy filling her. As her giggles subsided, she proclaimed, "Now that was worth coming home for."

He laughed and pulled her into the shelter of his arms, soothing her heated skin with gentle strokes of his hand and sweet kisses on her brow and temple.

After one such gentle kiss, precisely placed upon her lips, he settled his hand on her stomach. "I know about the baby."

She smiled, instinctively knowing the little life

inside her was alive and well. There was no reason to go to Billings. She could write to her mother, ask to have the baby clothes she'd worn as an infant be mailed to her. Turning, meeting his loving, adoring gaze, she whispered, "I know about the new stove you bought."

He threw back his head and let out a laugh that echoed off the ceiling. Hers did too, and it continued for some time. They were both so happy, so thankful, so in love.

After a long time spent simply laying together, holding each other, he asked, "Do we do anything about what we know?"

She'd been thinking about the same thing. The bits and pieces floating around the recesses of her mind were paradoxical, yet real. As real as he and she were. "You're thinking about Cindy, aren't you? The rumors in the future."

He shrugged. "Not as much as I'm thinking about Cliff and Nan. They'd tried to help me, they did help me. I'm wondering if I need to reciprocate."

God, she loved this man. He had such a good, caring, loving soul. Twisting onto her side, she ran the tip of one finger down the length of his arm and then up and over the ripples on his stomach and chest. "There is this thing called free will. No matter what others tell us, our own decisions, our free will, wins out. We all have it. Even Cindy."

She watched as his eyes went from thoughtful to bold, smoldering.

"And Vivi Anne knows the truth. No one in the future will ever believe you fathered anyone's children, other than mine."

He grinned. "I'm sure they won't, and there is this

other thing."

Beth frowned. "What other thing?"

"It's called staying in bed all day with your wife."

Heat bubbled between her thighs. "Oh?"

He lifted her hand and kissed each finger. "No matter what others say, it's a fabulous way to spend the day."

Suppressing a grin, but never her love, she brought a knee up between his legs. "I'm willing. Are you?"

"My will has never been freer."

Epilogue

Vivi Anne drew a deep breath as she took a hold of the door handle. The brick home before her didn't resemble the one in her visions, and there were several more barns, but this was the place. She'd just driven beneath the large *Rocking L* sign. Pushing open the driver's door, she stepped out of her truck. This was new to her. After a *job* of helping people unite, she rarely kept in touch, rarely needed to know more.

Of course, this case had been different. It had been her favorite.

"Can I help you?"

She twisted about, and despite all she knew, had to blink. And smile. Willowy, with frosted hair and sky-blue eyes, the young woman's resemblance to Liz was uncanny—even to a psychic. "Hello. I own an antique store up in Montana and believe I have some things that belong to you. To the *Rocking L*."

"Oh?" The young woman walked closer. "What sort of things?" Holding out a hand, she said, "I'm Ellie Livingston. Actually, it's Elizabeth, but because there has been an Elizabeth every generation, Beth, Liz, and Betty have already been used." She laughed and then frowned. "I have no idea what compelled me to say all that."

"I'm Vivi Anne, and—"

"I had a great-great aunt named Vivi Anne."

Vivi Anne had to blink several times at the special warmth filling her. With a gesture toward the back of her truck, she invited the woman to follow her. "I did a bit of research and think these may have belonged to your ancestor, Rance Livingston."

"My great-great grandfather. He started this place." Ellie grinned. "There's been a Rance every generation, too. His wife was Elizabeth. She went by Beth." Shaking her head, she shrugged. "I really am a chatty-Cathy today. Probably because I'm home alone. My parents flew down to Texas. An anonymous person sent a letter to the newspaper about a proposed nuclear dump site over on the Dixon place. My father, R.C., Rance Conrad, Livingston, is a state senator, and he won't let that happen, whether our families have been friends for years or not. Lou and Nate should know that."

"Yes, they should." Vivi Anne rolled back the tarp covering the box of her truck. Although their grandfather's parentage had never been an issue, Nate or Lou hadn't changed. Which was how it was supposed to be. "It's a saddle, and I think parts of a bridle and—"

"Halter," Ellie finished, unlatching the tailgate to get a closer look. "This is amazing. We all thought it was a family lore. The story goes that Rance had been making this saddle for Beth, but then she became pregnant, so he never finished it. They had a total of six kids and added on to the house after each one was born." She shook her head. "Sorry, the family history is just jumping out of my mouth today. Anyway, Rance swore he never finished the saddle because it was stolen." Running a hand over the leather, she frowned.

"It's so well preserved. Where did you get it?"

Not able to share the entire truth, Vivi Anne said, "In the back room of the antique store I recently opened."

"Montana, right?" Ellie asked.

A flash of a snow-covered mountain appeared as Vivi Anne nodded. "Billings."

Though she hid it well, Vivi Anne saw sadness welling inside Ellie.

With a wobbly grin, Ellie said, "I'm sure my father would like to offer you a finder's fee. Can you wait while I call him?"

"I don't want a finder's fee." The mountain flashed in her head again. A specific mountain. Mount Denali in Alaska. "Just wanted it returned to the rightful owners. Their family."

All the other items had been returned to Rance's barn when she'd put the trunk in the house, but these few things had been left in Montana. Lifting the saddle, she let Ellie collect the other items and then followed the woman toward the house, where she would enter and have a glass of iced tea. She'd thought her mission complete. Rance and Beth had lived long and loving lives together. Now she knew why these items had been left behind. Why she was here. Ellie Livingston needed to go to Alaska. To Mount Denali, the site of a plane crash.

Vivi Anne looked up to where a curtain fluttered in a second-floor window. She smiled, and winked. *Rest assured, Beth. Ellie's in good hands.*

A word about the author...

Lauri Robinson lives in rural Minnesota where she and her husband spend every spare moment with their three grown sons and five grandchildren. She's a diehard Elvis and NASCAR fan, and loves to target shoot pistols. Her favorite getaway location is the woods of northern Minnesota on the land homesteaded by her great-grandfather. Stop by and say hi to Lauri at: http://www.laurirobinson.blogspot.com